BELLA ANDRE

'The perfect combination of sexy heat and tender heart'
—Barbara Freethy, No.1 *New York Times* bestselling author

'Bella Andre writes warm, sexy contemporary romance that
always gives me a much needed pick-me-up. Reading
one of her books is truly a pleasure.'
— Maya Banks, *New York Times* bestselling author

'I can't wait for more Sullivans!'
—Carly Phillips, *New York Times* bestselling author

'Loveable characters, sizzling chemistry and
poignant emotion.'
—Christie Ridgway, *USA TODAY* bestselling author

'No one does sexy like Bella Andre.'
—Sarah MacLean, *New York Times* bestselling author

'A great combination of smokin'-hot sex, emotions and a great
secondary cast. I am absolutely smitten with…the Sullivan
family. I can't wait to read the rest of their stories.'
—*Guilty Pleasures Book Reviews*

'The Sullivans will be a great family to follow.'
—*Happily Ever After Reads*

BELLA ANDRE

The Sullivans

BELLA ANDRE

I Only Have Eyes For You

Published in Great Britain 2014
by Mills & Boon, an imprint of Harlequin (UK) Limited,
Eton House, 18-24 Paradise Road, Richmond, Surrey, TW9 1SR

© 2013 Oak Press, LLC

ISBN: 978 0 263 24575 2

024-0214

Harlequin (UK) Limited's policy is to use papers that are natural, renewable and recyclable products and made from wood grown in sustainable forests. The logging and manufacturing processes conform to the legal environmental regulations of the country of origin.

Printed and bound by
CPI Group (UK) Ltd, Croydon, CR0 4YY

New York Times and *USA Today* bestselling author **Bella Andre** has always been a writer. Songs came first and then non-fiction books, but, as soon as she started writing her first romance novel, she knew she'd found her perfect career. Known for 'sensual, empowered stories enveloped in heady romance' (*Publishers Weekly*) about sizzling alpha heroes and the strong women they'll love forever, nearly all of her novels have appeared on Top 10 lists at Amazon, Barnes & Noble, Apple and Kobo.

Her books have been *Cosmopolitan* magazine 'Red Hot Reads' twice and have been translated into nine languages. Winner of the Award of Excellence, *The Washington Post* has called her 'One of the top digital writers in America' and she has been featured by *NPR*, *USA Today*, *Forbes* and *The Wall Street Journal*.

If she's not behind her computer, you can find her reading her favourite authors, hiking, swimming or laughing. Married with two children, Bella splits her time between the Northern California wine country and a hundred-year-old log cabin in the Adirondacks.

Dear Reader,

For the past year, I have been living, breathing—and writing! —Sullivans. I can't thank you enough for the e-mails, tweets, Facebook and Goodreads posts you have made to let me know how much you've been enjoying their love stories.

As a writer, some books stick with you long after you've typed 'The End.' *I Only Have Eyes For You* is one of those stories that continues to make me smile every time I think of it.

The last man in the world that anyone expects Sophie Sullivan, a 'nice' librarian, to fall in love with is Jake McCann, a tattooed pub owner with a dark past. And yet the love story that began when she was five years old and he was eleven has never even come close to fading away…

The only woman Jake wants is the one he can never have. But even though he knows loving Sophie isn't the right thing to do… how can he resist? Especially when she's determined to prove to him that nice and naughty can sometimes overlap in the most wonderful way.

Happy reading,

Bella Andre

Prologue

Nearly twenty years ago...

Sophie Sullivan sat cross-legged on a soft blanket in the corner of the backyard, beneath the canopy of one of the smaller oak trees. Now that the rain had ceased to fall in Northern California and it was warm outside, her mother had made her this special area to take her books and read.

Last year, when she was four years old, Sophie had learned how to read. And books had changed her life.

When she was reading she wasn't the quiet Sullivan twin, she wasn't the one that no one ever noticed. She became a princess in a castle. Or a clown juggling under the circus big top. She explored jungles on elephants' backs and took trips to Mars on spaceships.

Reading took her anywhere she wanted to go. And Sophie found that she wanted to go absolutely *everywhere*.

Right now she was reading the most thrilling story about a girl named Pippi Longstocking who lived with a monkey and a horse and had a suitcase full of gold. Sophie had been so absorbed by her new book that her mother had asked her twin sister, Lori, to bring her a peanut butter and jelly sandwich to eat when she'd missed lunch with everyone else. Of course, Lori had taken a bite out of it before delivering the sandwich, so Sophie had to carefully pull off the teeth marks before eating the rest.

She loved her sister, but Lori also made her really mad sometimes. Everyone said they were lucky to be twins, and Sophie knew they were right, that it wouldn't be any fun at all to be the only female Sullivan. Still, she sometimes wished Lori didn't have quite so many *moods*.

Fortunately, Sophie was all alone in the backyard for now, and with a happy little sigh, she leaned back against the tree trunk and flipped the page to continue Pippi's adventure. Of course, in Sophie's family the solitude never lasted long, and when the sound of whooping and hollering in another part of the backyard sounded, she couldn't quite keep her focus on her book anymore.

She could tune out her six brothers and one sister just fine.

It was Jake McCann who was the real distraction.

He was the same age as her brother Zach, and she normally wouldn't have any interest in eleven-year-old boys. But from the first day she'd seen him walk through the front door with her brother, Jake had captivated her.

He was bigger, and tougher looking, than her brother. The bonus of no one really noticing her was that it was easy to listen in when her brothers whispered about Jake's dad being kind of scary and smelling funny, like when someone spilled a drink at their mother's annual holiday party.

It made her stomach hurt to think of anyone being mean to Jake, and she was glad that he could come over to their house so much, where everyone was mostly nice to one another. Jake never really talked to her—or paid any attention to her at all, actually—but just knowing he was nearby always made her feel warm and safe and happy.

Her brothers had been building a tree fort for a while in the biggest oak tree in their backyard. The fort was big and sprawling and from the ground

Sophie thought it looked really dangerous…but exciting, too. She'd never been up that high before in anything that wasn't a real building, and the fall to the ground looked really, really far. Which was why she hadn't quite worked up the courage to climb the ropes they'd knotted together to use as a ladder with some branches that stuck out here and there.

Jake's dark hair was a little too long, but when he laughed he tilted his face back and his hair shifted away from his eyes so that she could see all of his face at once.

Oh, my. He was so handsome, and intelligent, and just plain wonderful. She could have stared at him forever, and probably would have if he hadn't caught her looking just then.

In that moment that their gazes connected, Sophie's five-year-old heart told her with perfect certainly that he felt the same way about her…that he loved her, too. But then, so quickly she knew she must have imagined it, he scowled and called out to her siblings, "Last one up into the fort is a rotten egg."

Her brothers climbed over one another to get up onto the wooden platform, but her sister, Lori, was smaller and quicker than all of them, so she got up the tree trunk before anyone else could.

Jake was right after her, and then Sophie's brothers Gabe, Ryan and Zach followed behind. Her oldest brothers—Chase, Smith and Marcus—were off at baseball practice. Otherwise, the fort would have been bursting at the seams.

Standing way up high, her brothers and sister pretended to be looking out at the open sea through a couple of old collapsing telescopes that they'd found at a garage sale last month. Only Jake looked down at Sophie. He didn't say a word to her, but she could read the challenge in his gaze…and the silent question.

You're not scared, are you?

Her heart started beating extra fast as she thought about trying to climb the tree, about being up that high. She clutched the book tighter in her hands, the hard cover and pages slipping beneath her sweaty palms.

When the book slid from her lap, Sophie looked down at the drawing of the girl on the cover with the crazy red pigtails that stuck out straight.

Pippi wouldn't be afraid to climb up the tree.

Pippi would have even beaten Lori to the top.

Slowly, Sophie rose to her feet, the crumbs from her peanut butter and jelly sandwich falling from her T-shirt and shorts onto the blanket for the ants to devour. Her legs shook as she walked across the grass toward the big oak tree. Her siblings were all too busy playing Pirates to notice her coming over, but Jake's eyes stayed on her the whole time.

I will not chicken out. I will not chicken out. I will not chicken out.

Only, the closer she got, the higher the tree fort seemed. She'd never climbed a rope ladder before, and her hands were so sweaty now that she knew they'd slip right off just when she got high enough to fall and smash her brains open on the ground.

She was just on the verge of chickening out when she heard her name, spoken so softly she almost missed it. She looked up at Jake and knew she'd never forgive herself if she turned and ran back to her blanket and book.

He seemed to think she could do it. And she couldn't bear to prove him wrong.

Before she could freak herself out any more than she already had, she picked up her pace and all but jumped onto the rope ladder. She felt as if she'd turned into Pippi Longstocking's monkey as she clambered up the rope and tree limbs to get into the fort, moving too fast to let fear grab hold of her and toss her to the ground.

Her brothers and sister looked shocked when they saw her head poking through, and Ryan immediately grabbed her arms to haul her up.

"You should have told us you were trying to come up," he said in full-on big-brother mode, since he was the oldest one in the yard.

Lori pointed to Sophie's leg. "Ouch."

Sophie looked down and realized she had a long scratch up her right shin. She had no idea when she'd gotten it and, even now, she was so flush with triumph from climbing the tree that it didn't hurt.

Jake didn't congratulate her on making it up into the fort—he even made a crack to her brothers about how they should ban girls under six in the future—but she knew he was proud of her.

And, she thought as she smiled and looked around, she was proud of herself, too.

Because the world really did look different from way up high…and more than anything, she loved getting to experience the adventure with the boy she would love forever.

One

Present day...

Sophie Sullivan surveyed the final wedding preparations with satisfaction. She'd spent the past several months putting together the details for her brother's wedding and it was wonderful to see it all come together so perfectly.

In less than two hours, Chase and his fiancée, Chloe, would be saying "I do" beneath rose-covered arches with three hundred guests looking on. The Napa Valley vineyard owned by her oldest brother, Marcus, was not only the perfect backdrop for the wedding, but was also where Chase and Chloe had first met and fallen in love.

The catering staff Sophie had hired was busy in the on-site kitchen. The florist was putting the finishing touches on the flowers that ran up both sides of the aisle and the beautiful bouquets at the center of each of the tables in the reception area. The weather was perfect with blue skies and a few puffy white clouds lazily floating by. The vineyards were bursting with green leaves and budding grapes, and the mustard flowers between the rows of vines were a stunning burst of golden color all across the seemingly endless hills of grapevines.

The bride and the other bridesmaids were already in the guesthouse having their hair and makeup done. Sophie should have been there getting ready with them half an hour ago, but she'd wanted to first make sure that everything outside was perfect. Which was why she was still standing out in the vineyard wearing jeans tucked into boots, a long blue sweater and a hat over hair she hadn't bothered with that morning because she knew the stylist would take care of it for her.

Sophie was a librarian, not a wedding planner, but she'd leaped at the chance to help plan Chase's wedding, and it had been so much fun. Well, apart from all those meetings with—

"Hey, Nice, looking good."

Every muscle in Sophie's body tensed at hearing the low drawl from behind her.

Jake McCann.

Her brother Zach's closest friend…and the object of twenty years of her unrequited love.

Of course, not once in those twenty years had she ever been anything more to him than Zach's little sister. What's more, she knew darn well that she wasn't "looking good" right then in clothes she'd put on to move furniture and heavy containers of flowers all morning.

Barely stifling a frustrated sigh, she replied, "My name is Sophie, not Nice," without turning to face him. She'd reminded him of this at least a hundred times over the years, but he still persisted in calling her by her nickname.

It was one thing when her brothers called her Nice…and it was another entirely when Jake said it. Especially when, in her secret dreams, she was naughty and wild and the woman he couldn't believe he'd lived without for so long.

She felt him move closer, his innate heat searing her even from several feet away. She'd always been overly attuned to him, instantly alert to his presence in a room. As a little girl, she'd made excuses to hang out with her older brothers just to be near Jake, keeping extra quiet so no one would remember she was there while they played in the tree fort or shot pool in the basement while making off-color jokes that she didn't understand until she was a great deal older.

The urge to turn and drink him in, to lose herself in the spark of wicked in his chocolate-brown eyes, was so strong she almost gave in. Of course, she knew every inch of Jake's face by heart, having spent most of her childhood staring at him when she didn't think he was looking. His jaw was square and his nose had a couple of bumps on it that she knew were from fights he'd been in.

So instead of looking at him, she forced herself to keep her gaze trained on the outdoor seating area, watching the florists make final adjustments to the arrangements and the caterers rush trays of food in from their vans to Marcus's industrial-size kitchen. Regardless of what she actually felt for Jake, Sophie's pride insisted that she do her best to act as if she didn't care one way or another if he was there or not.

"Hard to believe the day has finally come." He paused, and she could hear the humor mixed with a faint disdain in his voice as he finished, "A Sullivan is actually taking the plunge."

Sophie was known as the clearheaded, soft-spoken one in the family, the one who always thought things through before taking action. She'd never been prone to outbursts or to giving in to crazy inner urgings. That was her twin sister Lori's territory, which was why Lori's nickname was Naughty and Sophie's was Nice. But Sophie rarely felt levelheaded anymore around Jake.

How could she when her heart always beat too fast at the thought of what it would feel like to be in his arms…or because he was making her angry with some macho comment? Usually both at the same time. Just as he was doing right now. He was utterly infuriating but so darn desirable that even though she knew she had to be crazy for wanting him the way she did, she'd never been able to stop the way she felt.

Hating how out of control he made her feel, her fingers curled into fists as she lost the battle with acting aloof and whirled around to face him.

Unfortunately for her traitorous hormones, Jake was more gorgeous than ever in his tuxedo. His crisp white dress shirt opened up just enough at the neck for her to see the dark hair curling up at the vee of his chest. His tattoos were covered up, but just knowing they were hidden behind a thin layer of fabric sent a kick of forbidden desire rushing through her. God, what she wouldn't give to see his tattoos up close, to have hours to run her fingers over his naked skin and study the ink imprinted into his skin.

"Chase and Chloe are in love," she told him in a sharp voice made even sharper by her disappointment with herself for not being even the slightest bit unaffected by Jake's good looks. "Their wedding is going to be beautiful and perfect and incredibly romantic."

It was even more beautiful and perfect and romantic that Chloe was pregnant and absolutely glowing. Sophie couldn't wait to babysit, to endlessly spoil her niece or nephew. Jake's mouth moved up into a half smile at her emphatic statement. "It's going to be one hell of a party, at least."

What was wrong with him? Sophie wondered for what had to be the thousandth time in twenty years. How could he look at a lifetime of love and only see the party?

Then again, given the fact that he blew through women at a shockingly fast rate, it wasn't hard to guess that he was one of those imbeciles who didn't believe in love. A rich, good-looking guy like Jake McCann would just be in it for the sex. She should know better than to give him even five minutes of her time. And yet…if it were that easy, if love was that rational, then she likely would have found another man to fall in love with years ago.

Unfortunately, when it came to her feelings for

Jake, rational had absolutely nothing to do with them, and never had.

Even worse, thinking about sex and Jake at the same time always made her go hot all over, and now was no different. Sophie was neither a virgin nor a prude, despite what people might otherwise assume about librarians. On the contrary, if people knew just how well-read she was on the subject of sex, they would likely be shocked. Especially Jake.

Wouldn't it be something to shock Jake, who clearly thought he had written the book on seduction?

Darn it, by now she should know better than to let her fantasies run away with her where Jake was concerned, even if her body had stupidly fallen in lust with him from the first stirring of teenage hormones. And still, she couldn't help but breathe in his scent, a faint hint of hops and something she'd never been able to categorize beyond *night* and *darkness*.

She moved to straighten an already perfectly straight chair. "I checked over the bar setup earlier and it looks like everything is in place." She'd planned on hiring a professional bar service for the wedding, but Jake had insisted on covering that aspect of the wedding himself. He owned a chain of Irish pubs, and despite the fact that he was incredibly successful with his businesses, she hadn't been quite sure how he'd pull off a bar at a formal wedding.

Now that she'd seen what he'd done, she grudgingly had to admit, "You've done a good job with it. A really good job."

She could feel his dark eyes on her as he said, "So have you, with this entire wedding." Again he gave her that half smile that made her stomach do flip-flops. "You sure I can't hire you to run my pubs? I could always use someone like you to whip the things into even better shape."

A burst of pleasure at his compliments shot through her, warming her all over. That was the problem with Jake. Even when she was irritated with him, even though he'd never return her feelings for him in a million, billion years, she couldn't help but be charmed by him. Sophie and every other woman on the planet, it often seemed.

Still, knowing she'd never forgive herself if she melted into a gooey puddle of lust in the middle of Marcus's vineyard, she simply told him, "I'd miss my books too much, thanks."

All her life, Sophie had had stacks of books in every room and she'd recently embraced the digital age and gotten an e-reader that fit in her purse. She'd gone to Stanford University and come out with a combined degree in English literature and Library Science that she'd put together herself with the help of an adviser who loved books just as much as she did. As soon as she'd graduated from college, she'd applied to work for the San Francisco Public Library. She knew she could have made much more money working for a university library, or applying her research and cataloging skills to one of the high-tech startups throughout the Bay Area, but she'd always wanted to be a librarian. Even if her apartment was on the small side and she'd never be rich, she hadn't regretted her decision for a second.

Knowing that prolonging her close proximity to Jake in this überromantic setting would only mess with her head, she said, "I'd better get over to the guesthouse." But just as she was turning to go, a sudden gust of wind whipped her baseball cap off her head.

Jake reached out and caught it by the brim before she even had time to react. "Got it."

He moved in front of her and slid a lock of dark hair that had caught on her mouth back under the hat as he settled it into place. Her cheek tingled from the gentle brush of skin on skin and she nervously licked her lips. She couldn't remember the last time he'd touched her. It wasn't that he wasn't an affectionate man, it was just that he'd always seemed to steer clear of touching *her*.

His hands stilled on the brim of her hat, his dark eyes turning almost jet-black as his gaze held on her mouth. Neither of them moved for several moments, but then, suddenly, he was stepping back from her, the slightly cool wine-country air pushing in where his heat had been just seconds before.

"You might want to tighten it down so it doesn't blow off again," he told her before quickly scanning her outfit with a frown. "Aren't you one of Chloe's maids of honor? What are you still doing wearing that?" Still working to catch her breath from the shock of his touch, it took far longer than it should have for her to register his question. She couldn't miss the mocking tone, however.

Months ago, when Jake had volunteered to run the bar at Chase and Chloe's wedding, she'd impulsively decided to teach him a lesson about his arrogance, along with the way he insisted on continuing to look at her as little more than a child, rather than a fully grown woman. She'd planned to make him want her, to somehow figure out a way to make him desperate with longing…before she scorned him, leaving him high and dry for the first time in his life.

But had she made good on those big plans to attract and then reject Jake in the past four months? *Ha!*

"Yes, I am," she finally replied, her words a hard snap of breath and teeth. "Everyone else is getting dressed, but I needed to check on a few final things first."

The perfect planes of his face shifted again from frown to scowl, before settling back into indifference. "Now that you know everything is perfect, you'd better go get pretty, then, shouldn't you, princess?"

Jake's harsh words landed with a hard thud between them. She didn't know if he'd intended to hurt her with the implication that it would take some time, along with a good amount of effort, to pretty her up...but whether or not that had been his intent, that was exactly what he'd just done.

A few minutes ago she'd felt proud of what she'd accomplished with Chase and Chloe's wedding. Now, that pride was all but erased by the way Jake looked at her and clearly found her so wanting, so utterly devoid of female allure. Because even though she knew better than to care, even though she knew better than to give him the power to hurt her, a handful of his careless words did more damage than anything else ever could have.

Had she imagined that hunger, that longing, in his eyes just moments ago when he'd touched her cheek and she could have sworn that he was thinking about kissing her?

Or had she simply wanted to feel those sparks so badly that she'd manufactured a split-second connection that would never actually be there between them?

Oh, how she hated the way he'd just talked to her—like she was still a little girl rather than a fully grown, successful, adult woman. *Princess.* He'd called her *princess.*

Somehow that was worse than Nice. At least her family nickname had been born of love.

In one fell swoop, all the resolve she'd had such a hard time holding on to where Jake was concerned gathered up inside her, settling in just over her breastbone. What she wouldn't give to shock him, to show him that he didn't know a darn thing about who she really was, that the "nice" girl he'd seen grow up, that the "princess" he saw when he looked at her, was more than woman enough to run him in circles.

Growing up in a family of extraordinary siblings, Sophie had known better than to try to compete with them. She'd never glide across a dance floor like her twin, Lori, who was a choreographer. Sophie would never lead a team to a national championship like her brother Ryan, who was a professional baseball player. She didn't save people's lives on a daily basis like her firefighter brother Gabe. And she'd never be passionate enough about photography or cars or vineyards to turn them into successful careers and businesses like her brothers Chase, Zach and Marcus had.

But as she stood with Jake in the middle of Marcus's vineyard barely an hour before Chase and Chloe's wedding, Sophie couldn't have been happier that she was so passionate about books that she'd read thousands of novels. Enough, she hoped, to pull together a quick plot that would give Jake a taste of his own medicine…and, at long last, a run for his money.

"You're right," she said softly, "I should leave soon to get *pretty*." The words tasted like grit on her tongue and she could have sworn he almost winced as she repeated them back to him. "But there's something I've been meaning to ask you first."

"What's that?" he asked in an easy voice. One she thought sounded a little too easy, like he was trying to force himself to seem completely nonchalant and unaffected by her.

"Well," she said slowly, "I just found out that

an ex-boyfriend of mine is one of Chloe's last-minute guests."

It was true, she'd dated the guy—Alex—for a few months last year. He was good-looking and nice enough, but when she couldn't bring herself to go to bed with him, his eyes started wandering to other pretty girls whenever they went out. If she'd cared about him, she knew she would have been upset about it. Instead, she'd quite easily decided to let him loose so that he could go after one of those other women. But while he had to know the two of them weren't going anywhere, he hadn't appreciated being dumped, even though she'd tried to be as gentle as possible about it. The word *tease* hadn't passed his lips, but she'd known it was what he thought about her.

That made it a little easier for her to spin the truth a bit for Jake's benefit. "He ended up being a bit of a jerk and he's someone I'd really like to make jealous." She slowly lowered her eyelashes as if she still wasn't over the pain of being left so callously.

Although she'd only been in the chorus of a handful of elementary-school stage productions, she tried to channel the way she imagined her movie star brother Smith would play this scene on-screen. With pathos. And a faint hint of shame at the way she'd never managed to be good enough for her ex no matter what she did.

She waited a beat before lifting her gaze to Jake's again. "Would you help me?"

He stared down at her, clearly unable to believe what she was proposing. "Hold up a second, Nice. You want *me* to help *you* make some loser ex-boyfriend jealous?"

She gritted her teeth at his use of her nickname—and the fact that he immediately assumed any boyfriend of hers had to be a loser—but forced herself to let it go. For now.

"You didn't bring anyone to the wedding, right?" A few weeks ago he'd told her he was coming stag so that he could keep watch over his staff at the bar. Sophie figured it was also a good way to make sure he had his pick of hot single guests for an after party in his bed. She forcefully tamped down the surge of jealousy at that vision as she said, "Please, Jake, will you help me?"

But he was already shaking his head. "No one will ever believe it. And your brothers would kill me if they thought I was looking at you that way."

Damn his bad reputation and her own, which was virtually pristine. And damn her brothers for being so protective.

Jake was right. They would tear him to shreds

if they ever thought he'd so much as had an impure thought about her or Lori. But she refused to give up now, not with his disdainful, *You'd better go get pretty, then, shouldn't you, princess?* comment still running through her head.

"Are you kidding?" she said with a laugh. "Of course none of them would believe it. You?" She laughed harder. "And me?" She shook her head as if the whole idea were utterly preposterous…even though she'd written their love story a thousand times in her dreams. "We've all seen the kind of girls you go for. I would be surprised if half of them can even spell their own names."

When he scowled, she belatedly realized she might have gone too far.

Oops.

"Don't worry," she reassured him, "we'll make sure none of my family or friends see us. Just my ex."

"Does this guy have a name?"

The way Jake looked right then, as if he was going to tear her ex apart with his bare hands, told her it wouldn't be fair to give him Alex's name.

Thinking fast, she said, "I don't like saying it aloud."

Her answer didn't seem to make him any happier as he growled, "Did he hurt you?"

She was glad she hadn't had too much to eat for

breakfast. Otherwise, it would have threatened to come back up as she moved her hand over her heart and said, "Only here," in an overly theatrical way.

Sophie was certain anyone else would have seen through her terrible acting job, but Jake was so bound and determined not to notice anything about her it looked as if she was actually going to get away with this.

Knowing it was make-or-break time, she played her final card. "Please, Jake. You're the only one I can ask to help me get a little revenge on a big jerk." She leaned in close to his ear and said in a hushed voice, "It will be our little secret."

God, he smelled good, so good she wanted to rub her lips over the faint stubble on his cheek. Instead, she forced herself to shift her weight away from him.

He ran one hand through his hair and shook his head as if he already knew he was going to regret helping her, then finally said, "Fine. If you're that desperate, I'll do it. Although I still don't think this plan of yours has much of a chance of working."

"Oh," she said softly, the word *desperate* grating along with *princess* and *Nice,* "it will work all right. I'll make absolutely sure of it."

What the hell had just happened?
Jake McCann knew how he was supposed to

feel about Sophie Sullivan. He was supposed to love her the way a guy loved his little sister, to watch over her, to make sure she was safe and happy. He was supposed to be blind to the way Sophie had filled out over the years. And he was supposed to hope she found a nice, easygoing guy who would always be careful with her.

He shouldn't have been appreciating her curves beneath her jeans and sweater as she'd stood in the middle of the vineyard and surveyed the wedding preparations. And when he accidentally touched her while putting her baseball cap back on her head and her eyes had gone all dreamy, he sure as hell shouldn't have felt the crazy urge to drag her against him and kiss that soft mouth and find out just how soft her curves would feel pressed against his hard muscles.

But, even knowing those things, he couldn't manage to drag his eyes off her as she walked away, couldn't stop thinking about how soft her cheek felt against the pad of his thumb and the way her hair slid like silk through his fingers.

Damn it.

How long had he worked to deny the way he felt about Sophie?

How many years had he told himself his need for her was nothing he couldn't work out of his system with other women? Women who were good for a few hours in the sack, but who didn't have an ounce of Sophie's natural elegance. Her brains. Her gentleness.

And how the hell was he going to make it through an entire wedding with Sophie when his self-control had been slipping a little more each time he saw her over the past few months as he'd been helping her with putting Chase and Chloe's wedding together? Sitting close to her as she ran through the wedding plans with him, breathing in her sweet scent, wondering if she would taste just as sweet against his tongue, had been slowly driving him crazy. Day by day she'd crept into his thoughts, his dreams, and every time she stayed longer.

Sophie had always been special, even as a little girl. Not only the prettiest thing he'd ever seen in his life, but also so smart she blew him away even at five years old. And she was brave, too. So much braver than she gave herself credit for. As the smallest, quietest one in a family of eight kids, she wouldn't even flinch as she walked into the middle of flying elbows and knees. And somehow, like magic, the sea of limbs would part for her, as if her silent power was so much bigger than her brothers' muscles or her twin sister's constant hollering.

Just a few minutes ago, as he'd been standing in the middle of Marcus's vineyard with Sophie near enough to pull into his arms, Jake had been caught between two impossible choices. Reach out and finally claim her the way he'd fantasized about taking her for far too long…or push her away for her own good. Because it was one thing for a McCann to be friends with a Sullivan girl. It was another thing entirely to think that he could claim her for himself, and keep her forever.

He'd always known that wasn't possible, that Sophie deserved better than the son of an abusive drunk who poured beer for a living. Unfortunately, knowing that hadn't made the wanting go away.

His chest clenched with regret as he remembered Sophie's wounded expression after he'd made those cracks about her clothes and needing to be made pretty for the wedding. She was the last person in the world he wanted to hurt, which was exactly why he'd made sure to keep his distance as much as possible over the years.

Jake hated to think that some guy she'd dated had done a number on her, and actually had the nerve to show up at her brother's wedding. She deserved to be with someone who would give her everything. A house in the suburbs and a white picket fence. A handful of cute kids with big brains like their mother.

He pushed his knuckles hard against his sternum, trying to physically shove away the tightening in his chest that began with the images of Sophie being picture-book happy with some other guy. Jake wasn't sure about her plan to make her ex jealous, but he was already planning to get the guy alone and teach him a lesson about what happened when somebody messed with a Sullivan.

Just then, Chase stepped out onto Marcus's terrace and called Jake's name, jolting him out of his thoughts.

Chase's brothers were all groomsmen and Marcus had gotten a special license so that he could officiate the ceremony. Jake was the only non-Sullivan to be given the honor of standing up with the groom, even though Chase had plenty of cousins who could have been chosen.

The ninth Sullivan. It was always how they'd made him feel, like he was one of them. Back when he was a kid and he'd hung out at their house, Jake had pretended he was home. And the truth was, Mary Sullivan's house had been the only real home he'd known until a few years ago when he'd bought his own place. By then his Irish pubs were booming and he was able to easily afford the kind of house he'd only dreamed of having before.

Jake was happy for Chase on his wedding day. The first time Jake had met Chloe, he'd been struck by what a perfect fit they were for each other. Sure, he had been surprised by the way his friend had fallen so quickly, and by how happy he was about the whole husband/father thing being dropped into his lap. But just because Jake wouldn't ever let himself get tied up in that ball and chain, he would always support a Sullivan.

Being a groomsman at Chase's wedding and running the bar was all part of giving back to the family that had helped raise him when his own family hadn't given a damn.

The two men shook hands and exchanged a hug. "How're you feeling on the big day?" Jake asked.

Chase grinned. "Good." His grin widened. "Really good."

Jake had seen Chase and Chloe together enough to know this was one seriously happy dude. Chase didn't seem to have one regret about giving up having his pick of hot models and finally settling down.

"Have you seen Chloe?" Chase asked. "Do you know if she needs anything?"

As soon as Chloe had announced her pregnancy, Chase had become a carbon copy of every other overprotective dad-to-be. It was exactly the kind of crazy behavior Jake would never understand. Which was why he made damn certain none of his sexual partners could get knocked up.

"I was just talking with Sophie," he told Chase. "Sounds like everything is under control with the girls."

"Good." Chase nodded, then grinned at him. "Come inside. Smith is telling us about an orgy he walked in on a couple of weeks ago at an awards show after party. I'm guessing it's a warm-up for his speech after the wedding."

Jake grinned, then said, "So you're really not going to miss all of that, huh?"

Chase didn't hesitate before shaking his head. "Chloe is worth so much more."

In companionable silence, the two men headed for the house, and Jake could hear the Sullivans laughing as they walked inside. He loved the family as if they were his own. He would take a bullet for any of them.

Especially the dark-haired beauty he couldn't manage to get out of his head.

Or his heart.

Two

"There you are! We were just about to send out a search party for you." Kalen, the makeup artist Chase usually worked with on his photo shoots, grabbed Sophie the second she stepped into the guesthouse. "Everyone else is putting on their dresses already." She looked carefully at Sophie's unpainted face. "Fortunately, all you need is some light mascara and lipstick." As Kalen laid out the products she was planning to use on Sophie, she added, "I swear, all of you have such good genes. I wish I could have worked on your mother when she was a model. She's so beautiful now, she must have been absolutely extraordinary when she was younger."

"Next time you're over at the house, you should ask her if you can see her scrapbooks," Sophie suggested. "I used to spend hours going through them when I was a little girl. I could hardly believe the woman in the pictures was my mother." And while Sophie had been going through her mother's scrapbooks, her sister, Lori, would be playing in front of the mirror with her mother's eye shadows and powders and lipsticks.

Normally, Sophie would have agreed with Kalen to keep her face close to bare. She'd never been all that comfortable in makeup. Sophie had always been more interested in reading aloud to Lori from the books she'd found on makeup application, rather than being in the makeup chair herself.

"Actually," she said, her heart pounding hard at what she was about to do, "I was hoping you could work a little of your magic on me."

Kalen raised an eyebrow. "Magic?"

Sophie nodded, forcing herself to admit, "There's this guy…"

"A guy, huh?" Kalen gave Sophie a slow grin. "Well, in that case, I'd be happy to work a little of my magic on you. He won't know what hit him." She called out to the hairstylist friend she'd brought with her. "Jackie, can you come here for a sec?"

A few minutes of hushed conferencing later—

in which Sophie made it clear that she didn't want to look overly made up or trashy, just a whole lot sexier than she normally did—the three women had formulated a plan.

Sophie sat back in front of the mirror and tried to ignore her rapidly beating heart as they transformed her from Nice into someone entirely different.

Kalen and Jackie had just finished doing Sophie's hair and makeup and were helping her change into her bridesmaid's dress without messing up their brilliant work when Lori walked into the room.

She'd always moved quickly, but one look at Sophie had her stopping dead in her tracks, and going as still as Sophie had ever seen her twin.

Lori stared at her in shock. "What the heck have you done with my sister?"

The two of them hadn't been getting along so well for the past year. Sophie hated to see the way Lori was letting that jerk she'd been dating in secret walk all over her. Everyone saw her twin as so fierce, so fearless, but Sophie knew Lori was simply better at hiding her emotions than the rest of them.

Every time Sophie had tried to bring up the situation, instead of confiding in her, Lori had blocked her out of her life more and more. Lori was a master of sharp, sarcastic barbs, as Sophie knew all too well, and she'd been lashed out at one too many times in recent months. But beneath everything that had come between them in the past year, she loved her sister.

How could she not, when they'd always been two halves of a whole?

Today was one of those days when Sophie needed her twin's reassurance. Lori was the only one who could automatically understand everything about her on a DNA level.

In the heat of the moment, when the way Jake had treated her had pushed her into finally making the decision to shake things up, it had seemed so empowering to let Kalen and Jackie get creative with her look. But for someone like Sophie, who'd always been perfectly happy disappearing into the background, this hair, this makeup, this attitude, was a big departure.

What if people laughed at her?

What if Jake laughed?

She'd die. Oh, yes, right then and there in the middle of Chase and Chloe's special day, in front of three hundred people, she'd wither up and drop dead.

Lori moved closer, then did a full circle around Sophie standing perfectly still in her deep pink satin strapless dress. She'd been the last one to meet Chloe at the bridal store to pick out her maid-of-honor dress. Although it was definitely more conservative than Lori's, Sophie had forgotten how well the satin hugged her curves, closer than anything else she owned, that's for sure. It was classic movie-star-style, à la Marilyn Monroe's "Happy Birthday, Mr. President" dress, with a long slit up one leg. Her dark hair had been blown out so that it looked impossibly glossy and soft as it fell around her shoulders just to the upper swell of her breasts.

Finally, Lori said, "You look amazing, Soph."

Sophie breathed a heavy sigh of relief. "Thank God."

"But," Lori added with a slight frown, "you don't exactly look like you." Her frown deepened. "Did Kalen convince you to do this?"

Sophie shook her head, knowing that if this all went horribly wrong, she had no one to blame but herself. "The makeup was my idea. So was the hair."

Lori frowned again. "I don't get it. I mean, you look absolutely gorgeous, but you've never wanted to try anything new before. Why now?"

Sophie forced a shrug, as if it didn't matter to

her at all if her sister got it or not. Even though it did matter. So much. "I just wanted to see what it would be like to look different for one day."

"Hmm." Lori scanned her again, head to toe, and Sophie knew the exact moment the truth hit her sister when her eyes grew big and she started shaking her head. "Oh, no. Please tell me you didn't do this to try to get J—"

Sophie leaped toward her sister to cover Lori's mouth with her hand before Jake's name left it. God forbid any of their brothers overheard their conversation, or figured out what she was planning. She wished she could tell Lori her transformation had nothing to do with Jake, but even though they'd been at odds recently over Lori's current jerk of a boyfriend, Sophie couldn't lie to her twin.

"I know what I'm doing."

Lori yanked Sophie's hand from her mouth. "You don't have a clue what you're doing, Soph. You've never played games with a man before, and he's definitely the wrong man to decide to mess around with. I love J—"

"Lori!"

"—him like a brother, but that doesn't mean I don't see his faults. Especially where women are concerned." Lori pinned her with a hard gaze. "Please don't do this. Not today. Not with him."

Sophie had never thought to admit this to anyone, not even to her sister, but now she found herself saying, "You don't know what it's like to be invisible." She instinctively lifted her chin and pushed back her shoulders. "I'm sick of it."

She hoped her twin would understand, but instead of encouraging her, Lori said, "You love to tell me when and where I'm screwing up." Sophie tried to interject, but her sister put her hands on her shoulders and made her turn around to face the full-length mirror. "This time you're the one who needs to listen. Don't do this, Soph." Lori squeezed her shoulders tight. "Don't. Do. This."

Sophie stared at the incredibly sexy woman staring back at her in the mirror. She'd never have been able to pull this together without professional assistance.

It was now or never.

And she was sick to death of the *never* she'd been living her whole life.

"I have to."

Lori looked as serious—and worried—as Sophie could ever remember seeing her. "The boys are going to be beside themselves seeing you looking like that. I mean, they're used to me playing up the goods, but you… Nope. They aren't going to like it. Not one bit."

Sophie figured it was a good test to muster up the bravado to say, "Too bad."

Finally Lori almost smiled, but then she asked, "What's going to happen if your plan backfires?"

Sophie's heart stuttered in her chest at the thought of just how many things could go wrong with her brilliant plan to teach Jake a lesson for ignoring her all these years. Still, she thought she sounded confident and secure as she assured her sister, "It won't."

And even though she could still feel the heated imprint of Jake's fingers against her cheek where he'd touched her, she told herself it was the truth. Because if there was one thing everyone knew about Sophie Sullivan, it was that she never, ever lied. Not to anyone.

And certainly not to herself.

Ellen, Marcus's winery manager, who had helped Sophie with plenty of the wedding details, popped her head into the room. "Wow, the two of you are gorgeous." She spent a few extra seconds looking at Sophie, a faint hint of surprise on her face, before saying, "Beyond gorgeous, actually."

Sophie momentarily forgot about her transformation as she asked Ellen, "Is everything going well out there?"

Ellen smiled. "Perfectly. The guests are gathering, the string quartet sounds great, the weather is perfect and the bride is simply radiant."

Sophie breathed a sigh of relief. "Good. I want Chase and Chloe's day to be perfect."

"It will be," Ellen promised her. "I've helped put on dozens of weddings at the winery, and I have to say, I think this is going to be the very best." She looked down at the iPad she brought everywhere with her. "It's nearly time to give the bride her big send-off. Are you both ready?"

Sophie's heart jumped in her chest at the thought of making her grand entrance. She was as ready as she'd ever be.

She joined the other women—Lori, Marcus's pop-star girlfriend, Nicola, Gabe's girlfriend, Megan, and the other two bridesmaids, who were old friends of Chloe's—out on the porch. As co-maids-of-honor, Sophie and Lori had had a fierce match of rock-paper-scissors over which of them would walk out first with Marcus, the oldest Sullivan.

Sophie was certain that Lori had cheated. Her twin always did. But now she was glad that she wouldn't be the first to walk down the aisle. It was even better that her brother Smith was her partner when she made her entrance. Everyone would be oohing and ahhing over the movie star in their midst. At least long enough, she hoped, for her to settle a little better into her brand-new sex-goddess persona.

Just as Lori had predicted, their brothers stopped and blinked at Sophie in surprise as they walked onto the porch. Surprise, unfortunately, quickly turned into scowls.

"Sophie?"

Her oldest brother's face looked like thunder and she had to force herself to hold her ground in front of Marcus, rather than take a step back in retreat—and go running back inside to wipe the makeup off her face and brush her glossy, blown-out hair back into the more casual style they were all used to.

"What the h—"

His girlfriend, Nicola, who was a pop star he'd fallen for six months earlier, put her hand on Marcus's forearm just in time.

"Hey, gorgeous," Nicola teased, "I hear you own this joint."

Thank God Marcus was powerless to resist his stunning girlfriend, especially when she was going up on her toes to whisper something into his ear that had him dragging her off to a private corner of the porch and kissing her.

Sophie made a mental note to do something really nice for Nicola in the future as payback for that quick save. Maybe a new e-book reader with a hundred fantastic books preloaded on it for those long hours between tour stops?

Unfortunately, her brother Gabe was only a beat behind with his, "Why are you wearing all that makeup, Soph?"

Megan, who had become one of Sophie's closest friends after the two of them had reconnected a handful of months ago, shot Sophie a sympathetic look before moving into Gabe's line of vision.

"Summer needs help with her basket of flower petals. She's asking for you, Gabe."

Sophie's firefighter brother had fallen hard for her friend and her daughter after saving both of them from a deadly apartment fire several months ago. He didn't stand a chance of holding focus on whatever Sophie was up to when Megan's seven-year-old daughter needed him.

Too bad Ryan, Zach and Smith didn't have girl-friends on the porch to distract them.

Wearing his tux as well as he did his baseball uniform, Ryan looked between her and Lori. "You guys aren't going to do that twin-switch thing again, are you?"

Her brother Zach just looked plain confused. "Whatever is going on here, I don't want to know about it." But then he added with a fierce scowl, "Swear to God, Nice, if anyone even looks at you crosswise I'm going to pound his head into the dirt until he's fertilizer for Marcus's vines."

"What about if someone looks at me?" Lori asked, obviously trying to pull their brothers' attention away from her twin by acting affronted.

Zach rolled his eyes. "You can handle yourself," he retorted.

Hating the way everyone was acting, even if it wasn't exactly unexpected, Sophie said, "So can I."

"Like hell you can," Smith said.

Her second oldest brother, who had millions of fans around the world, had been watching her silently until then. Although they were about as different as two Sullivans could be—he thrived in the limelight and she wanted to stay as far from it as she could—she'd always been especially close to Smith. As long as she could remember, he'd been the one to make sure her voice was heard at the dinner table and that she was included in the older kids' games.

He took her hand. "Let's go practice our walk down the aisle, Soph."

She'd been so steamrolled by her brothers, she finally realized who was missing. "Where's Jake?"

"He had a last-second emergency with the drinks," Smith replied, and then, when they were on the other side of the porch, he said, "You look beautiful."

"Thank you." But she knew better than to think he'd pulled her away from the rest of their siblings just to compliment her.

"But I'm confused about the new makeup and hairstyle." If anyone knew about transforming into a brand-new character, it was Smith. Which was why he was even more suspicious than her other brothers. "What's going on?"

She swallowed hard. "I wanted to look pretty for the wedding."

"You were already pretty. Before—" He gestured to the hair, the makeup, the dress.

Her heart squeezed at the way her brother looked at her, as though she were a little girl he needed to keep saving. Didn't he see? This was exactly why she needed to do this. So that everyone would stop thinking of her as sweet little Nice.

Little did he realize—little did any of her brothers realize—that they were only feeding her resolve with their overprotectiveness.

A part of her desperately wanted to confide in Smith, to try and take some comfort from her big brother's strong arms. But she knew better. If she told him what she was doing, he'd likely lock her in the guesthouse until the wedding was over. And then he'd go tear Jake limb from limb.

Sophie wanted that pleasure all for herself, thank you very much.

"I'm walking down the aisle on a movie star's arm," she forced herself to say. "Who knows where this picture will end up?"

Unfortunately, Smith didn't even come close to believing her. "Since when did you care about any of that?"

Since never, she thought, but that was beside the point.

She leaned forward and wrapped her arms around him. "I'm so glad you're here. I've missed you while you've been away."

She felt his kiss on the top of her head. She hadn't had a father past the age of two, but she'd never felt as if her life had been empty. Not with so much love all around her, not with Smith and Marcus and Chase to hug her, not with Zach and

Ryan to tease her, not with Gabe and Lori to play and argue with.

"I missed you, too, Nice." Smith pulled back, looked at her again. She wondered why it didn't rankle when Smith used her nickname, but she wanted to deck Jake for saying it. "I just didn't expect to come home from Australia and see that you've changed."

"I'm still me," she insisted in a soft voice.

Only, the truth was, she was barely an hour into her "transformation" and things were already different. She'd never had conversations like this with her brothers, for one. And while she wasn't at all certain she'd ever try this particular look again, despite her worries over making a big fool out of herself in the slinky dress and towering heels, there was a part of her that liked the change. Heck, hadn't the waitress at her favorite Thai restaurant even said to her the last time she was there, "Ordering the same old thing?"

Sophie suddenly realized she'd gotten stuck in a rut. A *nice,* comfortable rut.

Footsteps coming toward them had Smith smoothing her hair back into place. "You really do look great, Soph. Different, but stunning." This time his words were accompanied by the brotherly pride that shone from his eyes. Of course, the concern was still there. "And if you need to talk to me about anything, anytime, I'm always here for you." He lifted her chin up with a finger so that he could look directly into her eyes. "You know that, don't you? That I'll come home from any set, anywhere in the world, if you need me."

She squeezed his hand, and was saved from starting to bawl her eyes out in her brother's arms by Ellen's arrival.

"Smith and Sophie, we need you with the rest of the group now." Fortunately, Ellen was in enough of a rush that she didn't see Sophie work to quickly compose herself. "Marcus and Lori will lead everyone off the porch and down the aisle and I'll give you the go-ahead when it's time for you to head down after them." She noted Sophie's heels and said, "Careful on the stairs. They've felled more than one bridesmaid, I'm afraid."

A few seconds later when Ellen gave them their signal and Smith shot her a wide smile, Sophie couldn't help but return it full force. She'd been looking forward to Chase's wedding for what felt like forever, and even though her family had freaked out a little, she knew she'd never looked better.

As they walked through the vines out to the rose-strewn aisle—with Smith keeping a firm grip on Sophie's arm to make sure she didn't fall face-first off the steps into a bush—she didn't have to fake her radiant smile.

Watch out, world, she thought, *Sophie Sullivan is about to cut loose.*

And, hopefully, Jake McCann wouldn't know what hit him.

Three

Jake gave a few last-minute instructions to the staff he'd brought in to work the wedding, then stepped out from behind the bar just as the string quartet started playing the wedding march. A cute little blonde girl skipped down the aisle, tossing flower petals into the air. Charmed, the crowd laughed and admired Summer, the daughter of Gabe's girlfriend. Marcus and Lori came next, the oldest Sullivan and one of the youngest. Lori took her place as one of the maids of honor and Marcus moved to the center in preparation for officiating the ceremony.

Yet again, Jake could hardly believe this day had come. There were a few things he'd always been sure of in life.

Beer always tasted better from the tap.

Ryan Sullivan's fastball could be counted on to take the Hawks to another World Series as long as he was on the pitcher's mound.

And the Sullivan boys weren't going to be heading to the altar anytime soon.

Ellen caught sight of him and frantically waved him over to his place by Brenda, the bridesmaid he'd be escorting. A staffing emergency at one of his pubs meant he hadn't been able to attend the rehearsal dinner, so he hadn't met her yet, but he hoped Chloe had good taste in friends. At this point, the only way he had even the slightest chance of working Sophie out of his system after a long day together at the wedding was to make sure he ended the night in bed with a woman who was her polar opposite.

He was almost to the bridesmaid when his heart—and his feet—stopped cold.

What the hell had Sophie done to herself?

Jake blinked to try to fix his vision as Sophie and Smith rounded a row of vines and continued walking down the aisle. When he was still seeing things a few seconds later—crazy, insane things— he ran a hand over his eyes.

But nothing changed the fact that Sophie was looking like walking sex in a silky pink dress and high heels. She sure wasn't wearing the jeans and baseball cap anymore. But the dress wasn't the only thing different about her. What had she done to her hair? And why did her eyes look so big, her mouth so red?

His body reacted to the shockingly sensual picture of her before he could stop it, all of the blood that was supposed to feed a brain that knew not to *ever* look at Sophie Sullivan like that—especially in front of all six of her brothers—shooting south.

Ellen's hand at his elbow jolted him. "It's almost your turn to head up the aisle, Jake."

He heard what she said, knew he needed to join the rest of the group, but even as he held out his arm for Chloe's friend, he couldn't take his eyes off Sophie.

The view from the back didn't help his current problem, damn it. Sophie Sullivan had a perfect ass and right then she was showcasing it to three hundred people in that dress that slipped and slid over her curves so tightly he knew she couldn't possibly be wearing anything under it.

An urge to drag her away from the wedding, away from all those hungry male eyes drinking her in, to make her change back into her normal clothes—clothes that covered her up the way she should be covered!—came so fast, Jake was hard-pressed to ignore it. He couldn't stand knowing dozens of guys in the audience were drooling right now, even the ones who were married and had no business thinking those kinds of thoughts about little Sophie Sullivan.

Although…she didn't exactly look young and innocent, didn't seem quite so untouchable anymore, did she?

Ellen said his name again—this time a little louder—and he took it as his cue to start walking down the aisle. Gabe and Megan, who were in front of him, impeded his view of Sophie for a few seconds and he had to crane his neck to keep his eye on her as she took her place beside Lori beneath the rose-covered arches.

A moment later, Sophie looked up and caught him staring at her. Jake tried to look away.

And failed.

The woman on his arm had to tug him to keep his feet moving in the right direction. The last thing Jake saw before taking his place beside Gabe in the lineup was Sophie's soft mouth turned up into a sensual, utterly feminine smile.

Sophie had always loved weddings and, despite her nerves, she couldn't help but get caught up in the romance of it all. Of course, Sullivan Winery was quite possibly the most glorious wedding venue she'd ever seen. The budding leaves on the vines, the mustard flowers blooming in every free patch of soil, the rolling hills, the bright blue sky above, the masses of flowers in pots and displays at the end of every row of seats—these were all breathtaking additions to the celebration of love between Chase and Chloe.

Marcus was doing such a beautiful job officiating Chase's wedding. She was so glad he'd agreed to do it and one day, when she got married, she hoped it would be Marcus standing up in front of her and her groom, too.

Sophie could tell her oldest brother was as choked up as the rest of them, but his voice was steady and solid as he asked Chase and Chloe if they would love, honor and comfort each other.

She had to reach for Lori's hand and hold it tight as she waited for that perfect moment when her brother declared his love to his bride. It felt as if the entire world stood still as Chase turned to Chloe and smiled at her. Sophie's chest squeezed tight at the undying love radiating out from her brother to his bride.

What, Sophie wondered, would it feel like to have a man look at her like that? As if she was absolutely everything to him?

Chase said, "I will love you forever, Chloe,"

and a soft sigh left Sophie's lips as a tear slipped down her cheek. A few moments later, as Chloe made the same vow to Chase, more tears fell down Sophie's cheeks, one after the other. And as Marcus pronounced them husband and wife, everyone cheered, but none louder than quiet Sophie Sullivan.

Jake had never cared much for weddings. As far as he was concerned, they took up too much of a perfectly good weekend and were a waste of hard-earned money. Especially given that at least half of the unions ended in divorce.

For some reason, though, this wedding was different. He'd spent enough time with Chase and Chloe to think they actually had a shot at making this thing work. With that kid in her belly, he sure hoped it would.

Not, of course, that he was paying much attention to the actual wedding taking place...because he couldn't take his eyes off the groom's sister.

When Sophie walked up the aisle, he'd been struck stupid at how sexy she was in that dress. He almost hadn't recognized her as the sweet Sullivan who was always hanging around his heels when they were kids. But then, as he'd watched her during the ceremony, she'd transformed again.

Still ridiculously sexy, but sweet again, her eyes big as she listened to the vows, leaning in toward the bride and groom as if she wanted to become a part of their happiness. And in that moment when she'd reached out to grab Lori's hand, he'd had a split second of wishing it had been him she was grabbing for instead.

And that he could be the one to hold her.

Jake felt as if someone had reached a fist into his chest, grabbed hold of his heart and squeezed until it was nothing more than a messy pile of blood and veins. He'd never be able to erase the memory of the hope, the longing and the love in Sophie's eyes as she watched Chase and Chloe pledge their love to each other.

Before he knew it the ceremony was over, the guests were clapping and the happy couple was walking back down the aisle together while the string quartet played a classic Italian love song that harkened back to their mother's roots. Sophie took Smith's arm and walked down the aisle, her perfect little backside swaying in time to the music.

Jake was suddenly pulled from his reverie when he heard his name being called. "Earth to Jake," Gabe said, elbowing him in the ribs. "Wedding's over. Time to go eat cake."

Four

There was only one sure cure for Jake's sudden bout of insanity. He'd tend the bar...and then he'd find himself a willing single woman who didn't have anything to do with the Sullivan family. And he was going to steer completely clear of Sophie for the rest of the wedding. A little distance from all those soft curves and those plump red lips would help him get his head back on straight.

"I've got this," he told Sammy, one of his best bartenders who worked at the original McCann's in the city. "You can circulate with the trays."

Fortunately, the wedding guests were thirsty, clearly wanting some vino or hops to begin celebrating. Pouring drinks for strangers was as natural to Jake as breathing, and he immediately got into a rhythm in the middle of the vineyard as the meal was served and people kept a running line behind the bar between courses. He couldn't remember a time he hadn't been drying clean glasses, rearranging bottles. As a kid, when his dad had been the one running the taps, Jake had been in the back loading and unloading the dishwasher for a few extra bucks while the cooks at whatever pub they were at slung together plates of fish and chips and colcannon.

When the female guests flirted with him at the bar, he flirted back. So what if none of them were even half as pretty as Sophie? The Sullivans might be pairing up one after the other as if they'd been infected by the same virus, but Jake had had his shots.

Love wasn't going to take him down.

He knew better than to think that love meant a damn thing when the going got rough and it was easier to split. No wife, no kids, plenty of pretty women, but no rings, was what Jake's future held. He'd play with all the kids the Sullivan clan was bound to pump out, would enjoy being Uncle Jake, but he wouldn't make the mistake of thinking he'd ever be a good husband or father.

McCanns didn't come with those genes. He knew it for a fact since his father had been nothing but a worthless drunk, and had come from a long line of them back in Ireland.

"You haven't had anything to eat yet."

The slightly husky female voice reached out and grabbed him a split second before he looked straight into Sophie's eyes. Her soft sensuality in that pink dress and the sweet smell of her perfume were a one-two punch straight to a gut that hadn't yet recovered from watching those tears slip down her cheeks, or the radiant smile that had followed.

Without waiting for an invitation, she put a full plate on the back table for him and moved around the bar to stand next to him. "Scoot over. I'll help out while you eat." She bumped her hip into his, causing him to become rock-hard in an instant, his body not giving a damn that she was Off-Limits.

How could her brothers have let her out looking like this? What were they thinking? Didn't they care even a little bit about their sister's welfare?

He thanked her for the food in a gruff voice, and then while he was standing there losing his mind over her, Sophie took drink orders and deftly poured glasses of wine and mixed drinks for the wedding guests. She was a librarian, not a bartender. She shouldn't be so good at serving drinks.

And no librarian should ever be this hot, either, Jake thought as he clamped his jaw so tight his temple started throbbing. He'd let her help for five minutes, and then he'd send her back to her table to celebrate with the rest of her family and make sure she stayed there for the rest of the reception.

Even if he had to tie her to her seat.

The beer bottle nearly slipped from his grip as Jake was hit with a crystal-clear vision of Sophie tied to his bed, naked and begging for him to touch, to taste, to—

"I hear you're a librarian," a male voice said to her. "Read any good books lately?"

Jake surfaced from his triple-X daydream just in time to notice a guest leaning on the bar and looking down the top of Sophie's dress.

She didn't seem to notice any of that as she smiled back at the guy. She was too innocent to realize when a guy like this was aiming for one thing and one thing only: to get into her panties.

Panties Jake was almost certain she wasn't even wearing.

"Mmm," she said in that seductive voice, still slightly hoarse from her tears during the ceremony. Of course, Jake could barely remember Chase and Chloe's vows as he was slammed with another crazy vision of Sophie lying naked beneath him, crying out his name again and again until her voice gave out altogether.

Completely unaware of what Jake was doing to her in his mind, Sophie replied to the guest, "I'm always reading great books." Her smile was utterly beautiful. Too beautiful for Jake to keep trying to ignore as she continued the conversation asking, "What do you like to read?"

The guy shrugged, not seeming to care that there was a huge backup of thirsty people bottle-necking behind him. "I'm a doct—"

"What are you drinking?" Jake broke in.

The guy shot him a look that said, *Can't you see I'm about to score here?*

"Corona," he said to Jake before turning back to Sophie's phenomenal breasts, and then, several beats later, he finally refocused on her face. "As I was saying, I'm a doctor, so I don't have too much time to read. But when I do, I usually read thrill-ers. Medical thrillers, to be more specific."

Jake couldn't believe it when Sophie leaned over the bar and said, "Oooh, how exciting. Medical thrillers always leave me breathless."

Didn't she get that this loser was way beneath her? And that he'd found a way to brag about being a doctor within thirty seconds of meeting her? She should be throwing a drink in his face, not giving him a better view of her perfect body as she leaned down to grab a bottle of beer. Dr. Dickwad looked like he'd hit a home run, was counting the minutes until he could strip that dress from her tanned skin and find out if she tasted as good as she smelled.

Like hell. Jake would kill him first.

Jake snatched the bottle from her hand and shoved it at the guy. "Here's your beer. Time to let everyone else get a drink."

He could feel Sophie frowning at him as he pinned the guy with his hardest look. If she couldn't pick good from bad, he was going to have to save her. Whether she wanted him to or not was irrelevant.

Although the guy flinched at Jake's silent promise of violence, it didn't stop him from saying, "Be sure to save a dance for me, gorgeous," before he walked away.

Jake held on to his control by a very thin thread. Nothing would feel better than to jump over the bar and tackle the guy to teach him what happened when he flirted with the wrong girl. A girl who was too sweet, too pretty, too damn perfect, for him to even think of touching one hair on her head.

"You're not dancing with him," he growled. "Not tonight. Not ever."

Sophie's eyes widened slightly at his pronouncement before she tilted her chin up and told

him, "I'm a big girl, Jake. I'll dance with whomever I want."

Serving the customer always took priority. But
not this time. Turning his back on the crowd still
in line, he slid between Sophie and the bar, then
forgot his rule about not touching her as he put
his hands on her shoulders and gripped her hard.

"No. You won't. He's not good enough for you."

Fire flashed in her eyes, but her voice was soft
as she said, "It's so sweet of you to be concerned,
Jake. But I can take care of myself."

Rationally he knew she was right, that she'd
done a great job of taking care of herself for
twenty-five years. But he couldn't get the picture
out of his head of Dr. Dickwad's hands on her
curves, his smarmy mouth on hers.

Still, one thing remained irrevocably true. "Your
brothers would kill me if anything happened to
you." They'd also kill him if they ever suspected
the way he was thinking about her.

"Actually," she said as she looked over his
shoulder, "I think my brother's guests might kill
both of us if we don't keep serving them drinks."

He wanted to grab her tighter, pull her closer,
find out if the rest of her skin felt as soft, as perfect, as her shoulders had beneath his palms. Instead, very reluctantly, Jake removed his hands

from her bare skin and shifted back into position. But even though he didn't spill a drop and his fingers didn't slip on any more bottles, his attention was wholly focused on Sophie. Which was why he saw her shoot a glance at the a-hole who had been flirting with her just before saying, "I think he looks perfectly harmless. In fact…"

Jake tossed an empty bottle into the bin beneath the bar with a loud crash. "In fact what?"

"Since you don't want to help me out with my plan to make my ex jealous, maybe I should use that guy instead."

"Sammy," Jake called out across the reception area, motioning for his employee to take over the bar again. He didn't wait for Sam to make it to the bar before wrapping his hand around Sophie's wrist and pulling her out from behind the bar. He didn't stop walking until they were hidden behind a large storage shed, just on the edge of the reception area.

When he turned to face her, her face was flushed and he thought she looked as beautiful as he'd ever seen her. The shock of being this close to all that beauty, and to her sleek and soft curves in the pink dress, had him barking out one short word at her.

"No."

She tossed her hair over her shoulder as she informed him in a sassy voice, "There are thousands of other words in the English language other than *no,* you know."

He ignored her sarcasm and told her flat out, "You are not getting within a hundred feet of that guy again."

She looked down at his hand where it was still clamped around her wrist and tried to yank her arm from him, but he held fast. Anger flared in her eyes. Eyes that had been full of happy tears, full of pure joy, just a short while ago.

"You can't tell me what to do."

"Like hell I can't."

This time she managed to yank her arm away from him, but when she started to walk away, he couldn't let her go. Not when she was bound to do something stupid, like kiss a smarmy doctor. And maybe even offer him her body, those sweet curves slipping and sliding beneath him as she gave herself to him.

Furious at the picture of anyone touching Sophie like that, instead of just grabbing her wrist or her shoulders, this time Jake wrapped his arms all the way around her and pulled her into him. He held her tight, her chest pushing into his forearms, her height matching his so that her hips fit perfectly between his open legs, her soft hips pressing into his groin.

God, she felt so good. So perfect. Like she was meant to be his.

"Let go of me," she said from between clenched teeth.

"No."

His new favorite word was muffled by her hair, so soft, so silky, against his chin and lips. And the truth was, he couldn't have let go of her for the world. Not just because he didn't want that other guy touching her...but because he'd never wanted to hold anyone more than he did Sophie.

How long had he dreamed of holding her? Too many years to keep count. And yet, he'd never had a clue just how incredibly good she would feel in his arms, her dangerous curves pressed into him, her chest rising and falling against his arms.

"I'm not going to let you go until you promise me you'll stay away from him."

Now it was her turn to say, "No."

He shifted his hand enough to slip a finger beneath her chin and turn her face so that he could look into her eyes. "Promise me, Sophie. It's for your own good."

Sophie yanked her face away from his hand, then her whole body, and when she turned to face him head-on, her eyes were flashing. "I can't be-lieve *you* just said that! Especially since you of all people have *no idea whatsoever* what's good for me."

"Wanna bet?"

In an instant Jake had pulled her back into his arms so that her breasts were pressed up against his chest, his mouth on hers before he could put the brakes on his desire. He was too angry, too frus-trated with himself for wanting her this much—and her infuriating stubbornness—to be gentle.

Lips weren't enough. He needed to feel her tongue slick against his. He needed to slide one hand into her hair to tilt her head at just the right angle to take what she'd been about to offer some other worthless guy. He needed to grip the lus-cious curve of her hips with his other hand to drag her in closer.

Somewhere in the back of his brain, he knew he was moving too fast for her to possibly enjoy the kiss, let alone keep up with him. But even though she should have been fighting him, her arms had slid up to twine around his neck and she was moaning softly against his mouth as her tongue pressed out to slide against his.

Sweet Lord, Sophie was everything he'd ever wanted in a woman. Her scent, her taste, the feel of her. He'd wanted to touch her for so long that now that the impossible was finally happening, he couldn't stop his hand from creeping up from her hip to her waist, to the bottom of her rib cage and then—*holy hell, she felt good*—the curve of one breast in his palm.

She gasped into his mouth, shivering with pleasure as his thumb crested the aroused tip, and Jake knew he was barely a breath away from lowering her to the grass and pulling her dress up her long legs, until he could touch and lick and—

What the hell was he doing?

Knowing Sophie didn't stand a chance of fighting off a guy like him if he put her in his sights, his gut churned with self-hatred as he abruptly released her, so quickly that she stumbled back in her heels.

Even though he knew better than to ever touch her again, he couldn't let her fall. As soon as he knew she was steady on her feet, he forced himself to let go, the need to pull her back into his arms so strong it felt as if it was clawing at his insides.

Sophie's mouth was swollen from his rough kiss, her cheeks were flaming and her eyes were shining with what he assumed were budding tears. He expected her to slap him, or at the very least to turn and run to her brothers to tell them what had just happened.

So that they could kill him.

Which was exactly what he deserved for daring to kiss those too-sweet lips.

But she didn't run. And she wasn't crying. Instead, she stood in front of him looking more beautiful than she ever had before. One part vulnerable, the other part stunned.

"No one has ever kissed me like that," she said in a breathless voice, "like you couldn't get enough, like you couldn't stop yourself and I was driving you crazy." She stared at him, her blue eyes filled with amazement. And desire. "All these years and I never knew it would be like that."

Jesus, it was hot when she replayed their kiss like that. But his chest twisted at the way she was acting—like he hadn't been mauling her, like he hadn't been seconds away from ripping her dress off and taking something from her she should never, ever give a guy like him. After all these years, she was still enough of a romantic to have made him out to be something other than the bastard he really was.

Jake knew the truth. He came from a long line of bastards.

"Sophie," he said in low, remorseful voice. "I

never should have kissed you. Especially not like that."

He'd been a crazed man without any self-control at all. A few more seconds and she would have been beneath him on the grass, her pretty dress hiked up around her hips and pulled down beneath her breasts, getting wrinkled and stained with grass smears while he took her without caring what he was ruining. Not just her dress, but *her*.

If he'd done that to her, if he'd marked her with his out-of-control lust, he wouldn't have waited for her brothers to kill him.

He would have done the job himself, with pleasure.

She'd tried to run from him earlier. This time when she turned from him, he'd make himself let her go.

Only, instead of making any move to get away from him, she was moving closer as she said, "We were both part of what happened." Her voice was soft, but surprisingly firm. Her eyes were clear and steady on his as she surprised the hell out of him, yet again, by actually saying the words, "I've wanted you to kiss me for a long time. A very long time."

As she took another one of those deep breaths that had her almost popping out of her dress, Jake knew this was the universe paying him back for every bad thing he'd ever done. He felt as if his collar was too tight, even though it was unbuttoned and he wasn't wearing his tie anymore.

She moved even closer. Too close. But he couldn't make himself back away from her. Not when every last cell in his body wanted to erase the distance and go back to that place where she was finally in his arms.

Perfect. She'd felt so perfect.

"Sophie," he said in a voice made raw by desire and his unsuccessful attempts to shove it down, "don't—"

Her hand pressed flat onto his chest, right over the heart that was nearly leaping from it, made him lose track of what he'd been about to tell her, that she couldn't talk about wanting to kiss him. Because they were completely off-limits for each other. Always had been, and always would be.

Her eyelids closed for a moment, almost as if she were counting the beats of his heart, before she opened them again and said, "My brothers were losing it before the wedding when they saw me." Jake couldn't help but be impressed by her courage as she gestured to her dress, her hair, her face, with the hand that wasn't touching him. "They kept asking me what was going on and I told them it was nothing. I told them all I wanted was to have fun with the hairdresser and makeup artist. But I was lying to them." She looked him straight in the eye. "I did it for you, Jake. To see if I could finally get you to notice that I was alive. To let you see that I'm not a little girl anymore with a silly crush. That I'm a woman and a person who knows her own mind. Who knows exactly what she wants. *And who.*"

Jake didn't have any experience with this kind of honesty, with a woman opening up her heart to him like this and laying it at his feet. He could run a business worth millions. He could pilot a seventy-foot yacht through rough waters after three sleepless nights. But he couldn't keep up with the beautiful girl standing in front of him.

He knew his limits, knew that despite the success he'd had with his pubs, he was still just the dumb son of a bartender. Sophie deserved better. She belonged with a guy who had as many college degrees as she did. One day, Jake knew, he'd be here at her wedding, watching her walk down the aisle, even though the vision of Sophie in another man's arms—in another man's bed—had him seeing red.

Hadn't he known better than to let her get too close?

"The dress, the makeup, they look great, Nice." He purposefully used her nickname, wanting her to remember who he was to her. "But they don't change the fact that you're going to have plenty of crushes on guys before you find the one who's right for you."

Something flared in her eyes, a look he'd seen flashes of over the past few months. "Do you really think so?" She ran her tongue over her full bottom lip and his blood pressure spiked another ten points. He could have sworn she was purposefully screwing with him when she leaned a little closer and said, "Do you really think I'm going to feel that way again kissing some other guy?"

Didn't she realize there was nothing she could have said that would have gotten to him more? He couldn't have her, but damn it, there wasn't another man alive who was good enough for her, either. The thought of anyone else kissing her the way he had—the thought of her actively going out there to look for that kind of treatment—made him want to lock her up in a tower.

There was no way she could still be a virgin at twenty-five. But Jake still felt as if he'd taken something from her with that rough kiss. That he'd dirtied up her innocence by shoving his tongue in her mouth and putting his hands on her.

He couldn't argue with her about the kiss. Not when he was damned sure there'd never be one as hot…or as sweet. So he told her the truth instead.

"You deserve better." And yet, he couldn't seem to make himself step away from her.

Sophie cocked her head to the side and frowned at him just as Lori hurried around the corner of the shed.

"There you are, Soph! I've been looking everywhere for you."

Lori skidded to a stop when she realized her twin wasn't alone.

"Jake? What are you doing with—" Sophie's sister didn't finish her question as she frowned, looking between the two of them.

There was no way Lori could miss the fact that Sophie was standing really, really close to him with her hand still pressed to his chest, and her mouth swollen from his rough kisses.

The Sullivan boys were definitely going to tear him apart with their bare hands for this.

But Lori? Jake knew damn well that her punishment was going to be even worse to make him pay for kissing her twin. She and Sophie had always been so close, two halves of a whole, whether they wanted to admit it or not. Lori would protect Sophie with everything she had. And if she thought

Jake was a threat to her twin, she wouldn't care that they were friends. She would tear him limb from limb first, and ask questions later.

"The speeches are about to start," Lori informed them both. "Everyone is wondering where you are, Soph, especially Ellen." She pinned Jake with a look so sharp it could have sliced right through him. "And you, too."

"Okay," Sophie said in an overly bright voice. "Thanks for letting us know. We'll be there in just a minute."

But instead of leaving them alone, Lori put her hand around Sophie's forearm and pulled her away from Jake. "You can't go back looking like this." She ran her hands through Sophie's hair, fixing the mess Jake had made of it when he was pawing her. She brushed off a smudge of lipstick at the corner of her sister's mouth, and shifted the dress an inch to the right. "That's better. And, seriously, you should get back there before Ellen has a heart attack thinking some unruly loser of a guest was stupid enough to pull you off into the vines."

Sophie was silent for a moment. "You're right. I don't want anything to fall through the cracks today. It wouldn't be fair to Chase and Chloe."

"I'll be there in a sec," Lori said. "I need to talk to Jake about something."

"He kissed me, which you've clearly already figured out," Sophie told her sister, her expression stubborn as she faced Lori. "Now you two don't have to talk about it because I've told you everything that happened. Let's go." She grabbed her sister's hand and made sure they walked together past the shed.

Yet again, Jake was impressed with Sophie. Lori had a will strong enough to push most people around. He'd always assumed Sophie was the beta to her sister's alpha.

Had he gotten it wrong all these years? Had he made the mistake of underestimating Sophie just because she didn't feel the need to be the center of attention like the rest of them?

"Oh, no!" Sophie exclaimed. "That little boy is about to knock over the chocolate Eiffel Tower." She quickly moved toward the long food table and the hungry boy, leaving Jake alone with Lori.

He was a dead man.

"What the hell was going on back there?" Lori narrowed her eyes and snarled, "What were you doing to my sister?"

Jake wished he knew. One moment he'd been trying to protect Sophie from some worthless wedding guest who only wanted her in his bed...the next she'd been in his arms and he'd been kissing her as if his life depended on it. Nothing had ever felt more right.

Or had been so wrong.

Lori took a step closer and he had to fight the urge to take a step back in retreat. "If you hurt my sister, I will hunt you down and take great pleasure in hurting you. Badly." She smiled at him, a turning up of the lips that promised a great deal of future pain should he ever screw up again where Sophie was concerned. "And you'd better believe that I'll keep you alive just so that I can send my brothers in to finish you off." She cleared the expression of fury from her face before saying, "Now walk me back to my table and make it look believable that you and I were off getting into our usual trouble."

She slid her hand into the crook of his arm and pinched him hard, just in case he needed a reminder that tangling with Sophie was where the real trouble was.

Bigger trouble than any a screwup like him had ever been in before.

Five

After righting the fondue tower in the nick of time, and pointing the little boy toward a bowl of Hershey's Kisses, Sophie went to wash her hands and to take a few extra moments to compose herself. She put her hand on her belly as butterflies flew at the memory of how deliciously sensual she'd felt in Jake's arms. He was even yummier, even more dangerous, even more potent, than she'd dreamed he'd be.

If only Lori hadn't come searching for them, then maybe Sophie could have gotten past Jake's all-too-clear remorse. "You deserve better," was what he'd said to her just after the sweetness of his kiss had shot straight past her heart, all the way to her soul. At the very least, she wished she'd had time to convince him that his guilt and remorse were both misplaced.

She'd wanted that kiss just as much as he had. And they were two full-grown adults who could kiss whomever they wanted.

In any case, for the next few hours, she needed to push Jake's kiss to the back of her mind and concentrate her attention where it should be: on making sure Chase and Chloe's wedding was absolutely perfect. Later, she'd relive those moments when all her dreams came true, when she'd been in Jake's arms and it felt like the sun was never going to stop shining, and it seemed utterly impossible that he might not actually want her beyond that kiss.

She let the guests' laughter warm her before she headed to the big round table she was sharing with her siblings and their significant others. Noting that her mother, who was sitting with her close friends, had a worried look on her face, Sophie made sure to stop by her seat.

Mary Sullivan was dressed in a beautiful floor-length lace-and-silk dress in a soft coral that perfectly set off her coloring, and Sophie stopped and stared at her mother for a few moments. She knew her mom had been a model before marrying their father and having eight kids, but sometimes Sophie forgot just how pretty she was. Not just pretty, but glamorous, too. No one believed her mother was in her seventies, and Sophie hoped she'd look half as good when she was the same age. Clearly, Sophie noted as she looked around and saw half a dozen gray-haired gentlemen appreciating her mother's beauty, she wasn't the only one who had noticed just how attractive the mother of the groom was. Funny, though, she couldn't remember her mother ever dating anyone.

"It was a beautiful wedding, wasn't it, Mom?"

"It was," her mother agreed. "You are a natural at wedding planning. Everyone can't stop talking about all of the perfect little details you thought of to celebrate Chase and Chloe." But Mary Sullivan was too perceptive as she added, "Jake was your perfect partner, it seems."

Sophie's eyes widened at what her mother had just said. She knew there was no way that she could know what had just happened with Jake—and that *perfect* had been the exact word for it—but somehow her mother's comment was incredibly on point, nonetheless.

She worked to keep her voice easy as she said, "He's doing a great job with the bar setup and service. In fact, I should probably get back to—"

Her mother stopped her with a soft hand on her arm. "You've done enough work already, Sophie. Have some fun."

"I am," she told her mother. And she was.

Because kissing Jake McCann was the most fun she'd ever had in her life.

Lori and Jake walked by just then, arm in arm, Lori laughing at something he'd said, then punching him in the shoulder, hard enough that Sophie was fairly certain he was hiding a wince of pain behind his smile.

"I want Jake to celebrate with the rest of us," Mary said, "not feel like he needs to work during Chase and Chloe's wedding. He's family."

Her mother had never asked her about her feelings for Jake, but Sophie had never been able to hide anything from her. Especially not now, when she was feeling more than she ever had for the man who had stolen her heart when she'd been a little girl, and had taken more of it every year that passed.

"I know how much you love to dance at weddings, and Jake is the perfect height to be your partner," Mary Sullivan suggested before kissing her daughter's cheek.

Sophie felt her eyes grow wet. Of course, at no point had her mother commented on her makeup, her hair or the dress the way Sophie's brothers had. She'd simply seen beneath everything on the outside straight to what was going on inside.

"I love you, Mom."

"I love you, too, sweetheart." Mary Sullivan kissed her again. "Now, be sure to tell your brothers to keep those speeches clean."

Budding tears gave way to laughter as Sophie said, "Would it be bad if I told Zach and Ryan they're needed on the other side of town instead?"

Her mother laughed with her at the idea that her brothers would even think about staying in line when given the chance to say something shocking about Chase in front of such a large crowd.

Sophie quickly stopped by Chase and Chloe's seats. "Is everything going okay so far?"

Chloe hugged her tight. "It's the most beautiful wedding in the world. I can hardly believe it's mine."

"Thanks, sis," Chase said. "You're one heck of a wedding planner."

Sophie didn't bother to hide her wide grin. She adored Chloe and was beyond thrilled for Chase. "If it's okay with both of you, I think we should get rolling on the speeches."

After they agreed, Sophie walked up to the table where her brothers and sister were waiting. Before anyone could ask her where she'd been for the past half hour, she gave the microphone to Marcus. "We're going to start the speeches now. You're first. When you're finished just pass the mic to the next oldest. Jake will go after the boys, then Lori and I will go last."

Smith was frowning as he looked between her and Jake. She'd known her family was going to be watching her very carefully when she walked back into the reception area, and that even the slightest indication that something had happened to her would send all six of her brothers on a rampage. Especially given her new look for the wedding. She knew they were already suspicious that something was going on. She took her seat and flashed a bright smile at Smith, thankful when Marcus stood up and all eyes turned to him.

"This is a big day for the Sullivans."

The guests immediately stopped talking and focused their attention on Marcus. The oldest of all the Sullivans, he'd stepped in to help take care of his seven younger siblings at fourteen when their father passed away. He was the one they all automatically looked up to, and Sophie was beyond pleased that he'd finally found love of his own with Nicola. Together, they were splitting their time between Marcus's winery in Napa Valley and Nicola's tour bus as she put on pop concerts around the world.

"I'm sure there are some who thought the day would never come when one of us would say, 'I do.'"

As the crowd laughed at his on-point observation, Sophie worked like crazy not to stare at Jake, who was seated next to Lori at the far end of the large table.

"Now that it has, I know there isn't a single one of us who is surprised." Marcus turned from the crowd to face Chase and Chloe. "Chloe, if I had tried, I couldn't have found a partner more perfect for my brother." The bride's eyes were already filling with tears as her new husband threaded his fingers through hers. "Chase, I'm as happy for you as I've ever been. And so damn proud. Our father was one of the best men I've ever known and you've always reminded me so much of him. He would be as proud of you, Chase, and he would love you, Chloe, as much as the rest of us do."

Marcus's strong voice broke slightly on the last word and he looked up toward the sky and paused like that for a few long moments. Sophie could hear sniffles throughout the reception area. Out of the corner of her eye, she could see her mother beginning to cry, but Sophie knew if she actually looked at Mary, she'd dissolve into a wet puddle, too. Smith gripped Sophie's hand hard and she squeezed back with all her strength, the two of them holding on to each other as Marcus continued.

"One other thing I'm absolutely sure of—" Marcus paused again to smile at Chase and Chloe, and turned to briefly look at each of his brothers and sisters, before focusing on his mother "—is that he's here with all of us today."

Marcus was holding his hand over his heart by now and Sophie knew why. That place was exactly where they all held the memories of their father. He'd passed away when she was only two, but she'd heard so many stories about him over the years, and had each of his pictures memorized, that she felt she could remember him just as well as any of her older siblings.

"We can't wait to meet the first of the next generation of Sullivans," Marcus concluded.

Then the applause started and everyone got to their feet to toast not only Chase and Chloe, but also the baby growing inside of the beautiful bride. Chase's hand rested possessively over his wife's gently rounded stomach as he kissed Chloe, and Sophie leaned into Smith's shoulder as she whispered, "They're so beautiful together, aren't they?"

Smith kissed her forehead, then said, "They really are, Soph. He did good."

A moment later, Smith took the mic from Marcus. As he stood up, everyone let out a collective gasp. It wasn't just that he was an incredibly famous movie star. Smith had always had a huge presence, had always been mesmerizing, especially when he was decked out in a black tux with tails. Even when he'd been a teenager, all he had to do was walk into a room and every eye would be on him. Not because he was a show-off, but because he had an unstoppable charisma and charm. Fortunately, he was also a truly good man. Sophie was sure every woman at the wedding—taken or not—was dreaming about what it would be like to have Smith Sullivan give her a second glance.

"My brothers and sisters like to tell me I live in a world of make-believe," Smith said in the voice that a billion people around the globe could have recognized with their eyes closed. "I don't know what they're talking about. My life is perfectly normal."

Laughter rolled through the crowd as Ryan and Gabe shook their heads as theatrically as possible.

"One thing we can all agree on," Smith continued when the laughter subsided, "is that there's nothing imaginary about the love between Chase and Chloe."

Oh, my. Sophie knew her big brothers could be big softies. But had any of them ever let anyone but the family see just how sweet they could be before? Especially Smith, who had to guard himself from the pressures of fame and from strangers who thought they knew the real man when they definitely didn't.

And yet, in this moment, for the brother he loved, Smith was pure emotion. If he was willing to risk baring his soul for a few moments like this, Sophie knew she didn't have a prayer of being anything but a big old splashy puddle by the time the microphone landed in her hand.

Smith raised his glass. "To your forever."

Everyone clinked their glasses as Smith toasted the bride and groom and Chase nodded at his brother with a big grin in acknowledgment of the beautiful wish he'd just made for them.

Ryan was next as he took the microphone from Smith and stood up. Any of the women who hadn't just lost their hearts to Smith would have been hard-pressed not to give it up to the pro baseball player. Sophie couldn't think of the last time she'd seen Ryan or Zach in a tux. Both of them had complained when she'd informed them that that was what they were going to wear as groomsmen. Knowing her brothers and the way they charmed absolutely any woman they came into contact with, Sophie made sure to let the rental company know she'd be extremely upset if they caved and gave her brothers alternatives to the tuxes.

And she'd been right to hold firm. All of her brothers looked absolutely fantastic. Sophie shot a glance at Lori, silently acknowledging that the two of them didn't look half-bad, either. Their mother, Mary, was pure elegance, of course.

"Guys like me tend to look at life as a game."

Sophie could see how much the crowd loved Ryan's easy manner. He'd always been the most relaxed and easygoing of them all. On the baseball field he took no prisoners, but even then, he made it all look so easy. So effortless. It was the same now, as he surveyed the guests with a lazy appreciation.

"It helps if early on you realize that some games are gonna go better than others." Ryan shrugged. "A year ago, if you'd asked me for my thoughts on the game of love, I would have told you to ask some other sap."

Surprised laughter burst from the crowd and Sophie had to shake her head and roll her eyes at Ryan, before catching her mother's gaze and grinning. They'd predicted just this, hadn't they? It was nice to know there were some things you could count on, she thought with a grin that she didn't bother repressing.

"But I've watched my brother and his bride pretty closely since they first found each other and, even for a guy like me, there's no denying that if life is a game, I'm betting on their chances at taking home the pennant." He lifted his glass to Chase and Chloe. "To both of you."

Sophie couldn't believe Ryan had actually made her tear up. He was supposed to be the comic relief. Fortunately, Zach was up next. He'd practically been born with a wrench in his hand and he'd turned his love of classic cars and racing into an enormously successful chain of Sullivan Auto stores.

Zach grinned as he took center stage, knowing darn well that none of the women in the reception could even remember Smith's or Ryan's names anymore. How many times had one of Sophie's girlfriends told her they'd never seen anyone as gorgeous as Zach? She was certain plenty of flat tires had been faked on his behalf, if only for the chance to get close to him for a few minutes. All of her brothers were good-looking, but Zach pulled together the very best features of their mother and father into one shockingly handsome package.

Her brother could be utterly insufferable and arrogant. Yes, at times, Sophie had to admit Zach was pretty darn close to being the dictionary definition of both those words. Still, despite his endless teasing, she couldn't help but love him.

"Let this be a lesson to all of you who aren't keeping up with your auto maintenance," Zach said to the group. "Flat tires and totaled cars can lead straight to something truly shocking." He paused for effect, then lowered his voice and said, "Marriage."

The guests all laughed, but even though Sophie was on the verge of laughing, too, she made herself shoot her brother a hard look. Noting it, he grinned unrepentantly at her before turning to the bride and groom.

"But seriously, this is a great day and I couldn't have picked a better girl for my brother. To Chloe, for being brave enough to take the plunge with a Sullivan." Zach raised his glass and everyone followed.

Gabe pretended to tackle Zach as he pulled the microphone from his hand, but he instantly sobered as he turned to Chase and Chloe. "All my life I've looked up to you, Chase. But never more than today, when you had the courage to make vows of forever with Chloe."

Trust Gabe to get right to the heart of it. Her firefighter brother had always lived a life of risk and bravery. Just a few months ago he'd finally found his own true love in Megan and her daughter, Summer, two hearts and souls that were just as brave as his.

"Just as you've always been there for me, I want you both to know that I'm here for you. Anything you need, anytime, don't hesitate to ask. Because I'll move heaven and earth to make sure that it's yours."

Chloe blew Gabe a kiss as everyone applauded. Sophie felt bad for the men in the audience whose wives were now looking at them with new— higher—expectations after hearing from the firefighter.

Sophie had been trying to prepare herself for the moment when Jake took the microphone to make his toast. She told herself not to stare at him for too long, but not to look away too many times, either. She needed to behave like everyone else in the audience…rather than like someone who was hopelessly, irrevocably, in love with the man standing before them.

"I was ten years old when I first met Chase

Sullivan. I was in his backyard, and I told myself I didn't want to be there any more than I thought anyone else wanted me around."

Sophie forgot all about trying to act normal. What was Jake doing? Sure, everyone else was pulling out the stops, but that was what brothers did for one another. Jake had always held his cards much closer to his chest than the rest of them, even Zach. Sophie fell even more in love with Jake as she watched him unexpectedly open up in front of hundreds of strangers.

"I still remember watching the football come sailing from out of nowhere straight toward my puny little head."

One look at the large man standing before them and it was absolutely clear to everyone that nothing about Jake had ever been puny. Sophie shivered as she remembered how big, how strong, his muscular body had felt pressed into hers while he'd been holding her.

"Somehow I managed to catch the football before it nailed me right between the eyes." Grins turned to laughter as Jake turned to Chase. "Your aim has always been dead-on, buddy. That day, as I was surrounded by a whole gang of Sullivans, I realized there was nowhere else I wanted to be. Now, years later, things are no different. It's an honor to stand up for you today." He turned to Chloe, and said, "After witnessing firsthand the way your new husband and the rest of this motley crew took in a scared kid more than twenty years ago, Chloe, you'll be pleased to know that you've chosen to spend the rest of your life with one of the best men I've ever had the honor of knowing. There's a saying in Ireland that seems appropriate for today.

If you must lie, lie in the arms of the one you love.
If you must steal, steal away from bad company.
And if you must drink, drink in the moments that take your breath away.

Sophie couldn't pull her gaze from Jake's chiseled face as he raised the glass of specially brewed McCann beer that, she was surprised to suddenly realize, had just been delivered to all the guests' place settings during the other toasts. That he'd planned such a beautiful toast for her brother and his new wife simply stunned her with its poignancy, as did his final words as he lifted his glass.

"To one of those moments."

Sophie wasn't the only person choked up by

Jake's incredibly heartfelt toast, as she realized each of her siblings was taking a moment to process not only the beautiful Irish saying, but also everything Jake had just revealed about himself.

A few moments later, Lori gave the crowd a saucy grin as she stood up. Sophie could always count on her twin sister to win over a crowd, not only with her beauty, but with her confidence and nearly constant laughter. Laughter that started in her eyes, moved to her mouth and zipped all the way down to her wildly painted toenails.

Putting her hand on her hip as if she were mad about something, Lori said, "I'll have all of you know that I always figured I'd be the first Sullivan to get married." She pouted into the laughter, somehow managing to look beautiful even as she playfully pushed out her lower lip. "And if anyone had told me that my big brother was going to up and steal my thunder, I would have reminded him that little sisters know how to exact our revenge." She winked in Chase's direction.

Sophie had to admit that her twin knew how to work a crowd. It was why she was such a great choreographer. Lori understood what people wanted, and she was talented enough to give it to them. After the deep emotions from her brothers and

Jake, Lori's seductive playfulness was just what the doctor ordered.

"Good thing my love for you, Chase, is only surpassed by my thrill at calling Chloe my *sister*." Lori raised her glass to the bride. "Welcome to the family, sis. We're thrilled you're officially one of us now."

Knowing it was her turn to speak, Sophie's heart started pounding an out-of-control beat as Lori sashayed across the reception area to give her the microphone. She wasn't comfortable speaking in front of people, had always been able to rely on a crowd of charismatic Sullivans to take the focus at a public gathering. Sure, she read stories to children at the library every day, but children never judged, never critiqued. They simply listened and enjoyed.

When she didn't immediately take the mic, her twin pulled her to her feet and shoved it at her, leaving Sophie no choice but to grab it before it fell to the floor. Sophie knew she must look like a deer caught in the headlights, with all of those people staring at her, waiting for her to say something beautiful and moving like every one of those who had spoken before her.

Oh, no.

She didn't know where to look, wanted to disappear into the floor. But then, just as she thought she was going to suffocate from being unable to take a full breath, she looked up and found Jake's eyes on her.

You can do this, he seemed to be saying to her. And there was such belief in his unwavering gaze that Sophie had no choice but to believe, too, if only for long enough to make her speech and sit down.

"Hi." She wasn't used to hearing her voice echoing out of speakers like that and it took her aback, until she locked on to Jake's dark gaze again.

You're not really afraid of this bunch, are you?

She suddenly remembered the way he'd looked down at her from the tree fort in her mother's backyard, so many years ago. Her legs had been trembling the same way they were now, but she'd seen that challenge in Jake's eyes and she'd risen to it.

She would rise to it again, darn it. She'd put this whole wedding on, hadn't she? She could certainly make it through one small speech.

"I love weddings," she finally said, not letting her voice waver. "Big ones. Small ones. If it's about love, and forever, you've got me. Right here." Sophie put her hand over her chest, then looked at her siblings. "Growing up in this family where everyone has an opinion about absolutely everything, it wasn't always easy being an incurable romantic." Her brothers and twin grinned along with the rest of the guests. "But if I'd ever been even close to being cured—" she paused and faced Chase and Chloe "—the two of you made me believe in love all over again."

The word *love* immediately made her think of Jake and she had to steel herself not to look at him…even though she could feel his dark eyes burning a hole into her.

She raised her glass to the couple. "I'd like to make a toast to my beloved big brother Chase, and my brand-new sister, Chloe, for writing one of the most beautiful love stories I've ever known."

Everyone got to their feet again and she didn't bother to stop her tears from coming as she beamed at her brother and his bride.

And then, finally, it was time to give the microphone to her mother. Mary Sullivan kissed her on the cheek and whispered, "You were absolutely perfect, honey," before she took the mic and faced the happy couple.

"I can't count the number of times people have remarked on how hard it must have been to raise eight children, but I've always thought I was the luckiest person in the world." She reached up to her hair. "Even if I had to start coloring my hair in my thirties to cover up the grays that seemed to come in by the second."

The laughter was mixed with sniffles already and Sophie was utterly enraptured by the love flowing around the room, wrapping them all up together in a soft cocoon.

"Although today I'm officially welcoming Chloe into my family, she's been in my heart since the very first time Chase spoke of her and I heard the love he felt for her. And when I was finally fortunate enough to meet her, I fell just as much in love with her as my son did. I love you both."

Just as Sophie had planned, the music started at the tail end of her mother's toast. Smith immediately pulled Sophie up out of her seat and into his arms. Her big brother was a fantastic dancer and she'd always loved dancing with him, since the time she'd been a little girl, standing barefoot on top of his shoes as he twirled her around the living room.

She'd cried more today than she had in years, but they had all been good tears. Tears of joy, of pure love. Now she was laughing, feeling so light, so full of that love, as her brother dipped her and then drew her out for an extended twirl that left her breathless.

Especially when she landed straight in Jake's strong arms.

Six

Jake had never seen anyone more beautiful than Sophie Sullivan. If he'd been charmed by the purity of her emotions during the wedding ceremony, her reaction to her siblings' speeches had to be the sweetest thing he'd ever witnessed.

But it was her laughter as she danced with Smith that took him over the edge, straight to a place he knew damn well not to go.

Sophie was simply irresistible. Not just because of her curves and her gorgeous face, but because of the very thing that should have had him heading as fast as he could in the opposite direction: she couldn't even begin to know how to hide her emotions.

No other woman had ever felt this right in his arms, and when the song slowed and she put her head on his shoulder, he had to pull her closer, had to breathe in her soft scent, a hint of champagne and flowers.

Jake could feel Smith's gaze on him, hard and threatening, but in that moment Jake simply didn't care if he was going to pay for his transgressions with Sophie. She was too warm. Too soft.

And too damn sweet for him to figure out how to let go of her, yet.

"Oh, Jake," she whispered in his ear as they moved to the music, "this is so perfect."

He was so attuned to the soft press of her breasts against his chest, to the feel of her breath over his earlobe, he didn't hear the warning bell in his head until several beats had passed.

He knew what he needed to do. He needed to pull away, needed to make it clear that *perfect* was never going to be in the cards for the two of them.

But Lord, all he wanted was to steal a few more short moments with the first—and only—girl who'd ever looked at him with love in her eyes. He was amazed to realize that her feelings hadn't gone away with the years. Instead, they'd grown so big that he'd felt it in her kiss, in the way she held on to him like he really was a hero, instead of typecast as the villain.

He knew better, though, and even though his

gut twisted at what he was about to do, even though he couldn't bring himself to release her just yet, he made himself say, "You threw a great party. Got everyone wrapped up in the fantasy of happy-ever-after." He put his hands on her waist and tried not to think about how good, how right, how *perfect,* she felt against him. "But that's all it is." He wasn't just reminding her, he was reminding himself, too. "Just a fantasy."

She stiffened in his arms. Only she didn't bite as quickly as he wished she would.

Instead, she said, "Jake, please, you don't have to do this. I know you're concerned about how my family would take our relationship, but—"

"We don't have a relationship, princess. And we're not going to."

She blinked at his low words, her body going even stiffer against his. Still, she didn't walk out of his arms. And something that looked like resolve settled deep in her gaze as she stared at him.

"I know why you're trying to push me away," she said softly, "but you're wrong. I could have never fallen for you if you weren't worth it."

Too late, Jake realized what he'd done. He'd let Sophie tell herself one lie after another about him over the years. He should have made sure she knew the truth a long time ago.

"I've done things that would make you physically ill," he told her. Not just all the back-alley fights he'd been in as a teenager, but the fact that he'd had to hold a knife up against his drunken father during a beating that could have ended in a totally different way. And then there was the secret he'd kept from everyone but her brother Zach, who would take it with him to his grave. He could never make the mistake of allowing Sophie in close enough to uncover it.

But if he'd thought his admission would convince her to stop caring for him, he was wrong. "Jake—" her arms tightened around him, pulling him closer as she spoke "—you don't have to be afraid to share your past with me. I lo—"

"Never." He had to cut her off before she said the fatal word. "That's *never* going to happen."

He wrapped his hand around her wrist and dragged her back to Smith, who hadn't taken his eyes off the two of them since they'd started dancing together.

"What about how you were going to help me make my ex jealous?"

He didn't look at her, couldn't look at her, or he'd lose hold of his resolve. "We both know there is no ex."

He waited for her to insist there was, almost

wishing she would keep up the charade. But that wasn't the girl he'd known nearly all his life.

"You're right," she said softly. "I did date someone here, but he isn't at all important to me. I'm sorry I lied to you." She sighed. "I didn't know any other way to try and get your attention."

Why couldn't she be cold and calculating like other women? What was he supposed to do with that honesty? Other than crush it flat…along with the spark he hated to see extinguished in her eyes when he couldn't resist stealing a glance at her beautiful face.

Smith's face was carved in granite by the time Jake and Sophie made it off the dance floor. "Sorry to interrupt your dance, Smith," Jake told his friend. A friend who he guessed might never speak to him again, simply because he'd had the gall to dance with Sophie. "I've got to man the bar the rest of the night. She's all yours."

Jake turned on his heel and forced himself to walk away from Sophie, straight through the throng of dancers, not caring who he knocked into as he made his way over to the bar. But her scent was still on him, and he couldn't shake the phantom feel of her curves pressing into him as they'd danced.

He didn't need to look back to know that Sophie was staring after him with those big beautiful eyes. Eventually, she'd realize he'd done the right thing—for once—by walking away from her. One day soon, she'd find some perfect guy and they'd all be standing around toasting true love while she beamed back at them in a white wedding dress.

Smith had looked like he wanted to kill Jake.

Jake wished he would give it his best shot…and put him out of his misery.

Hours later, Sophie was exhausted and exhilarated all at the same time. The wedding had been absolute perfection and Chase and Chloe were spending the night at the guesthouse before heading to the coast of Thailand in the morning. The catering crew had nearly everything cleaned up and she, Jake and Smith were the only ones left on-site.

Smith hadn't needed to stay to help out, but she knew what her brother was doing. He was babysitting her, making sure she didn't do something stupid with Jake. If her brothers had their way, she would still be an untouched virgin.

Jake shoved the final keg into the back of his black van, then walked over to her and Smith. "That's it for me. Unless you guys need anything else?"

She wasn't fooled by the way he referred to her as one of the "guys" and she didn't think Smith was, either. The only one with the wool pulled over his eyes right now was Jake, and that was only because he was so desperate to "do the right thing."

No wonder everyone always said men were stupid. He wouldn't know the "right thing" if it hit him between the eyes…which she had been more than a little tempted to do with one of her heels when she'd seen him flirting with a couple of the attractive female wedding guests.

"Sophie and I have it covered, Jake," Smith replied.

Normally Smith would have asked about Jake's pubs. Likewise, Jake was always interested in hearing about whatever movie Smith was filming. Tonight, however, the two men were saying as little as possible to each other.

Sophie thought they were both being utterly ridiculous.

"Okay, then." Jake nodded in their direction. "Good night."

He left without hugs or handshakes for either of them, and when the two of them were alone in Marcus's vineyard, Smith immediately started in with, "I know you don't want to hear what I have to say, Sophie—"

"Then don't say it."

Of course, he had to say it, anyway, just as she'd known he would. "He isn't the right man for you."

She glared at her brother. She loved him, but sometimes he could be stubborn and pigheaded... and just plain *wrong*.

"How can you say that about one of your best friends? You grew up with Jake. We all did."

"That's exactly why I *can* say it."

Smith reached for her hand and when he made her look at him, with the moon shining down on the only two people left in the vineyard, she didn't see the movie star everyone else saw. Instead, Sophie saw a father figure who had cared for her—and loved her—every moment of her life.

"You need to let him go, Soph."

"I know he's been with a lot of women, but—"

"More than you could ever add up, but what I'm talking about goes way deeper than that." He ran his free hand through his hair before saying, "He can't love you back, Soph. He just can't."

Smith's words resounded with a forceful premonition of doom, of pain, of loss. She was almost frightened by the expression on her brother's face.

His phone rang just then, an urgent beeping that had him cursing and pulling it from his pocket. "Damn it, it's my director in Australia."

Smith was executive-producing his new big-budget movie, and she knew it had been nearly impossible for him to carve out these hours for the wedding. And yet, not once all night had he picked up his phone.

He turned his back on her as he told the director, "I can't talk right now, James. I'm in the middle of something important and I'll have to call you back." He listened for a few more seconds, then added, "You knew what she was like when you hired her. We all warned you. I'm leaving for the airport at first light. I'll deal with it as soon as I can."

But by the time Smith had disconnected the call, Sophie was gone.

Seven

"What the hell are you doing here?"

Sophie was standing on the front step of Jake's Napa Valley rental house, as if he'd conjured her out of thin air.

"I came to see you, Jake. To talk. To figure things out." Her gaze dropped to his mouth before she whispered, "And to kiss some more."

Jake had thought about Sophie every second since their kiss among the vines earlier. Working behind the bar all night, it had been torture watching her dance with an endless stream of men. Even knowing many of them were old family friends didn't stop the bile from churning in his gut and his hands from balling up into fists. He was an old family friend and look at what he wanted to do to her: rip her clothes off and take her again and again.

Working to ignore the way his body was responding to her nearness, he stepped out onto the front step and closed the door behind him.

"There's nothing to talk about. Nothing to figure out. And we're not going to kiss again. Ever."

She should have run at his harsh tone. Instead, she moved closer. Close enough to mess with whatever brain cells were still functioning in the bloodless zone of his brain.

"Jake, if you'll just let me come in—"

"I could have been in bed with someone else."

She couldn't hide her flinch at his harsh words, at the reminder that he had specifically *not* chosen to take her to his bed tonight. But instead of backing off, he watched as she pushed her shoulders back and her chin up.

"But you aren't…are you?"

"No." Damn it, he should have been. That would have showed both of them that all he needed was a warm, willing body, instead of wanting Sophie with an urgency that was nearly driving him insane. "But that doesn't mean I was waiting for you."

The corners of her mouth moved up at the words *waiting for you*. "Stop trying to deny what happened between us, Jake. You're not going to convince me that our connection isn't real."

She was right—the sparks between them had practically set the vineyard on fire. Convincing her he didn't want her wasn't going to work. He'd have to make her run a different way.

He'd kill anyone who harmed even one hair on Sophie's head. Already, he knew it was going to be a very long time before he forgave himself for that kiss…and for what he was about to do to her now.

Just because pushing her away was a necessary evil didn't mean it wasn't evil, damn it.

He purposely raked his gaze down her body, lingering on her breasts and hips far longer than he needed to. "You're too innocent for me, princess. Why don't you leave before something happens that you'll regret?"

It was partly that innocence that drew him to her, of course, but she didn't need to know that. Not when he was on a mission to get her to leave before his control shattered.

But instead of rising to his taunts, she simply smiled at him. "One of the perks of being a librarian is endless access to books." She licked at her lower lip, slowly, deliberately. "All kinds of books."

Suddenly, Jake couldn't get past the image of

Sophie poring over *The Kama Sutra,* memorizing all those variations on lovemaking with her big brain. It was wrong. So damn wrong.

And yet, his body seemed to think it was impossibly right.

"Reading about sex doesn't mean a damn thing, princess." He forced the sneer, hating himself more with every word out of his mouth. "It's what you've done—" he dropped his gaze to her incredible breasts again "—and what you're willing to do that counts."

"I'll do anything."

Oh, hell, no. That wasn't what she was supposed to say.

Jake had never been backed into a darker corner. Not even with his drunk father had he felt so helpless, so out of control. He needed to pick the reins back up, rather than let the beauty standing before him keep taking him for a ride they shouldn't be on in the first place.

"Anything, huh?"

She nodded, but her face was flushing again, a flush that moved down her neck to the soft swell of her breasts rising up above the top of her dress.

"I already told you," she reminded him in a soft but firm voice, "you're not going to scare me away, not matter how hard you try. You can't scare me because I already know the real you."

The real him? He'd show her the real him, all right.

"How many times have you been blindfolded? And I'm not talking about Pin the Tail on the Donkey."

"I know you're not," she shot back.

"How many, princess?"

She looked him straight in the eye. "Are you sure you want to know?"

Damn it, he hadn't seen that coming. Before she could actually give him her answer, and knowing he could barely handle the thought of Sophie in bed with another man, he tried again with something she couldn't possibly have done.

"What about sex in a public place?"

Sweet, *nice* Sophie Sullivan smiled at him. Actually goddamned smiled as she said, "Define public."

Jake sucked in a hard breath, feeling like he'd just been punched—repeatedly—in the gut. Still, he had to try one more time, one last-ditch effort to make Sophie see what a mistake she was making with him.

"Okay," he said as easily as he could between clenched teeth, "so maybe you've played around a little bit. But you and I both know what a guy like me needs isn't something a girl like you wants to give."

"Wanna bet?"

The last thing he expected was for her to throw the same words back at him that he'd said before he grabbed her and kissed her. He shouldn't want to do it again, shouldn't be a heartbeat away from shoving her up against the front door and ripping off that silky dress so that he could make good on showing her he meant every word he'd just said.

"I'm not a soft, gentle lover like the guys you've been with before. You make the mistake of taking one step inside this house," he warned her in a hard voice, "there's no going back."

As if in slow motion, Jake watched as Sophie reached for the doorknob, turned it and took that fated step into the house. He was paralyzed. He couldn't do anything but stare at her as she moved farther into the house, her hips swaying with every step she took. When she reached the living room, while still in full line of sight from the front step, she paused for a moment before turning around to face him.

Her face held hope, desire—and something that looked too much like love—as she reached for the zipper on the side of her dress and began to pull it down.

No.

God, no.

He needed to put a stop to this right now. But instead of barking out an order to stop acting crazy, instead of turning away as if he didn't care one way or another if she undressed in front of him, he was struck stupid yet again. It was as if she'd cast a spell over him, one he couldn't break if it meant he missed one single second of her shockingly gorgeous unveiling.

He'd guessed earlier she wasn't wearing anything under the dress, but he hadn't ever expected to confirm it in person. In seconds, the dress would fall and he wouldn't have a prayer of doing the right thing.

"Sophie," he said, her name a ragged plea from his lips.

A plea to stop…and a plea to let him *finally* see all of her.

A plea to leave…and a plea for her to promise she'd never, ever give up on him, no matter what happened.

The zipper came all the way down and she held the dress in place with steady hands. Her eyes were huge, but he didn't see fear, didn't see nerves, in them.

Only anticipation.

And a desire strong enough to match the lust eating him up from the inside.

A moment later, she let her dress drop to the wood planked floor, and stood before him wearing nothing but a pair of pink heels.

"I'm yours, Jake."

Eight

"Holy hell, you're beautiful."

Jake's words took the chill away from her naked skin just moments before the front door was slamming shut and she was in his arms. His mouth covered hers, taking, claiming, branding her with a kiss that blew every other kiss she'd ever had away. His hands cupped her hips, and as the kiss spiraled more and more out of control, he dragged her naked body into his. He trapped her legs between his spread thighs, the thick bulge behind his zipper throbbing and pulsing against her.

She wanted to touch him everywhere, wanted proof that this moment was real and not just a dream she was going to wake up from, frustrated and alone. He was holding her so tightly against him that her forearms were pressed up against his rock-hard chest, but she could splay her hands against him, could rub the pads of her fingers over his chest through the fine cotton of his dress shirt.

But it wasn't enough for her. Sophie was desperate for more of him, for more of this kiss and the chance to slide her hands up over his shoulders, up his neck, to cup the planes of his beautiful face. When he began to rain kisses over her cheeks, her chin and then into the hollow of her neck, she threaded her fingers into his hair, then arched her head back and pressed her breasts harder into his chest as he pressed kisses to her skin.

And then—*oh, God, how long had she waited for this moment?*—she felt his mouth move lower, and lower still, until his tongue curled over the tip of one breast.

She'd never felt anything like this, had never known what it was to step inside a bolt of lightning and become light and flames and heat. The explosions started deep in her belly, down low where everything was throbbing with arousal, waiting for Jake's savage possession.

She'd been so nervous as she'd gotten into her car and drove to the house she knew Jake had rented for the weekend, but she hadn't let herself falter. Not even when her legs had been trembling so hard as she walked up to the front door that she'd had to brace herself for a moment with both of her hands on either side of it.

It's now or never, Sophie, was what she'd reminded herself.

And, oh, as she gasped his name, was she ever glad she'd chosen *now.*

Jake moved one of his hands from her hip to cup and tease the other breast, just as he slid his other hand between her legs. She dropped her gaze down to his dark head, only to find that he was looking up at her, too, and in that instant that their gazes connected, Sophie lost hold of the thin thread that had been holding her together.

Her eyes fluttered closed as she came apart against him, her hips instinctively rocking into his hand as she rode the shockingly unexpected climax. His sensual touch, the warmth of his fingers in her most intimate place even as he moved his mouth to her other breast, his stubble scratching against her chest in the most deliciously rough way, sent her spiraling off even higher, from a prelude of pleasure to an encore that came out of nowhere and seemed to just go on and on.

Her legs would have buckled if not for Jake slipping one arm beneath her knees and the other around her rib cage as he lifted her off the floor. He didn't give her any time to think as his mouth came down over hers again, his tongue thrusting against hers. And as he carried her through the living room and down the hall, she felt so incredibly sexy, naked with only her heels on in his strong arms.

She heard him kick open a door and the next thing she knew he was lowering her onto a soft velvet bed covering. His mouth still over hers, she realized he wasn't kissing her anymore, that he was taking her wrists in one of his large hands and lifting her arms above her head, holding them firmly in place. Holding her right where he wanted her.

She'd been bluffing out on the front steps, of course. She hadn't ever been blindfolded, hadn't had public sex. Not because she was afraid to do those things, but because she'd never had the right man to do them with.

Until tonight.

Until Jake.

She tried to wrap her legs around him, wanted him to take her, to make her his, but he wouldn't let her lead, instead using his body to still hers beneath his.

Held deliciously captive beneath his strong muscles, she watched his beautiful mouth say the words, "Let me love you." His mouth moved to her earlobe as he licked at the skin behind it before biting into the sensitive flesh. "I just want to love you."

Love.

He wanted to love her.

Her muscles melted like butter beneath the sweet stroke of his free hand down the side of her body, from breast to waist and hips to thigh, and she opened up for him again, for the sweet slide of his hand between her legs.

He raised his head to look down at her as he cupped her, his heat melding with hers until she didn't know where she ended and he began. Sophie had to arch her hips up into his hand, searching all over again for that pleasure he'd given to her mere minutes ago.

"That's it," he urged her as she rocked against his hand while she tried so desperately to take herself back over that incredibly high peak. Her inner muscles clenched and pulled at his fingers as he thrust them into her, sometimes fast, sometimes excruciatingly slow.

"Please, Jake," she begged him, the plea falling from her lips unbidden.

"Anything," he vowed. "Anything for you."

And then his mouth was back on her breasts oh-too-briefly before he was moving lower, kissing and biting at the skin stretched taut over her stomach. Somewhere in her head she knew what was going to happen, that he was going to put his mouth between her legs and taste her. Of course she'd fantasized about what it would be like to be so intimate with Jake, but she'd never actually believed it would happen.

His hands moved to her inner thighs, gently pushing them apart. "Show me how beautiful you are. Let me taste your sweetness."

No one had ever talked to her like this during sex, like he was a starving man and she was a feast laid out before him.

"Beautiful." He breathed out against her aroused flesh and a shiver took her over. "So damned beautiful." And then he was lowering his head down, then down farther still, until he was covering her, breaking her apart one slow swipe of his tongue at a time.

She should have been prepared for her climax this time, should have known it would send her reeling, should have been able to take it in and hold on to the feelings of extreme pleasure to mine later in her memories. But she didn't have a prayer as his stubble rubbed over her slick and damp curls. He sucked her aroused flesh between his lips, and as he tugged at the incredibly sensitive ball of nerves, her limbs shook and her heart pounded so hard it nearly jumped through her ribs and skin as she came for him. Her cry of pleasure sounded through the bedroom, the tall ceilings and large glass windows echoing it back.

When the currents of pleasure finally subsided, never leaving her completely, Sophie knew a deeper exhaustion—and satisfaction—than she'd ever had in her life. Her eyes were heavy, so heavy that even as the mattress shifted beneath Jake's weight, she couldn't quite manage to open them to see what he was doing.

Soon, she felt the bed move again and knew he was back with her. She reached for him, her eyes still closed. But when he grabbed her hands in his and lowered his mouth to them instead of letting her touch him, she had to push her eyelids open.

The most beautiful sight in the world awaited her.

Jake was a bronzed, perfectly formed god, kneeling between her thighs, his head bowed down to her hands as if in prayer. A tattooed tail of an animal she guessed was a dragon traveled across his rib cage from his back. She'd seen the band around his arms when he'd worn short sleeves, but she'd never had the chance to appreciate the artistry that shifted and pulsed with the tightening of his muscles.

She couldn't focus on his tattoos for very long tonight, though. Not when he was also shockingly erect, his shaft already covered with a thin layer of latex. For several moments, she couldn't tear her eyes from it, could hardly believe anything that big could ever fit inside her.

But when he raised his gaze to hers, she was rocked by what she saw in his dark eyes. Not just desire, but something fierce.

Possessive.

"I shouldn't do this." Each word from his lips was raw. Broken. His face was ravaged with conflicting emotions. "But I can't walk away this time. I need to have you, Sophie."

"Yes," she urged him, "take me. *Now.*"

He was shaking his head, but even as he did, he was letting go of her hands and moving to cup her hips to pull her closer. When he was nearly against her and she was holding her breath waiting for the precious moment when they finally became one, he stopped and gripped her hips so hard she knew she'd have bruises in the morning.

And then he thrust into her, so hard and deep that his name burst from her lips on a cry of the deepest pleasure she'd ever known. Being claimed by the only man she'd ever truly wanted was a thousand times better than she'd ever dreamed it would be.

She reached up and put her arms around his neck to pull his face down to hers. Their mouths came together in a desperate kiss as she met him thrust for thrust.

"I love you," Sophie whispered against his lips, causing Jake to still above her so suddenly, so sharply, the sudden shift of his body actually kicked her over the edge she'd been teetering on again since the first moment she looked up and saw him poised to take her.

"I love you so much, Jake." She wasn't afraid to tell him anymore. Not now that he'd shown her how he felt about her with his body, worshipped her with it. "Always," she vowed even as waves of pleasure washed through every cell in her body.

"Forever."

As if her words of love had broken the dam that held him immobile, Jake moved back into action, pushing into her so fiercely that the top of her head hit the cushioned headboard behind her as he exploded inside of her at the exact moment her name left his lips.

Of all the things Jake would never forgive himself for, taking Sophie in such a savage way would always be at the top of the list. And yet, even as self-hatred grew inside of him like a festering virus, she was so soft, so sweet, in his arms as she slept that he couldn't stop himself from breathing in her scent, from soaking up her warmth.

Jake was no stranger to hot sex. He'd been enjoying women of all shapes and sizes since he was a teenager. But sex with Sophie had been so much bigger than anything he'd ever experienced, so much more than just *sex*.

He'd loved her nearly all his life. Loved her so much, in fact, that he tightened his hold on her even as he faced what had to happen next. He never should have let the sight of her beautiful naked body send him all the way over the edge the way it had. But when she'd unzipped her dress and let it fall to the floor, when he'd finally been given everything he'd wanted for so many years, he'd been unable to fight the beast inside of him that wanted Sophie.

Needed Sophie.

Craved Sophie.

The moonlight streaming in through the windows was bright enough for him to see her face as she shifted with him, her soft mouth curving up into a satisfied, contented smile even in her sleep.

If only he could be worthy of a woman like her.

Jake carefully moved his arms from around her and slipped from the bed. She made a sound of protest, a small frown appearing between her eyebrows, and he thought for a moment she might wake up and catch him sneaking out.

Open your eyes, princess, he silently urged her.

If she called him back to bed, he wouldn't hesitate to go back to her, to take her again, to repeat what he couldn't deny were the best moments of his life. Not just watching her come more beautifully than any other woman on earth, but the rare moments of peace he'd felt when he was holding her in his arms.

Instead, she settled deeper into the pillows, wrapping her arms around one and pulling it close. His chest was so tight he could barely breathe as he quietly pulled on his clothes and packed his bag.

It was time to leave. He'd be back in the city in ninety minutes. Less, probably, because he'd likely be the only car on the road at three in the morning.

But all Jake could do was stand in the middle of the bedroom and stare at Sophie. He knew how soft her skin was now, knew exactly what her curves felt like in his hands, could still hear the sweet little gasps and moans she made as she came for him.

Just as he hadn't been able to stop himself from

jumping her when she was naked and offering herself to him in the living room, he couldn't stop himself now from moving to the edge of the bed and kneeling down. With infinite gentleness, he ran his hand over her hair, then down to her face. She nuzzled her cheek into his palm even as she slept and he had to close his eyes on a sharp pang in the center of his chest that felt like it was tearing him wide-open.

One day she'd have a husband and kids. She'd belong to someone else, to someone who would love her and take care of her the way she deserved.

But for a few stolen hours, she'd been *his*.

Sophie woke up alone in the big bed at first light, still able to feel the imprint of Jake's hands, his mouth, on her skin. She listened for the sound of the shower running, but the rental house was suspiciously quiet. Maybe, she tried to tell herself as she sat up, he'd gone out to get breakfast. Because he couldn't have just left like that, could he? Last night had meant something, she was sure of it. Otherwise, she never would have declared her love for—

Her thoughts stuttered, then stopped entirely, when she realized his clothes, his shoes, his bag were all gone.

For a moment she couldn't process it, couldn't let herself believe that it could possibly be true. And when she heard her phone buzzing she leaped on her bag and pulled it out, praying that it was Jake saying he'd needed to go pick something up, but would be right back.

Instead, it was Smith calling. To check up on her. To make sure she hadn't done something stupid like drive to Jake McCann's house in Napa to seduce him.

The phone fell from her numb fingers unanswered.

Oh, God, the evidence was right there before her eyes…and she had to face it. Had to face the bitter, horrible, awful truth.

He'd left her.

Sophie pushed the sheets back and stepped, naked, onto the hardwood floor. The splendor of Napa Valley rolled before her as she stared out the large bedroom window, but she didn't see the beauty.

All she saw in the glass was a woman who should have known better than to love the one man who wasn't capable of loving her back.

He'd tried to push her away, tried to convince her to go, but she'd been so sure there was something more beneath his kiss. Something bigger than just desire, a deeper emotional connection than she'd ever had with another man. The kind of love that existed between Chase and Chloe. Marcus and Nicola. Gabe and Megan.

She'd been wrong.

Nine

Two and a half months later...

"Gabe and I are engaged!"

The women in Lori's living room exclaimed in surprise as they jumped up to hug Megan. Sophie smiled and gushed along with everyone else as her friend gleefully showed the group of women her new diamond engagement ring from Gabe. But even through all the laughter, the joy, Sophie remained numb. Cold all over as the conversation went on around her in a buzz.

Of course she was happy for her good friend and for her brother. Sophie was absolutely thrilled that they were about to embark on a new life together as a family, along with Megan's seven-year-old daughter, Summer.

But right now Sophie wasn't able to feel much of anything at all.

Lori jumped up off the couch in her living room and came back from the kitchen with a bottle of champagne. "Time to celebrate!" She held a smaller bottle of sparkling apple juice in her other hand for Chloe, who was looking more gorgeous than ever with her baby bump.

Lori filled a glass for everyone as they all sat down. The five of them—Lori, Megan, Nicola, Chloe and Sophie—had begun to have these girls' nights a few weeks before Chloe's wedding. Sophie loved spending time with a group of women this amazing. On paper, they didn't necessarily make the most sense: a choreographer, a CPA, a pop star, a quilter and a librarian. And yet, they were totally in tune with one another.

"To Megan and Gabe!"

Sophie reached for her glass and was just raising it to her lips when she stopped and quickly put it down. The sweet, bubbly liquid splashed out against the rim and onto the coffee table.

"When did he ask you?" Nicola asked. "We need all the deets, right, girls?"

Megan blushed. "Actually, he asked me at Chloe's wedding."

Everyone blinked with surprise. "But that was,

let's see, how long ago was it?" Lori paused to calculate.

"Two and a half months," Sophie said, the number burned like a hole into her brain.

"That long?" Lori turned on Megan. "Why didn't you tell us that night?"

"We didn't plan on keeping it a secret for so long, I swear." Megan looked at Chloe. "Gabe took me out into the vines and dropped to one knee. He told me he'd been carrying the ring around for weeks, that he wanted everything to be perfect when he asked me." Megan couldn't contain her glow. "He had already asked Summer if he could be my husband. And her daddy." She sniffled and giggled at the same time. "The two of them are already keeping secrets from me. I'm in such big trouble from here on out," she said, but it was clear to all of them how happy Megan was, not only to have finally found the love of her life, but also to have a true partner and father to help raise her daughter.

"That is ridiculously romantic," Lori said, "but you still should have told us. Right, Soph?"

Sophie nodded, hoping her smile looked natural. "Right."

"It was your day," Megan said to Chloe. "And

then I guess we were enjoying keeping it to ourselves for a little while."

"No problem," Chloe said, "just as long as you tell us the second you get pregnant."

Sophie choked on the breath she'd been taking. Her eyes immediately started watering as she fought to breathe normally.

"Sorry, the champagne must have gone down the wrong pipe," she said before jumping up from the couch and heading for Lori's guest bathroom.

Ten weeks, two days and fifteen hours—that's how long it had been since those hours in Jake's arms when he'd given her more pleasure than she'd ever dreamed was possible...then disappeared in the middle of the night.

It also happened to be exactly enough time to figure out that her period wasn't missing because it had always come at random intervals or because she was stressed out over work.

No, there was a much more scientific—and shocking—reason why she was so late.

She was pregnant.

Standing in front of the oval mirror over the sink, Sophie stared at herself and tried to see if she looked different yet. But the hollows beneath her eyes, the increased prominence of her cheekbones—neither of those things had anything to do with the baby growing inside her.

No, those were the result of nothing more complicated than self-pity.

How, she'd asked herself a thousand times in the eight hours that had passed since she'd taken a half-dozen pregnancy tests—one from every manufacturer on the market—*had it happened?*

She already knew the answer to that, of course. Jake had used a condom, she remembered that clearly. But evidently there was a reason for those disclaimers on condom packages.

Despite the shock of seeing that blue line over and over—along with the word *Pregnant* on that one test that had practically shouted at her—it wasn't lost on Sophie just how ironic it all was.

She was *Nice!*

The only time she'd ever let herself do something crazy, the only time she'd ever thrown caution to the winds to take what she so desperately wanted, she ended up totally paying for it.

How many lies had she told herself, all because she'd wanted that night with him so badly? The list was ridiculously long, but yet again she made herself go through each bullet point, knowing it was the perfect way to remind herself of the truth.

Lie: If she loved Jake enough, he'd eventually love her back.

Truth: She could spend every second of the rest of her life showering him with love, and he'd never love her. Oh, he'd like her, all right, just as he liked the rest of the Sullivans. But love wasn't something Jake McCann was ever going to sign up for. He'd even told her that straight to her face.

Lie: The only reason he felt funny about falling for her was because he was such close friends with her brothers.

Truth: Could she have been any more delusional? He hadn't fallen for her. He'd simply taken what any guy would have taken after she threw it at him—her naked, willing body.

Lie: He didn't think he was good enough for her, but once she convinced him that he was, they'd have their happy-ever-after.

Truth: Jake was one of the most confident men she'd ever met. If anything was ridiculous, it was that she'd thought he could ever be happy with a boring, *nice* librarian. It wasn't that he didn't think he was good enough for her. He just didn't want her. Period.

Lie: Their mind-blowing kisses, the shockingly great sex, had to mean he loved her, too.

Truth: Sex wasn't magic. Orgasms didn't connect to emotions. And she was a pathetic fool for ever thinking anything else.

Lie: She could have one incredible night in Jake's arms and then go back to her normal life without anything else changing outside of those wickedly perfect hours.

Truth: Everything had changed.

And still, despite the undeniable list of truths she'd just laid out for herself, Sophie couldn't stop remembering the way he'd looked at her that night. Had she imagined the fierce possession? The emotion he hadn't been able to hide? She'd thought he was touching more than just her body. She'd thought he was reaching all the way into her soul.

Stop it, Sophie!

She needed to accept the truth that Jake McCann probably looked at every woman he slept with like that, and that their hours together had nothing whatsoever to do with touching souls. Just body parts.

She still couldn't believe she'd actually told him she loved him. Always.

Forever.

God, she wanted to curl up into a ball on the bathroom floor and never come out again. Stupid Sophie Sullivan with stars in her eyes blinding her to reality. And now look what had happened.

She was pregnant.

With Jake's baby.

A knock sounded on the door. "You okay in there?"

It was Lori. Sophie quickly splashed some water on her face and flushed the toilet to make it seem like she'd actually used the bathroom.

She opened the door and faked a smile. "Isn't it exciting about Gabe and Megan?"

"Of course it is." But Lori wasn't smiling back. "I need to talk to you after everyone leaves, so stick around, okay?"

Sophie immediately worried that something was wrong with her twin. Had she been too pre-occupied with her own shocking news that she hadn't paid close enough attention to whether Lori needed her support?

The door had barely closed behind the other women when Lori turned on Sophie. "Spill it, sis."

The wineglass Sophie had been washing in the kitchen sink slipped from her fingers and shattered on the white porcelain. In the past, Sophie had always been the voice of reason, the shoulder for her twin to cry on.

This time, everything was turned around.

She braced herself on the rim of the sink. She wasn't going to cry.

Not. Going. To. Cry.

But when Lori moved behind her and wrapped her arms around her shoulders, tears started streaming down Sophie's cheeks as fast and thick as the water still pouring from the faucet.

Everything she'd been trying to hold in, to deal with by herself, burst apart inside of her. She felt as if she was breaking apart from the inside out, as though she were about to shatter into as many pieces as the glass in the bottom of the sink.

Her sobs racked her body so hard that if Lori hadn't been holding her up, she couldn't have stayed upright. Somehow, Lori turned off the water and got them both over to the couch, where Sophie held on to her twin for dear life. Their endless fights over the past year receded to nothing.

All that mattered was knowing she wasn't completely alone.

When Sophie had finally stopped crying, her body feeling completely wrung out, Lori said, "Hold on a sec," and came back a few seconds later with a roll of toilet paper. "Sorry, this is the best I've got."

It was more than good enough for Sophie to blow her nose on and wipe her face dry.

"Wow." Lori looked at her. "You're really a mess."

Her twin pointing out the horribly obvious shouldn't have made Sophie laugh, but she couldn't hold back a choked giggle. "You think?"

Lori reached for her hand. "It's just that you've never been like this. You're freaking me out."

"You're not the only one." Although the truth was that *freaking out* was a pathetic, ridiculous understatement of what she was feeling.

"What did Jake do to you?"

Of course Lori would immediately figure out what—*who*—was at the heart of her sorrow. Only Sophie couldn't exactly say, *Oh, you know, not much besides making the sweetest, most sinful love imaginable to me and then leaving me in the middle of the night, knocked up...and completely lost without him.*

She opened her mouth to give her sister an answer, but nothing came out.

"You were with him, weren't you? That night, after the wedding."

Sophie nodded. She could at least do that.

"How was it? No, wait." Lori held up her hand. "Forget I asked. It would be too much like hearing about one of our brothers' sex lives."

Only, Jake wasn't their brother. Just because he'd practically grown up in their house didn't change the fact that he wasn't actually one of them.

"I'm just going to assume it was awesome," Lori said.

Sophie knew what was expected of her here, so she managed another nod.

"Super awesome?"

Sophie sighed, finally responding verbally with, "Yes." But those thrilling details of their few stolen hours together, while still important, had faded into the background as soon as she'd found out—

"I'm pregnant."

There. She'd said it. And, oh, if Lori could see her own face right now.

"Hold on." Lori looked as shocked as Sophie had ever seen her in twenty-five years. "I thought you just said you were p—" She shook her head. "I can't even say the word, Soph."

"I haven't gotten my period since before the wedding."

"Have you been seeing him in secret all this time?"

Sophie snorted. "Are you kidding me? We did

it once—" *one spectacular time* "—and then he snuck away in the middle of the night." Leaving her alone in that big bed in that big house in the Napa Valley hills with nothing to hold but a pillow.

"I'm going to kill him." Lori leaped off the couch and grabbed her cell phone from the kitchen counter. "I'm going to rip his heart out through his throat. Better yet, I'm going to make sure he can never get anyone else pregnant ever again."

Sophie grabbed her sister a millisecond before Lori was able to find Jake's number on her phone's contact list. "Stop! You can't call him! He doesn't know yet."

Lori's finger stilled over her phone. "You haven't told him?"

"No. We haven't even spoken since that night. I only took the tests this morning." Sophie forcefully pried the phone out of her sister's hand. "I love you for having my back. But I've got to deal with this myself."

She didn't feel great by any means, but after the long cry—and confessing the news to her sister— she felt better. Stronger.

Like she might actually be able to face Jake without crumbling.

"I can't believe this," Lori said. "Here you've been all over me for a year to break this thing off with you-know-who because he's 'bad for me' and one night is all it takes for you to get in big trouble."

It could have sounded like gloating in another context, but Sophie knew it wasn't. It was simply Lori stating the crazy irony of their situation.

"I never thought something like this would happen to me," Sophie said.

And still a voice in the back of her head was saying, *Even if you knew how this was going to end up, you would have done it, anyway. You would have given up everything, anything at all, for the chance to be with him.*

"It could work, you know," Lori said, halfheartedly. "Maybe he'll step up to the plate. Maybe the two of you can actually make this work." She looked down at Sophie's stomach. "Well, the three of you, I guess."

Sophie knew better than that. "I don't want him to be with me only out of duty." She took a deep breath, letting oxygen fill her lungs and help rebuild her strength. "I want love."

She could see in Lori's eyes confirmation of what all her siblings had known: Jake didn't believe in love. Sophie could try the rest of her life to convince him, but it would just be a waste.

"Oh, Soph." Lori scowled. "I'm still going to kill him. Just as soon as you give him the news."

It would have been so much easier if Sophie could blame Jake for everything. But even now, she had to be fair. "It wasn't all his fault. I tricked him into sleeping with me. I made it impossible for him to walk away."

"Are you kidding me?" Lori let go of her hands and stomped on the wooden floor in her fury. "How could you possibly have trapped a guy like Jake into sleeping with you? Did you cement his feet to the ground and hop up on him while he begged you to stop?"

Sophie was beyond glad for the way her sister always made her laugh. Even in the worst of times. "You said you didn't want details," she reminded her twin.

"Right. Okay. No details. But you don't have the kind of experience he does with the opposite sex. Seducing you would have been like taking candy from a baby."

The word *baby* brought them both back to the most important issue at hand.

"You're going to have a baby, Soph." Lori's eyes were wide with wonder.

Sophie put her hands over her stomach, even though she knew there had to be something barely the size of a pea inside her. That was when it fi-nally hit her.

A baby.

Even though she was terrified, she suddenly couldn't help but be thrilled. She was going to have a little boy or girl with Jake's eyes, a child that would run her ragged, if Jake's energy was anything to go by.

"I'm going to love this child so much."

Lori actually looked like she was going to cry. "All of us will."

Oh, God. Her mother. Her brothers. She didn't want to think about how badly they'd lose it over this.

"Don't you dare tell a soul."

"But—"

"No one, Lori. Swear to God, you'd better let me deal with this—with Jake—the way I need to."

Lori frowned. "Okay," she said, very reluc-tantly. "But don't forget, you've got at least seven people backing you up on this. Six with really big fists."

Sophie smiled at her. "Thanks, Lori."

"Hey," her sister said with a smirk, "I'm just glad it's you and not me."

Now, there was the evil Lori she knew and

loved. "You almost cried there for a second," So-phie said.

"Did not."

"Did, too."

The familiar patter of their bickering helped center Sophie a little more. Enough that by the time she headed back outside, she decided she was strong enough to go and do what needed to be done.

It was time to tell Jake he was going to be a father.

Ten

The numbers on the spreadsheets covering the desk in Jake's home office blurred before his eyes. As difficult as words were for him to process, numbers had always been easy.

He shoved away from his desk, knowing any work he tried to do now he'd have to redo in the morning. The only reason he'd stayed home tonight was to power through some work. If he wasn't going to be able to get any of it done, he might as well be at one of the pubs manning the taps.

He grabbed his cell phone off the kitchen counter and saw a missed call from Zach Sullivan. For ten weeks he'd gone out of his way to avoid the Sullivans. He couldn't face Zach or Marcus or Chase or Gabe, not knowing what he'd done to their sister. It was the lowest he'd ever stooped, so low he still couldn't believe it. He kept hoping he'd wake up and it would all be a crazy dream… but any time he managed to sleep, all he could see was Sophie and the look in her eyes when she'd told him she loved him.

Forever.

He knew better, knew she couldn't actually love him. She loved a fantasy version of Jake McCann that she'd probably been writing about in her journals since she was a little girl in pigtails.

She'd never forgive him for what he'd done and Jake knew he didn't deserve her forgiveness, just as he knew it was for the best that she steer clear of him from now on. Because now that he knew the taste of her, the feel of her…

He needed to get to the pub, where the noise and activity would distract him from thinking about her. He shoved his phone in his pocket, grabbed his car keys and yanked open the front door.

Sophie Sullivan stood on his front steps. "Oh, hi. I was just about to knock."

"What the hell are you doing here?"

It was exactly what he'd asked her when she'd showed up at his rental house in Napa. He knew coming at her so aggressively wasn't doing a damn thing to make up for the way he'd treated her, but it was the best he could do given that even looking at Sophie had his brain cells scrambling.

She looked uncertain and uncomfortable. Along with tired—at least as tired as he felt.

"Could I come inside?"

"Don't you remember what happened the last time?" He all but growled the words at her, but even though she paled and her eyes widened, she didn't make a move to leave.

"Yes," she said softly. "That's exactly what I'm here to talk to you about."

Jake didn't trust himself around her. Just as he'd expected—if he saw her again, one look would be all it took for him to be gripped with a fierce urge to drag her off and chain her to his bed.

God, he was sick, thinking even now about all the ways he could corrupt her.

Nice.

He had to remember she was nice…rather than the innately sensual woman who had writhed and cried out beneath him, desperate for pleasure when it turned out that beneath her sweet, innocent, *nice* facade was a naughty woman who—

"I don't have time for this tonight." The last thing he wanted to do was hurt her, but if she stayed, if she let him touch her again, he'd only end up hurting her more. "I've got to get back to the pub."

"Too bad," she said, "because you and I need to talk. Now."

She shoved past him, a fierce Sophie Sullivan he hadn't known existed until now.

As he shut the door and turned to face her, Jake was wholly focused on tamping down his reaction to how beautiful she was, how good she smelled, how much he wanted to pull her against him. He was so focused on hanging on to his almost non-existent control, that he nearly missed her next words.

"I'm pregnant."

The earth actually stopped spinning, nearly pitching him off the edge. His brain tried to hold on to what she'd just said, but he couldn't wrap his head around it. Couldn't believe he'd heard what he thought he'd just heard.

He stared at her stomach, her sweater and skirt tight enough at the waist for him to see that it was still flat.

"I probably won't start showing for a few weeks."

Panic gripped him at the thought of being a father. He'd never planned on having kids. Had made damn sure something like this would never happen.

"You're sure it's mine?"

She looked like he'd hauled off and nailed her with a fist to her jaw, rather than asking her a question. "The wedding was two and a half months ago." She worked visibly to calm down. "You are the only man I've slept with in—" she paused "—a long time. It couldn't have been anyone else."

Panic and shock still clawed at his guts, but it couldn't override the purely primitive male instinct to claim her and his kid that instant.

Relief swept through Jake at knowing she was his.

Only his.

She took a deep, shaky breath. "I came here to tell you what…what happened. You deserve to know, not to always wonder if my little girl or boy is yours."

Her words, and the image they conjured up, nearly brought him to his knees.

A little girl. Or boy.

His daughter or son.

"When will— How far—" Everything he tried to ask came out in a voice that was still too harsh.

"I think I'm right around twelve weeks. I'll have the baby this fall."

Jake had never marked time by anything other than business trips and vacations…and beatings when he was a kid. "Have you seen a doctor yet?" Again, the words were rough as he couldn't manage to temper the primitive instinct to claim her and the baby as his. *Now.*

Forever.

She looked surprised by his question. "I have an appointment for tomorrow."

"Good," he said, needing to get closer to her, her glow pulling him in the way it always had. Only he couldn't remember how to fight it anymore. "I'm coming with you."

"Wait." She shook her head, took a step back from him, widening the gap he'd just been closing. "I didn't just come here to tell you I'm pregnant. I also came to tell you that I don't want anything from you. And that no one needs to know you're the father."

"Like hell."

She looked shocked by his reaction. But despite her shock, she didn't budge an inch, even as he continued to close the distance between them.

"Why are you saying that?" she asked. "I thought you'd be happy to hear that I don't want anything from you. That way you can keep your free lifestyle."

The word *free* twisted on her lips until it sounded like a curse.

"I'm not going to let you walk away, Sophie. And I'm not going to let you tell your family, your friends, that some random guy did this to you." He pointed his index finger at his chest. "It was *me*."

Sixty seconds ago, he'd been trying to get her to admit it wasn't. But now the truth came out: he was desperate to claim this kid as his.

And her, too, a mocking voice in his head told him. *Finally you can have everything you've ever wanted. Even though you don't deserve any of it.*

"I know you've probably forgotten what happened that night, but I haven't." Sophie's frustration had morphed into full-on anger. It was another side to her that he'd never known existed. "You were gone as soon as you could sneak away, probably wishing for an escape hatch long before you actually left. We both know you have absolutely zero interest whatsoever in being with me. The fact that I'm pregnant doesn't change any of that. For so long, I wanted you to notice me. To see me. And you did, for one night. But then I realized that even though I got what I thought I wanted, it didn't mean anything." She shook her head. "It was great sex, but I want more than lust. I want undying love. I want that look that Chase gave Chloe when he promised to be hers forever."

He hated the way she was looking at him, with

none of the hero worship, none of the undisguised admiration, she used to have for him.

Jake had never felt like a hero. But in one person's eyes, at least, he hadn't been complete scum.

Until now.

Hurt spilled from every word she'd said. But he couldn't deal with that now, not when there were more important things to settle. He'd never had a mother and would probably have been far better off if he hadn't had a father, either. Kids weren't supposed to have ever been in the cards for him, but since he was just starting to realize that he wasn't in control of nearly as much as he liked to think he was, one thing was for sure.

He wasn't going to let *his* kid miss out on having a mother *and* a father.

"Now that you're having my kid, we're getting married."

Her mouth fell open. "Didn't you hear anything I just said?"

Yes, he'd heard her. Every brave, courageous word intended to push him out of her life.

"We can be in Vegas in a couple of hours, just get it done."

"I'm not going to marry you, Jake," she said, and then with a confused shake of her head, "of all the people in the world, I wouldn't have expected this from you."

How could she not understand that his upbringing was exactly why being a part of his child's life would be so important to him? Just because she was pregnant with a kid he hadn't planned on ever having didn't change the fact that he wasn't going to let that child grow up without knowing its father.

"You're pregnant with my kid." He reached for her, putting his hands on her shoulders before she could get any farther from him. This was his chance to finally claim everything he'd ever wanted. Not just Sophie, but a family. "*My* kid, Sophie. You can't keep it from me."

"No," she said, tense beneath his grip, "I wouldn't do that to you."

"It's exactly what you're threatening."

She shook her head, but she didn't try to pull out of his arms. "I'm not. I swear I'm not. I'm just trying to let you off the hook."

"Fuck being let off the hook."

She flinched at his foul language and Jake nearly cursed again as the thought of losing Sophie already tore his guts to shreds. But losing his child, too?

Not a chance.

Jake's desperation to keep them both took pre-cedence over everything else.

"One week."

"What?"

"I want one week to convince you to marry me."

"You seriously think you can convince me to marry you in seven days? You must be the most arrogant, self-absorbed—" She stopped midinsult, clearly trying to regain control. She took a deep breath. "Look, if you want to be a part of your child's life, I'm not going to keep you from him or her. But you and I both know we don't have to get married to be involved parents. I don't understand why you're acting like this…or how you could pos-sibly think I'm going to agree to your demands."

Because just a handful of hours with you in my arms made it so I can hardly remember what my life was like before you. I only know it wasn't any good.

Growing up, Jake's neighborhood had been rough enough that he'd quickly learned to do what-ever he had to do to make sure he walked away in one piece. Right, wrong, none of that mattered when your life was on the line.

This time, three lives were on the line—his, So-phie's and their child's—and he'd fight as dirty as he had to for them.

"You're the one who came to my house in Napa and took your clothes off." He let his reminder of who seduced whom sink in before saying, "You owe me at least seven days."

Sophie stared at him for a long moment, long enough that he knew he had her right where he wanted her. Finally.

"If I say yes, at the end of the week you'll agree to do this my way?" she asked.

No. He'd never be able to do that, could never in a million years not claim his baby or the mother of his child. But it wouldn't help his cause if she knew that going in.

Knowing he needed the week to work his magic, he nodded, just one more lie to add to the pile. But he wasn't done playing dirty yet, not when he knew using their sexual connection was his best chance to get her to change her mind. Even if he burned in hell for it.

"The bed is part of the deal, Sophie. It's non-negotiable."

"Obviously," she replied, shocking the hell out of him, yet again. "We'll have a bunch of sex for a week and then you'll leave again and I'll deal with the rest of my life." She shrugged as if she couldn't have cared less about it either way.

Jake belatedly realized his misstep. At the end

of the week, Sophie was going to use all the great sex they were bound to have to prove that's all there was between them. He'd never had to prove the opposite to a woman, had never wanted to.

It was one heck of a situation. Especially considering, he knew now, that it didn't matter how hard he tried not to touch her. He was barely going to make it another seven minutes, let alone seven days, without making love to her again.

"So we're agreed?"

"Fine." The one word from her mouth held a world of irritation. "I'll give you seven days, but you can't tell anyone in my family about us. About the baby."

It made sense that none of them knew yet. Because if they did, her brothers would already have hunted him down. And killed him. And then he'd never get this chance to try to convince her to be his. Forever this time, instead of just for one night he relived every single time he closed his eyes.

"Does anyone know apart from the two of us?"

"Only Lori. She wanted to do terrible things to you when she found out. Still does, actually."

It would definitely be easier for him to win her over in seven days if her family wasn't constantly interfering in their business, especially if her brothers put him in a full body cast. But Sophie's keeping something so big, so important, from the family that meant everything to her didn't sit right with Jake.

"You look different." *Glowing.* "Your mother will take one look at you and know."

Her face went white again. "Oh, God, you're right. I just won't see her." He could see her trying to convince herself that what she was doing was okay. "It's just a week."

The seven days she'd promised him started ticking like a time bomb, laughing at him as he tried to figure out a way to turn it off before it detonated. They'd talk about her family later. Right now he had the mother of his child to win over.

"Have you eaten?"

"This morning."

It was late, way past when she should have eaten dinner. "You've got to think about more than yourself now."

"Are you accusing me of doing something to harm—"

He cut her off. "No. I just want to make sure you eat. Sit down," he said, pointing to one of his bar stools. "I'll make you dinner."

"I thought you were needed at the pub," she said, throwing his earlier words back in his face. She turned and headed for the front door.

Jake didn't think before reaching out and pulling her against him. He knew being held by him was the very last thing she wanted, but she belonged in his arms.

"Seven days starts now."

Eleven

Some things were way too weird for Sophie to get her head around. Like the fact that after all these years of wishing and hoping and dreaming, she was finally sitting in Jake's kitchen.

Where he was cooking her dinner.

While she was pregnant.

With his baby.

No doubt about it, she had been sucked into *The Twilight Zone*.

The city lights from his third-floor loft, in what used to be the industrial part of the city, were spectacular. But she couldn't take her eyes off Jake.

He had a surprisingly full fridge for a bachelor and he certainly looked as if he knew what he was doing with the carrots, potatoes and onions. She was still angry with him for his Neanderthal demands, but she needed to eat. And she was perfectly fine with letting someone else feed her on a day that had been more trying than any other she could remember.

Of course, just because big dangerous Jake McCann looked impossibly cute cooking her dinner, Sophie knew not to read too much into what he was doing, or to confuse his concern for the baby's welfare with concern for her.

Now that he knew he was going to be a father, she could tell all he wanted was a healthy kid. She had no doubt he wouldn't blink twice at taking drastic measures to meet his goals, like tying her up and force-feeding her healthy meals.

If only the tying-her-up part didn't still sound so good...

"Are you too hot? Too cold?"

"I'm fine," she said in a clipped voice.

"Have you been—"

The most self-assured man she'd ever known suddenly looked like he didn't know what to say. Darn it, Sophie told herself, it wasn't the least bit adorable.

"Have you been sick?"

"No. Mostly I've just been tired." *But I thought that was because every time I tried to fall asleep I ended up thinking about you instead.* "That's why I didn't realize I was pregnant until today."

"Good," he said in a gruff voice as he refilled her half-empty glass of water and slid a plate of warm soda bread with butter melting on it toward her before moving behind the stove. "I'm glad you've felt okay."

It was hard to remember he didn't really care about her at all when he was being so sweet. How on earth was she going to keep her guard up for seven days?

And how the heck had he even gotten her to agree to a week in the first place?

Sophie still wasn't sure, although she didn't think she'd ever forget the expression on his face when she'd told him she didn't want anything from him and would deal with the baby all by herself without ever naming him as the father.

Jake had looked momentarily lost. Then angry. Then determined.

Maybe she should have come more prepared for his reaction, but she hadn't expected him to want a baby. Especially not hers. And frankly, she still didn't understand why he *did* want it. Jake was the ultimate bachelor. His night-driven life didn't lend itself to family dynamics.

Tomorrow, after a good eight hours of sleep,

she'd make herself face him down again and demand an answer. Tonight, however, she wasn't even sure how she was going to stay awake through this meal.

"I can't believe you know how to cook." The simple statement came out with such a bite, more than she even knew she had in her. Sophie couldn't understand how she could love and hate him at the same time…just that she did.

He gave her a half smile, not quite the smirk she was so used to. There was something in this smile that was different, almost as if he was a little embarrassed to be caught doing something that didn't scream *womanizing male*.

"I had to learn when the cook was sick and no one else was around to do it."

"I never thought about how hard it must have been to have your own restaurant," she said, assuming he was talking about buying and operating the first McCann's Irish Pub.

"Yeah," he said, "it was crazy knowing that running McCann's was entirely up to me. Win or lose, I was the guy to blame, but that's not where I learned to cook. I was ten. My dad was working the taps. I would hang out in the back, wash dishes for quarters. The cook was too drunk to fry up the orders. He passed out in the back and the customers were giving my father trouble. He told me to cook." Jake transferred the vegetables to a plate, then sliced the pork roast he'd heated up on the plate beside it. "So I cooked."

How long had she wanted to know something like this about Jake's life? How long had she dreamed of being close enough to him to actually hear stories of his childhood? Now that the moment had finally come, she was so mad at him. Too mad—and too tired—to really appreciate it.

He slid the plate in front of her and it smelled wonderful. "Standard Irish fare." There was a hint of defensiveness in his tone. "It's what I do best."

That, she knew, was where he was wrong. The food looked amazing, but she already knew what he did best. And while it involved plenty of heat, the kitchen wasn't the preferred location...and there were a heck of a lot less clothes involved.

The bed is nonnegotiable.

Over and over his earlier words played in her head, thrumming through her body, making every cell come completely alive, alert with wanting, despite how exhausted she was. She'd already accepted that seven days in close proximity with Jake would make it impossible to guard her hormones. Especially when she now knew *exactly* how good he could make her feel.

Only this time, she was smart enough to know she needed to guard her heart. No matter what.

Fortunately, the growling of her stomach stole her attention back from how close his bed had to be. She reached for the knife and fork. "Thanks for dinner."

It wasn't the most grateful she'd ever sounded, but it was the best she could do for now. Jake would just have to deal with it. But when she took a bite, she couldn't stop the moan of appreciation coming from her lips.

"You like it?"

He was smiling at her, and when she looked up at him, when she saw those dark eyes on her like that, looking so pleased with pleasing her, she lost hold of every thought…lost hold of anything but the sudden, desperate need to feel his mouth on hers again, taking her, possessing her the way he had during their one beautiful night together.

It didn't help when his smile changed, shifting to an intense look of desire that she was sure mirrored hers exactly.

Somehow she managed to pull herself together enough to say, "It's great." She took another bite, hoping that if she kept her mouth stuffed full, she could keep her lips focused on something other than wanting to feel Jake's pressing against them.

"Good. There's more if you need it."

She frowned. "Wait, aren't you having some?"

He shook his head. "I ate earlier."

"Oh." He really had done all of this for her. No man had ever cooked for her before.

Then again, no man had ever knocked her up, either. She supposed rustling up a meal was the least he could do.

Sophie was hungry enough not to care that he was just sitting there watching her eat. She'd never been one of those girls who picked at her food. Her hips and breasts were evidence of that, despite the laps she swam every day. Lori was quite a bit leaner, given her intense dance and choreography schedule.

But after several minutes, as her stomach went from empty to full, she realized she was going to lose the battle with keeping her eyes open. She put down her knife and fork and yawned, big and long.

"You're tired."

Jake, she'd noticed more than once, didn't waste words. But before she could do much more than nod, his arms were going around her and he was lifting her off the stool.

Her brain—and body—immediately flashed back to Napa, when he'd picked her up, naked and desperate for him.

"What are you doing?" She couldn't hide the panic that underlay each word.

He didn't break stride. "Taking you to bed."

Her breath lodged in her chest. Even wanting him as bad as she still did, she knew she couldn't have sex with him tonight. Not when she was feeling so tired and weak. On top of it all, it was as if every wall she should have up to protect herself was lying down taking a nap.

What would happen if she lowered the defenses she'd tried to put up? What remaining part of her heart—or worse, her soul—would she end up handing over to him on a silver platter?

"Jake, dinner was great, but I need to go home now."

"No." His bedroom was big and masculine, just like him. "Seven days, Sophie. You promised me the week." He moved to take off her shoes and she was so stunned by how gentle he was being with her that she let him.

"I know I did," she said when she found her voice. "But I thought they'd be like dates, that we'd meet up after work for a few hours."

"I want you here. With me."

It was everything she'd ever wanted him to say, and yet the words coming from her lips were, "What if I don't want to be here?"

He looked up at her from where he was kneeling by her now-bare feet, his eyes an unfathomable near-black. "Then I'll stay with you."

She swallowed hard, suddenly realizing his intent—and just what she'd signed herself up for.

Not just seven days, but seven nights.

Oh, God.

He got up and went to the bathroom, but was back in seconds. "There's a new toothbrush beside the sink. I'll be back soon."

Sophie knew she could put her shoes back on and leave, that she didn't have to go into his bathroom and brush her teeth before slipping into his bed. But she also knew Jake well enough to know that if she did that, he'd just follow her.

He wouldn't care about pounding on her apartment door loud enough to wake the whole neighborhood before she let him in. Not when he was so incredibly possessive, clearly wanting to take over her life by doing things like forcing her to eat dinner. It didn't matter that she'd been hungry enough to eat a horse. She didn't want anyone telling her what to do.

Especially not *him*.

But the craziest thing of all was that, instead of only being mad about his domineering behavior, she was aroused by it at the same time. So much so that she couldn't stop her old favorite daydream from playing in her head, the one where Jake's hard muscles were pinning her to the bed and he was looking down at her telling her exactly what he was going to do to her. And she was dying for it.

She shoved herself off the bed and went into the bathroom. "Stupid, stupid, stupid." She ranted at herself the entire way across the carpet to the tiled floor.

Her stupidity had already gotten her into this mess. She didn't need to compound it further by actually falling for his seven-day "let me convince you I can be there for you and the baby" game. Especially since any guy who kept extra toothbrushes on hand clearly needed them for a parade of women.

Furious at herself, she brushed her teeth hard enough to take off the top layer of enamel, then washed her face. He hadn't offered her any pajamas and she definitely wasn't going to get into his bed naked.

Wouldn't he just love that?

At least, she thought with a small measure of comfort, he didn't keep women's pajamas in his house to go with the toothbrushes. She'd never gone through someone else's things before—Lori was the snoop in their family—but Sophie didn't feel at all bad about opening his closet to look for a T-shirt. She hated sleeping in her bra, and she needed something to cover her in lieu of the white cotton she had on.

She found a black shirt and as she quickly pulled off her skirt, sweater and bra she tried not to appreciate the fact that the shirt smelled like Jake. A clean, masculine smell that went straight to her head.

Hearing footsteps, she all but threw herself onto his bed and beneath the thick covers, only to find his mattress deliciously comfortable. Clearly, from what she'd seen of his house so far, he bought the best for himself. She could only imagine how much a bed like this must have cost.

Oh, but it was worth every single penny.

She hadn't thought she'd be able to sleep a wink in his bed. But it was so comfortable…and she was so tired.

Before she knew it, Sophie's brain turned off and she was down for the count.

Jake stood in the doorway, so struck by the picture of Sophie asleep in his bed that he couldn't actually make his feet move forward. Yet again, he couldn't do anything but stare at her, watch as her chest rose and fell slowly, her hair spread out across his pillow, her expression so serene.

His chest clenched tighter as he finally moved into the room. Her scent was already everywhere, wrapping around him, winding through him, drawing him closer.

He could still barely process what had happened tonight, that Sophie had come to his house and told him she was pregnant. The fear he'd felt had only been eclipsed by one thing: pure joy.

For two and a half months he'd missed her every day.

No, he silently admitted as he started to strip off his clothes, he'd missed her every second. Not just because their lovemaking had been spectacular, but because he'd always loved being near her. Listening to her talk and laugh and even sing when she thought no one was listening. She danced, too, in the kitchen when she thought she was all alone, and even though Lori was the professional dancer in the family, Sophie was just as graceful, just as beautiful in motion. Jake had missed getting to watch Sophie with her family, the easy way she had with her brothers, the sparks that often lit between her and her twin, the way she pampered her mother more than anyone else.

Every moment of the past ten weeks he'd been

torn between knowing he wouldn't give up the memories of his night with Sophie for anything… and wishing they could rewind back to that place where she was still Nice and he was the ninth Sullivan who knew better than to even look twice at either of the Sullivan girls.

And now that she was pregnant?

It meant she was *his* whether she wanted to believe it or not. And not just for a few stolen hours anymore.

He wanted her. Badly. He hadn't just wanted her since the moment he'd found her standing outside his front door, hadn't just needed her for two and a half months, ever since they'd made love in the rental house in Napa. No, the truth was he'd wanted her so much longer than that. So long that he could hardly remember a time when he hadn't wanted her.

And he knew for damn sure that there would never come a time when he wouldn't want her.

Sixty seconds later he finished stripping his clothes off, pulled back the covers, slid in next to her and wrapped his arm around her waist to pull her into him, her soft curves fitting perfectly against him, her hips a soft, warm cradle for the erection that wouldn't go away. Jake slid one hand into her long hair, breathing in her sweet scent.

Maybe it shouldn't feel right to have Sophie Sullivan in his bed. But nothing had ever felt quite so right before.

"Good night, princess." He whispered the words against the top of her head, pressing a soft kiss there. Sleep claimed Jake long before he thought it would, with the one woman he'd never thought he could have safe and warm in his arms.

Twelve

Sophie felt so safe, so warm, as she floated in that in-between space between sleep and coming completely awake. She knew exactly where she was, knew precisely why she felt so good. Jake was holding her, his arms curled protectively around her shoulders, with one of his hands splayed flat over her stomach beneath the T-shirt as if he were trying to protect more than just her.

And he was completely naked.

She could feel the rigid flesh of his erection against the small of her back, the hairs on his thighs against the smooth skin of her legs, and as desire swiftly stole through her, she couldn't stop her half-asleep body from wanting to get even closer.

She'd assumed night would be her enemy, those

dark hours during the seven days she'd promised. But now she knew it didn't matter whether it was day or night, light or dark.

She was her own worst enemy.

Jake wouldn't have to ask her for a darn thing. Just to be near him like this, if only to know the sweetness of his touch for a few seconds, she'd give up everything.

Obviously hearing her secret admission, Nice Sophie came completely awake inside of her and started yelling at her to protect herself from being hurt any worse than she already was. Nice tried to remind her of the pain she'd felt for two long months, tried to hold on to those truths she'd made herself face the day before.

But Naughty Sophie, the part of her that had clearly been held down for way too long, wanted to go back to that place where Jake had been touching her, teasing her, taking her to heaven and back. She'd be careful this time. She wouldn't be foolish enough to blurt out her love for him—or even to admit that she felt it—no matter how good he made her feel.

Of course, when Jake softly blew the hair away from her neck and pressed his lips to the sensitive skin there, it was inevitable that Naughty would win the battle over Nice. Rather than trying to fight it, knowing it was pointless to even try to pretend she didn't want to be his lover for the next seven days, Sophie did what came naturally and arched her neck to give his mouth better access.

His low groan of pleasure rumbled from his chest to hers as he pulled her hips even more tightly against his, his hand never leaving her stomach. His tongue slid over her exposed neck and she shivered at the delicious sensation of being tasted. Savored. And when he blew over her damp skin, she felt her nipples become sharp points of need. Her breasts were more sensitive now, probably due to her pregnancy. And, oh, how she wanted his hand to move those few inches, up from her waist.

But then his mouth was back on her neck, nipping at her skin, causing a trail of thrill bumps in its wake before latching on to her earlobe, and the breath Sophie hadn't realized she'd been holding whooshed from her chest as his teeth bore down on the soft flesh.

More ready for sex that she'd ever been in her life, she instinctively pressed her hips into his erection, trying to widen her legs for him, so that he could take her. But his thigh between hers held her captive.

"Jake," she pleaded, barely awake and already begging.

"Shhh," he soothed, and she might have pressed her case for quick and fast if not for the fact that he finally started moving his hand.

Sophie went completely still, not wanting to do anything that would make him stop the sinfully slow press of his fingertips over her belly button and then her lowest ribs. But even as she tried to hold still, she could feel herself trembling.

How long had she dreamed of Jake touching her like this? As if she was the most precious thing in his world? As if he'd never let anything hurt her? As if he'd slay all her dragons for just one more moment with her?

As his fingers skimmed over her skin, it didn't matter that Nice Sophie was screaming at her to know better, to wake up and face reality. Naughty Sophie promised that reality could wait, and it would have to, because there was no way she could leave Jake's arms now, not when he was so close to touching her—

His hand stilled just below the swell of her breasts and she nearly groaned with disappointment.

"Soon," he promised her, and the wicked intent in his voice—along with the shocking tenderness of his promise—had her toes curling against the tops of his feet.

Her breath came fast as he rained more kisses and soft little bites down from her ear, over her neck, then across her raised shoulder. She could have sworn his erection was actually throbbing against her back by that point, that he was teasing himself just as much as her, but his own clear desire for her didn't make him move any faster. If he kissed his way up and down her body like this he would drive her nearly insane…every press of his lips on her skin taking her closer to the peak, but never all the way there.

At long last, his fingers recommenced their erotic journey, lightly brushing over the curve of both breasts until his hand was in position to touch both at once. The taut peaks ached from the slightest touch of his palm and she arched into his touch to try to get him to take more from her.

Everything. Jake could have everything from her in this moment. It didn't matter what it was, she would give it to him, just as long as he made good on his promise of pleasure.

"So soft." He cupped one breast in his hand so gently she gasped at the sensation of his slightly rough skin against her. And then he was pressing his mouth into the curve where her shoulder met her neck and her gasp turned back into more begging she couldn't control.

"Please, Jake."

From the way she couldn't stop her hips from rocking into his, he had to know what she wanted. Just to be taken like this, while he was holding her and she was in the sweetest heaven anyone had ever known.

But when her begging didn't get her any closer to her goal, Sophie realized Jake would always be in control when they were together like this. The thought shocked her, but not as much as the realization that she loved it.

And, oh, to be his, if only for a little while in his arms like this...her Nice inner voice had no choice but to go quiet. A moment later, even the newly unmuzzled Naughty voice was silenced as Jake pulled his T-shirt off of her and his tongue slid against her skin again, moving slowly down her spine just as he shifted his hand to fill his palm with her other breast and slowly pressed his thumb and forefinger over one nipple.

Her insides felt like molten lava, and even though he hadn't touched anything but her neck and back and overly sensitive breasts, Sophie felt herself going over the edge, hurtling toward an unexpected climax that claimed her breath, her thoughts, just as Jake had claimed all of them.

"Oh, oh, oh!"

As the gasping little noises left her throat, Jake's thigh muscles bunched and pressed between her legs and she rode him like a woman possessed. There was no room for embarrassment here. Nor was there space for the anger and hurt she'd felt earlier.

All that remained in the in-between early morning of his bed was exquisite pleasure. Pleasure that ran so deep, she was powerless to do anything but let it take over every cell, inside and out.

He slid his hand down from her breasts, thankfully moving faster on the way down than he had on his earlier trip up from her belly. "I need to touch you," he said as he hooked his fingers on the side of her panties and pulled them down her legs.

The unexpected climax only ratcheting up her need, this time when she moved to spread her legs, he let her. And then his hand was moving over her pelvic bone, softly sliding over her damp curls, not stopping like he had before when she'd been dying for him to caress her breasts. She could feel a slight tremor shake his arm as he came closer to her core, almost as if the self-control he'd had earlier—his obvious intent to torture her slowly and gently—was slipping.

"Sophie."

Her name fell from his lips as he covered her

with his whole hand. His raw heat shocked her, shook her, enough that her head fell back into the curve of his shoulder. Jake's big, strong body cradled her, cupping her sex, literally holding her in the grip of anticipation for what would come next.

"So soft," he said again. "So wet for me."

And then, before she could figure out how to take her next breath, his fingers were inside of her, filling her, stroking her core so perfectly that the pressure way down deep in her belly grew again. Her sex throbbed against his talented fingers and her breasts ached for more of his touches.

Finally, Jake let her back fall flat against the mattress, and for the first time since the night before, she got to look at his impossibly beautiful face, those eyes so full of heat, so dark and dangerous. She couldn't look away, could feel desperate words of love about to spill from her lips, even though she knew better, even though she'd vowed not to let it happen again.

"Jake, I—"

His mouth covered hers before she could say anything more, and his passionate kiss drove her thoughts away. She loved feeling him over her like this, like she wasn't the only one who couldn't get close enough, and she kissed him back with all of the love in her foolish heart, giving herself up to all the emotions she'd sworn never to let herself feel for him again.

Too soon, he took his mouth away from hers, but she instantly forgave him when he lowered his head to her breast, laving first one and then the other. While the hand between her legs continued to stroke her nerve endings in the most delicious way, his free hand slid over her other breast.

It was too much. The way her lips still tingled from his kisses, and now his mouth, his hands on her, covering her, caressing her, tormenting her.

"This feels so good, even better than before," she moaned as she arched up off the bed into his hands and mouth and taut muscles, needing to press even closer to the man who was loving her as no one ever had before. Waves of pleasure rolled over her, going on and on like the sea, dragging her out with them until she was doing no more than bobbing in and out of them, trying desperately to catch her breath.

But Jake wouldn't let her fill her lungs as his mouth came back over hers. His tongue swirled with hers, his hands moving to grip her hips. His skin felt even rougher against her softness, and she reveled in the slight scratch of his large hands, the calloused fingertips that so deftly played over her, inside of her.

He shifted so that his entire weight was over her and she instinctively opened her legs wider to give him room to settle between them. The head of his shaft slipped and slid over her sex and she arched into him again, but he held her hips still in his big hands, holding himself just as rigidly above her as he lifted his mouth from hers.

"You're absolutely sure you're pregnant?"

She didn't know why he was asking her that question. "Yes. I'm sure."

"I'm safe, Sophie. I just had a blood test and I swear I'm safe."

Somehow, through the lust-filled haze that clouded her brain, she realized what he was saying. He didn't want to use a condom. She didn't want anything between them, either, wanted Jake and Jake alone to fill her.

The thought made her so wild with need, she could barely get out the words, "I am, too."

"Thank God," he said, and the words really did sound like a prayer of thanks falling from his lips.

She held her breath, waiting for him to slam into her the way he had their first night together. Instead, he gently slid his hands out from beneath her hips. Not to fondle her breasts. Not to tease her skin the way he had just a little while ago. But to reach for her face, to hold her jaw so gently with those big hands that were capable of such strength.

He didn't kiss her, just stared at her with those dark eyes, and she was held completely in his thrall. "You're mine."

This time there were no sage, protective inner voices to stop her from agreeing. How could there be when they were all on the edge of anticipation?

"I'm yours."

The word *mine* sounded in the room again as he slowly entered her, his eyes still locked with hers. Sophie had never known such intensity, in or out of bed, as Jake's presence wrapped itself around her just as his arms had, cradling her, holding her steady when she otherwise would have broken apart.

She had to tell him, needed him to know. "I've never felt like this before." Pleasure so sweet couldn't possibly exist. And yet, she now knew it did. "I never knew."

It was what she'd said to him after their first kiss, and now she was saying it again as he made love to her in his big bed as the sun rose higher in the sky and washed over them.

"All those books, and you never knew."

Her eyes widened as she realized he was teasing her, the corners of his beautiful mouth curving up for a split second before he bent down to press one soft kiss against her forehead, and then each cheekbone, before moving lower to the curve of her neck, her collarbone, the upper swell of her breasts.

If their lovemaking after the wedding in Napa had been a fierce staccato of desire and unquenchable need, the way Jake now lingered over every inch of her skin was like a beautiful sonata, playing slowly as the soundtrack to their coupling.

She knew sex was simply part of their one-week agreement, had thought she could hold part of herself back from him while still finding pleasure in his touch. Only, now she had to face just how impossible that goal really was.

After loving him in secret for so long, to have him touch her like this, to know his intention was to convince her to let him be a part of her and her baby's life...it was too much for Sophie to resist.

And in the end, it was his tender attention, along with his unexpected smile, that had her crying out in the ultimate pleasure, his mouth capturing the sounds as he moved with her, taking her higher and higher with every stroke of his body into hers.

Together, they moved, sweat-dampened skin slipping and sliding, mouths taking and giving in equal measure as her inner muscles gripped him so tightly that he had to fall with her, just as far, just as hard, just as long. As she felt him explode inside of her, she leaped to an even higher peak she hadn't known to reach for, one where it felt as if the explosions would continue forever, ripples of pleasure that had no end.

She'd thought she needed fast and rough, had believed her urgency to be taken by him warranted nothing else. But she'd been wrong.

Because after everything that had happened, she'd needed to be loved.

And, oh, how Jake had loved her.

Thirteen

Jake lay over Sophie, pressing her into the bed, her slim arms wrapped tightly around his neck, her gorgeous legs wrapped around his waist. He could stay like this with her forever, never wanted to let go—

Oh, no! He scrambled off her, practically jumping out of the bed.

"Jake? What's wrong?"

"I can't believe I forgot." He grabbed pillows and shoved them under her knees while she stared at him like he'd lost his mind.

She tried to sit up, tried to reach for him again. "What are you doing?"

He put his hands on her shoulders and gently laid her back against the bed. "I was crushing you. I could have hurt you, could have hurt the baby."

He'd noticed this morning that her stomach had a slight swell to it. Not big enough that anyone would notice the change if they didn't know she was pregnant. But he knew, and that knowledge had already changed him. He'd never felt like this, so protective and pleased…and proud.

Sophie's laughter broke through his thoughts. "I can't believe you think that a little sex is going to hurt anything."

He couldn't believe she was laughing at him. Or that she'd taken what had just happened between them and reduced it to practically nothing. What had happened to the quiet, mild-mannered girl he'd known for so long?

"I wouldn't exactly call what we just did 'a little' sex."

Again, her mouth curved up with laughter, but when she saw that he was serious, she said, "I feel fine, Jake."

She clearly didn't understand. It was *his* kid in there. He'd planned to put her on her hands and knees, to take her from behind so she couldn't look at him with those big, hopeful eyes, and so he wouldn't crush her with his weight.

But he hadn't been able to do that. Because he had to look at her. Had to see that beautiful expression of pure joy come over her face when he came into her with nothing between them this time.

He shouldn't have wanted to hear her say she loved him again…but he had. More than he'd ever wanted anything in his life. Even worse, looking at her lying beneath him—so open, so giving, so sweet—had made crazy things rattle around inside his head. And his chest. He'd made himself cover her mouth with his before either of them could say something they'd regret later.

And in the end he'd lost all control, taking her without any thought at all to the life she carried inside.

"I'm pretty sure sex is perfectly fine during pregnancy," she told him in a reassuring tone.

"I'm going to ask the doctor."

Her frown came back. "Oh, no. No way. We are not doing this." She threw back the sheets and got out of the bed, giving him a mind-blowing view of her naked curves as she bent over to pick up her clothes.

Now it was his turn to say, "What are you doing?"

He was pretty sure she didn't remember she was completely naked as she faced him, clearly irritated. "I am not made of porcelain. I get that you're all freaked out, that you want to control everything around you, but I absolutely will not let you control *me!*"

"Wait a minute." He advanced on her. "I'm not trying to control you."

She lowered her voice into a bad imitation of his. "Seven days, Sophie. Of course you're moving in with me. And sex is nonnegotiable as long as you keep those pillows under your knees and worry about every single thing you do all day and night from now on to keep my precious baby safe."

He wasn't going to laugh. But it didn't help that she was not only the sexiest naked woman he'd ever seen, but also the cutest. Sophie had always seemed so serene, borderline submissive. But ever since the wedding, she'd been full of sparks and fire.

And it aroused the hell out of him.

Unfortunately, she saw his barely repressed laughter. "You should know, any progress you just made with me on your weeklong marriage quest has just been eradicated by that stupid smirk on your face."

She moved to whirl away from him and into the bathroom, but he reached out to snake an arm around her waist and pull her against him, the clothes and shoes she'd been holding falling to the floor. Her breath was coming fast as she looked up at him.

"I made some progress, huh?"

She made a furious little sound, then laid both of her palms flat against his chest and shoved, hard enough that he actually fell back on the bed.

"The orgasms might have won you a few points," she told him in a voice that could have cut through steel, "but the way you're acting now just put you back into negative territory. Way back."

With that, she reached into his closet, grabbed a long, blue-and-red-striped dress shirt, gathered up yesterday's clothes and shoes and stomped into the bathroom, slamming the door hard enough that his windows rattled.

Jake knew he should be worried about pissing her off, but the truth was he liked seeing this side of her. Not just because she was gorgeous with flushed skin and flaming eyes when she cut him down to size…but because he'd never expected her to be full of such fire.

Yet again, little Sophie Sullivan was surprising him. In—and out of—bed.

But the surprises weren't over yet, because when he heard the shower turn off and she came out of the bathroom a few minutes later, she was wearing his shirt like a dress, belted around the middle, stopping just above her knees, her legs bare in her heels. Her hair was wet around her shoulders and she looked as sexy as it was possible for a woman to be.

"You look beautiful."

On a disbelieving snort, she said, "I look like a poster from the eighties. But it's better than putting on dirty clothes." She wrinkled her nose. "I hate that."

"Wait a minute," he said as he approached her, "are you saying you don't have anything on under my shirt?"

Her eyes got big and she started backing away from him. "We should go soon. The appointment is in forty-five minutes and we still need to stop by my apartment so I can put on normal clothes."

"Forty-five minutes?" He pretended to think about it for a moment. "That should be enough time for what I have in mind."

A look of pure lust shot across her face. But a moment later, she had on her best librarian expression, the one that told him he was being too loud and unruly and was on the verge of being kicked out of the building if he didn't shape up right away.

God, how he loved the idea of making love to the prim and proper librarian...and turning her into the wild lover he now knew she was underneath it all.

She narrowed her eyes at him as if she could read his mind. Knowing her, she probably could.

"Go shower and get dressed, Jake."

He could tell how much she wanted to look down at his boxers to see if he was aroused... which he was. Hugely. But she determinedly kept her gaze on his face. "I'll be waiting for you in the kitchen."

It would have been so easy to grab her again, to push her up against the wall and be inside of her in five seconds flat. And boy, was Jake tempted to do just that, to fill his hands with her soft curves, to taste that sweet skin, to slide bare into her slick heat again.

But he'd been serious when he'd told her he needed to ask the doctor if sex was okay. So he let her run.

For now.

Oh, God, when Jake had been advancing on her, a beautiful naked lion about to pounce, those dark eyes full of enough sensual intent to take her breath completely away, it had been all she could do to walk away from him.

Especially when what she really wanted was to

throw her arms and legs around him for yet another trip to paradise.

Thank God he'd gone to take a shower. It would give her room to breathe. And to try to work off her agitation with him…and ever-present arousal.

Sophie was pacing Jake's kitchen when her cell phone rang. She was praying it wasn't someone from her family calling. Not because she didn't love talking to her mother or siblings, but because she hated the thought of outright lying to them. It was bad enough that she was going to make sure to avoid them for the next week.

But when she saw that it was Lori calling, she knew she had to pick up. After their talk last night, and the fact that Lori knew Sophie had gone to tell Jake about the baby, her twin had to be worried sick about her. And if she hadn't been so shell-shocked by coming face-to-face with Jake again, she would have remembered to call her sister to tell her that everything was okay.

Only, she thought as she pressed the talk button, how could she have possibly said that?

Lori didn't waste a single breath before saying, "Why didn't you call me last night? I swear I was about to come over to Jake's house and knock down his door."

Sophie had never doubted her twin's love for

her, not even when they'd been having their worst fights. But now, her sister's love helped fill up all of those parts of her that were scared and hollow.

"I'm sorry, I can't believe I forgot to call you. It's just that when I saw Jake and told him—"

Lori cut her off. "What did he do? What did he say?"

Sophie looked at the closed bedroom door, and even though she could still hear the sound of the shower running, she lowered her voice as she said, "He was pretty surprised." That was pretty much the biggest understatement *ever*. "But…he said he wants to try to make it work, Lor."

"Wow," Lori said, and then, "that's good news, right?"

When Sophie didn't answer, because she simply didn't know how to explain everything she was feeling right then, her twin suggested, "I know you wanted to deal with Jake on your own first, but I really think you should talk to Mom about this. She'd understand, you know she would."

Sophie knew her sister was right. When they'd made bad decisions, even when they completely screwed something up, their mother had never acted disappointed in them.

Still, that didn't change what Sophie knew deep down in her heart: after two decades of being surrounded by her family, she and Jake needed these seven days to themselves.

"I can't talk to her." Her voice shook a little bit as she said, "Not yet."

"Well, then, maybe I'll just have to accidentally—"

"No! I've never told her about you-know-who even though I've wanted to every time I see what the relationship is doing to you." Sophie couldn't believe she had to remind her sister of the pact they'd made with each other when they were really, really young. They'd vowed never to betray each other's secrets. "So you can't tell her about me and Jake and the—" She put her hand over her stomach. "The baby."

She heard the shower shut off and she said, "Thanks for calling and don't worry if I'm out of touch for the next week or so, okay?"

Lori said a very reluctant, "Okay," and then Sophie hung up the phone and put it back in her purse.

In the clear light of day, she forced herself to go back over her list of all the reasons Jake was bad for her. He'd never love her the way she loved him. And after their one night together, when he'd touched her like she mattered—then disappeared—she knew better than to ever give weight to that hope again. If she hadn't gotten pregnant and come to tell him the news, she knew with absolute certainty that he never would have come after her. Rather, he would have avoided her completely, just the way he'd avoided numerous Sullivan family events in the past two and a half months that he would otherwise have attended.

Only, their lovemaking this morning had seemed different from their first night together. She hadn't had as many orgasms, but it had still been better. Because Jake really seemed to want her, not just that fantasy bridesmaid she'd had the makeup artist and hairstylist put together for him.

This morning, she'd felt like he was touching her because he couldn't bear not to.

Of course, he'd gone and ruined that theory right away when he jumped off her and shoved those pillows under her knees. Jake was the last person on earth she would have thought would go nuts over pregnant women, but it only confirmed the main fact she needed to remember at all times: he clearly wanted her for the baby, not for herself. And if some great sex was thrown in along the way to having that kid, who was he to say no?

She opened the fridge to see if there was anything in there that could settle her slightly nauseous stomach, but the smell of last night's leftovers had her slamming it shut a few seconds later, muttering, "I could probably be any pregnant woman and he'd be losing it over me. The big jerk probably has some kind of weird pregnant-woman fetish."

"What's that about fetishes?"

She spun around, hand over her heart. "I didn't know you were out here." Not wanting to have to explain herself, she picked up her bag and headed for the door. That was when she suddenly realized something strange. There were no books anywhere. Not on the coffee table or the counter, and especially not sitting around in piles on the floor like at her place, tripping her every time she went out to get a midnight snack.

But when he put his hand on her lower back, her questions about his lack of reading material fled as she focused her thoughts on ignoring how good his touch felt...and how nice his manners were.

It's because of the baby, she reminded herself.

He kept his hand on her back as they walked out to the car, and when he started gently massaging her tight muscles she could barely hold back a moan of pleasure at how good it felt. He knew exactly how to touch her, exactly how rough or gentle to be without her having to give him any guidance at all.

Simmering with the arousal she couldn't fight

no matter how hard she tried, as they drove in silence to her apartment, she noted that he drove the way he made love, his big hands controlling the wheel of his expensive car gently, but firmly.

Her body heated up and she squirmed in the passenger seat, pressing her thighs together to try and stop the ache. Of course, every second she was with him—and every time they made love—that ache only grew deeper. Stronger.

"I'm only human, Sophie." Jake's eyes flicked to her face, then her breasts and legs, naked beneath his shirt. "Keep looking at me like that and I'm going to pull over so we can take care of the problem."

"There's no problem," she assured him, but her voice was ragged enough that she knew it was clear she was lying.

How could she reconcile the Nice Sophie she'd been her whole life with the wanton woman in Jake's car who wanted to spread her legs wide for him and let him do whatever he wanted to her in the middle of downtown San Francisco traffic?

Thank God they pulled up in front of her apartment thirty seconds later. "I'll be back in a couple of minutes. You can wait in the car."

She shoved the door open and nearly fell out onto the sidewalk in her hurry to get away from temptation. She could only imagine how small her apartment would feel if Jake were in there with her…and how hard it would be to keep her clothes on around him so that they actually had a chance of making it to her doctor's appointment on time.

Jake knew he should be feeling guilty about the dirty thoughts running in circles in his head, about the fact that he'd been ten seconds from making good on his threat to pull over and put his hands and mouth all over Sophie.

But, damn if she wasn't the hottest thing he'd ever come across…and so transparent that she couldn't possibly keep her lustful thoughts from passing over her face one after the other as she sat next to him in the small interior of his sports car.

Two and a half months ago, she'd given herself to him without a second thought. Now, even though she clearly wanted him as much as he wanted her, he could see her intent was to withhold every part of herself that she could. Yes, she'd agreed to be in his bed, but even though that should have been more than enough for him, it wasn't. Not anymore. Not after having had all of her once before.

What, he wondered, would it take for Sophie to open up to him again? To trust him the way she'd trusted him in Napa?

A heavy weight settled in Jake's gut as he silently acknowledged her valid reasons for not trusting him. She would never believe him if he told her he wasn't the kind of guy who slept with a girl and then left her hanging for months. He'd always been clear with his lovers about expectations, about the fact that they couldn't have any. And he'd never slunk away in the middle of the night like a coward.

Until Sophie.

And he had no idea how to make it up to her.

No question, the sexual connection he and Sophie shared was as good as it got. Their desire for each other wasn't going anywhere, no matter how hard she tried to slam the brakes on it.

But that wasn't enough. He'd always liked Sophie, but now that he was seeing the different sides to her—the smart and the sexy, the complicated emotions and the simple pleasures she took from beauty and food, the spark that sprang from the serene—he realized he wanted her to like him, too.

And that, he already knew, was going to be the biggest hurdle of all, considering he'd be hard-pressed to come up with reasons why she should.

Sophie came back to the car wearing a soft, long-sleeved sweater dress in gray that did more for her curves than he figured she knew. She'd put on a little makeup and brushed her hair until it shone. She buckled her seat belt and sat with her hands primly clasped on her lap before telling him the address of her doctor's office in a tight voice.

He couldn't help but smile at the way she was trying so hard to rein in all that passion she'd been losing the battle to just minutes before. His lovely, foolish girl. Didn't she realize she should just give in already?

"We're going to be late," she snapped when he didn't start the car. But when she finally turned to him, whatever she'd been about to say fell away, confusion taking its place. "Why are you looking at me like that? What are you smiling about?"

She was so easy to rile up. He could already see he'd never get tired of putting sparks into her pretty eyes.

"Whatever you have up your sleeve," she muttered, "you'd better just forget it."

The truth was, he didn't have anything much up his sleeve for the time being. He wanted to get through this doctor's appointment first before he moved on to his next step in convincing her to marry him. But Sophie didn't need to know that. Especially not when he found he liked having her on her toes, anticipating what he was going to do next.

Whether she'd ever admit it or not, she liked it, too.

"Don't you wish you knew?" he said in as sensual a tone as he could muster around his grin, then sped off into traffic before she could say another word.

Fourteen

Sophie checked in with the receptionist, then sat on one of the padded leather seats in the waiting room and picked up a magazine. She was determined to ignore Jake. But, of course, that was nearly impossible, with all the other women in the room staring at him in wonder.

These women were all pregnant, for God's sake! What were they doing looking at a stranger like that?

It wasn't that she was possessive about him, she told herself, just that they were behaving inappropriately. Their husbands wouldn't be pleased if they knew the way their wives were practically bowing down prostrate before Jake's male beauty.

"So," he asked one of the women, "how's your pregnancy going?"

Of course, he couldn't just leave it alone, could he? The woman beamed at him as though he were the Second Coming.

"Really great." The woman leaned in close as if she were telling him a secret. "I'm having a boy."

Jake leaned closer and grinned at the woman. "That's great."

"I'm having a girl!" another woman from across the room piped in.

Jake smiled at her, too. "Congratulations." He nodded at the women. "There really is nothing prettier than a pregnant woman."

Sophie had never seen people look as happy as these women did after he made his proclamation. What was wrong with them?

And why did she feel so pathetically jealous?

"I knew it," she muttered into her magazine, and the woman closest to her raised an eyebrow.

"What do you know?" he asked, putting his hand on her knee.

Why did he have to be so warm? And why did she have to love being touched by him so much? Way too much.

She purposefully uncrossed and recrossed her legs so that he'd have to slide his hand away. *I knew you were one of those pregnancy fetish creeps,* was what she was thinking, but she simply said, "Nothing."

He leaned in close and she could feel his breath on her earlobe. "I'll find a way to convince you to tell me later, you know." His tongue flicked out against her earlobe before he pulled away and she barely swallowed a lust-filled moan before it escaped her lips.

Angry with herself for having absolutely zero control over her hormones around him, she hissed, "You're a pervert, that's what!"

His laughter at her crazy statement rumbled through the waiting room. "I can't wait to hear why."

"You know why."

He looked at her in confusion for a second and she had to nod her head in the other women's directions before awareness dawned. His laughter was loud enough this time to ring out through the room. "So that's what your muttering about fetishes was this morning. You think I'm into—" He broke off, laughing again. "I am, you know," he said, leaning in so close to her ear that his warm breath sent thrill bumps racing across the surface of her skin, "but only when the pregnant woman is you."

How did he do it? How did he melt her with every word? Every touch?

Reminding herself that she was supposed to be making him prove himself, she purposely lifted her magazine closer so that she could pretend to be engrossed in the article she hadn't even glanced at yet.

A moment later, when he'd finally stopped laughing, he leaned back over and whispered, "Might be easier to read this way."

His big, strong body was too close to hers in the small waiting room for her brain to figure out what he was talking about until he turned the magazine around in her hands.

Oh, my God. How embarrassing. She didn't normally care what a bunch of strangers thought of her, but then again, she'd always blended into the background, so no one had ever really noticed her.

Being with Jake, she was slowly realizing, was the opposite of being invisible. He had too much presence, was far too charismatic and charming— not to mention gorgeous—for her to stay hidden when she was with him.

It should have been easier to get lost behind him. But he wouldn't allow that, she realized as he put his hand back on her thigh and held it there, no matter what she did to try to shake him off.

For all his arrogance, he didn't seem interested in hogging the limelight. Instead, she got the strange sense that he was proud to be sitting there with her.

Even when she was doing dumb things like pretending to read a magazine upside down.

"When are you due?"

Sophie couldn't believe the woman in the corner asked Jake the question instead of her, like they had some special bond just because he'd smiled at her and said she was pretty.

Of course, it stung even more that Sophie hadn't needed much more of a reason than his smile to fall in love with him so many years ago.

"In the fall."

No one could miss the possessive note in his voice, or his clear joy at the prospect of having a baby. Sophie felt her heart soften despite herself.

Darn it, why couldn't he be more of a jerk all the time? Why did he have to keep having these moments when he seemed like the perfect guy? It would make it so much easier to hate him if he would just behave like a self-absorbed imbecile, rather than a sweetly concerned, übersexy father-to-be.

Then again, at least it helped her remember that the only thing he was really interested in was the baby. Not her. After all, he'd walked out on her without a second glance, but as soon as he'd heard about a child, he'd become the most possessive person on the planet.

"Oh, that's wonderful!" the woman exclaimed. "Congratulations."

Jake squeezed Sophie's thigh just above her knee and thrill bumps immediately ran up and down her legs at the intimate touch.

"Thanks," he replied. "We're really excited about it."

Amazingly, it was true. Despite the fact that she'd gotten pregnant by accident *and* the status of their relationship was completely up in the air, both of them really were excited about having a child. Even if the whole coparenting thing was going to be sticky from different households—especially if there was one of his playthings over when she went to pick up her kid at his house.

At some point after she had the baby, they'd have to have a talk about what was and wasn't appropriate for children to see. Yes, she'd be sure to let him know she expected him to keep all future dates and sexual partners away from their child, simply so he didn't confuse their son or daughter. If it put a damper on his sex life, he'd just have to deal with that, wouldn't he?

A nurse popped her head out of the door that led back to the examination rooms. "Sophie Sullivan?"

Sophie stood up and Jake moved with her, his hand on her lower back. The nurse looked between them, a question in her eyes.

How many times, she wondered, would she see those same silent questions? *This is the man you're with? How could you possibly pull that off? And how can I get one just like him?*

At least, she thought with a small measure of gratitude, rather than barging in and taking over absolutely everything, Jake was waiting patiently for her to explain why he was there.

Only, Sophie wasn't sure she could explain any of it at all, not without using words like *in love with him forever* and *never going to love me back*...and, of course, *crazy accident.*

Which was why all she said was, "He'll be coming in with me."

Without missing a beat, he held out his hand. "Jake McCann."

The nurse's eyes got big as she shook his hand. "I thought you looked familiar. You're on those great ads for McCann's Irish Pubs. Are you the owner?"

He nodded but, amazingly, didn't prolong the conversation about himself. Most of the guys Sophie had dated loved nothing better than to talk about themselves. Jake couldn't possibly be the exception, could he?

The nurse ushered them into the room and looked down at her chart. "Let's see, you're here to see the doctor about a possible pregnancy?" When Sophie nodded, the nurse asked, "When was the date of your last period?"

Feeling more than a little embarrassed about discussing this kind of stuff in front of Jake, she quickly calculated the date and told the nurse.

"Let's get your weight."

Great, just what every woman wanted, for the man she was sleeping with to see the number on the scale. She worked to keep her chin up as she slipped off her shoes and got on the scale.

"Looks like you've put on about ten pounds already."

Considering her stomach was still fairly flat, Sophie was pretty sure those extra pounds were all in her breasts and hips so far.

Obviously seeing her disgruntled expression, the nurse said, "Eight to twelve pounds is really normal for this stage of the first trimester. Especially with the first pregnancy, when you're not used to the changes in your body." She handed Sophie a plastic cup. "We'll need you to give us a urine sample and then go ahead and put this gown on so you're ready for the doctor."

Through it all, Jake sat in the blue chair in the corner, looking perfectly comfortable with being in a gynecologist's office. His dark eyes were tracking her every move, but she couldn't read his expression. Frankly, she didn't want to know what he was thinking. Because even though she was nervous about being here with him, she suddenly realized she was even more nervous about the pregnancy.

Now that she'd started to get her head around being pregnant, she really wanted this baby. She prayed that the doctor would say everything was all right after her examination. A healthy baby was all she wanted now.

You want Jake, too, she had to admit as she finished filling the cup and set it on the bathroom counter for the lab technician. It was why she'd agreed to give him seven days.

But she wanted so much more than just his body. She wanted his heart…and for him to open up a window to his soul.

Sophie sighed, knowing it was long past time to give up those dreams and focus on something real. Like the child inside her. And the fact that she and Jake were going to have to figure out a way to bump along together as parents during the next fifty years.

Sixty seconds later, she had her clothes neatly folded up and the cloth hospital gown on. She held it tightly closed in the back as she exited the bathroom, which was ridiculous, since Jake had seen her naked more than once.

The doctor was already in the room chatting easily with Jake and Sophie's heart skipped a beat as she watched him easily charm the woman who had been her gynecologist since she was a teenager.

"Sophie!" Marnie moved to fold her into a warm hug. "Well, isn't this a wonderful surprise?"

Sophie plastered a smile on her face. "Yes. Really wonderful."

Her doctor patted the padded table. "Scoot on up here and we'll do a quick exam to make sure everything is progressing well." She referenced Sophie's chart. "The HCG levels in your urine sample concur with twelve weeks."

Relieved that the tests she'd taken at home hadn't been wrong about the pregnancy, Sophie slid onto the table and put her feet in the stirrups, trying not to think about how strange all of this must look to Jake.

"Jake, why don't you come stand over here. It

will be easier for you to see the ultrasound monitor."

He moved to her side and put his hand on her shoulder. He smiled down at her and Sophie was amazed to find herself more comforted by his presence than embarrassed. She'd been planning to come here alone. But she was—suddenly—incredibly glad she hadn't had to.

Marnie reached for something big and thick and light blue. It already had a condom over it, and acute embarrassment swept over Sophie at the thought of Jake watching her doctor slide that into her.

"This shouldn't hurt," her doctor said, "although it may be a little cold at first."

The lubricated ultrasound wand slid in easily and she could have sworn Jake's eyes were twinkling at her predicament. The doctor typed in a password on the ultrasound machine and the monitor switched to a picture that looked like a night sky with faint clouds and stars.

"Now, let's see where the little guy—or girl—is hiding."

Sophie's heartbeat ratcheted up, but before she could reach for Jake's hand, he was sliding his over hers. They held on to each other tightly, neither of them breathing until Marnie smiled.

"Ah, there it is." The doctor pointed to a faintly throbbing white light on the screen. "That's the heartbeat."

Sophie's eyes filled with tears. There was a new heart beating inside of her, one that she and Jake had made together.

"Wow." Jake's hushed voice echoed her feelings exactly. "Amazing."

Marnie smiled at him, then Sophie. "Always. The size of the fetus looks perfect for twelve weeks, too."

Sophie assumed they'd be done now, but instead of pulling the wand from her body, her doctor said, "Now I'm just going to take a quick look to see if there is anyone else in here."

"Anyone else?" Jake repeated.

"While it's not likely, it's certainly not impossible that you've got—" The doctor gave a happy little shout. "Right here. There's another heartbeat."

Jake squeezed Sophie's hand so hard she almost yelped. But it was hard to register the pain when she was busy being totally shocked by what the doctor had just said. Marnie moved the wand around inside her some more. "Yes, looks like there are only two."

Only two?

Oh, God, when she'd been making those proclamations to Jake and her sister about doing it all herself, she'd been assuming she was only in for one baby. Not two!

Sophie shot a panicked glance up at Jake. His tanned skin was as pale as she'd ever seen it, even whiter than it had been right after she'd given him the news that she was pregnant.

Marnie slid the wand out, then handed her the picture that she'd printed. "For your scrapbook. Have you been taking prenatal vitamins?"

Sophie shook her head as she sat up, feeling light-headed. She was so glad to have Jake standing strong behind her. "I wasn't planning to get pregnant."

Marnie's expression didn't betray any surprise or condemnation. "Okay, then. Here's a prescription for the ones I like best for my patients." She handed Sophie a bag from inside one of the cupboards. "Here are a few other things you might find helpful. Although I have to warn you, please don't freak out when you read the *What to Expect When You're Expecting* book. I'm giving it to you to use as a resource, not to feed any fears you might have about pregnancy." She smiled at Sophie. "You're a healthy young woman, and if we look at your mother's history, we can be pretty sure you're going to have no problems at all."

Sophie worked to find her breath as her doctor asked, "Now, do you two have any questions for me?"

God, yes. Sophie had zillions of questions she needed answers to. Most of which started with, *How could this have happened to me when other people have one-night stands all the time?* But for now, she just shook her head and said, "I'll probably have some once I read through these."

Books had always made her feel better. She'd always thought that knowledge could cure practically any ill. This time, however, she wasn't at all sure books could work that kind of magic.

"What about you, Jake?"

"Does she need to be extra careful? You know, should she be careful not to overexert?"

Marnie shook her head. "Sophie should be able to live pretty much as she is now. Good food, lots of rest and exercise."

"What about sex?"

His question shook Sophie from her panicked state. Now she was mortified instead.

"I'm glad you asked that, Jake," Marnie said. "It's something that pretty much every newly pregnant couple wonders about. I promise you, intercourse isn't going to hurt a thing. In fact, a lot of patients say it's even better during pregnancy." She smiled at both of them. "Feel free to email the office with any questions. And I'll see you again in four weeks."

The door closed behind the doctor, leaving Jake and Sophie alone.

She didn't have the first clue about where to go from here. She'd thought she was past the point where the rug could be pulled out from under her. But hearing that she was pregnant with twins was a whole new level of rug-yanking.

She knew she should get off the table and put her clothes back on, but she wasn't sure her legs would hold her up.

"Can you believe it?" Her question was more of a whisper than anything, as if she was afraid to say the word aloud. But she had to. *"Twins."*

Jake hadn't moved from behind her and she wanted to lean into him and never let go. Thank God he was here. If she'd had to do this by herself she'd—

"That decides it. We're definitely getting married now."

"What?" Sophie jumped off the table, not caring that her cloth gown was gaping open completely in the back. "No!"

Jake's face was completely shut down. "Yes."

"But you promised me seven days."

"You're having twins, Sophie. You can't do this alone. Not with two."

She shook her head. "That's beside the point."

He looked frustrated. And just as shell-shocked as she felt. "Then what is the point? It's just seven goddamned days. We both already know you're going to marry me."

How could she say, *The point is that if you drag me to Vegas today and make me say "I do" because I'm carrying your children, then you never even have to try to fall in love with me.*

But didn't she already know better? Why was she still hoping for the impossible?

She could taste defeat, that horrible bitterness on her tongue that she'd become so familiar with in the two and a half months after Jake had made love to her in Napa.

"If you don't know why those seven days matter," she said in a shaky voice, "then you're the world's biggest idiot."

She was about to grab her clothes and head to the bathroom when she saw Jake's expression. He looked utterly furious. But there was more than anger there, she realized as she looked closer. He looked ashamed, too.

And wounded. Horribly wounded by her insult. She rewound through all the names she'd called him in the past day. None of them had made him react like the word *idiot*. If anything, he'd laughed the rest of them away.

"Jake, I—"

Jake's voice cut through her like a knife. "I'll wait for you outside."

He was gone before she could call him back, before she could apologize for calling him an idiot.

The bathroom mirror mocked her as she caught a glance of her wild eyes, her flushed skin. She of all people knew how powerful words were. It made her sick to think she'd just hurt Jake with them.

All she wanted was to love and be loved…and she'd never been further from it.

Jake didn't say another word to her until he pulled up in front of the library and she fumbled at the buckle, trying to get out of his car as quickly as possible.

"Sit still, Sophie." Each word was a bullet aimed straight at her. "You're going to let me get the god-damned door for you this time and every time after."

For all the times she'd pushed him before now, something told her not to keep pushing. Not right at this moment.

She cringed at what she'd called him. *Idiot*. It

was a word she'd never spoken to anyone else, not even in her angriest moments. He had to know she hadn't meant it, that she'd spat it out in the heat of the moment. Didn't he?

A few seconds later, he yanked open the passenger door and leaned in to unbuckle her seat belt. It took every ounce of self-control she possessed to hold herself rigid as his muscles brushed over her skin, as his scent filled her senses. He held out his hand to help her out of the car and she had no choice but to take it.

"Jake," she said softly, "I'm sorry for what I called you earlier. I was angry. I didn't mean it."

He didn't acknowledge her apology. "Eight o'clock tonight. Be waiting for me with your bags packed."

Before she could tell him where to shove his commands, he was pulling her into him and kissing her so hard but with such finesse that even as she tried to fight him her body told her just to give in already.

It was what she'd always wanted, after all.

Jake.

But that wasn't good enough, just fulfilling her body's needs. Not if her heart was left out in the cold.

He let go of her and was back in his car and

speeding away from the library before she could begin to process what had happened on the steps.

"Who was that?"

Sophie still had her hand over her mouth, which was tingling and warm from Jake's furious onslaught, as she turned to her coworker with surprise. She'd forgotten she and Jake had been out in public.

He always made her forget everything but him.

Janice didn't wait for her to reply before saying, "I didn't think there were any men out there better-looking than your brothers." She shook her head in disbelief. "Is that your boyfriend?"

No, Sophie thought with an edge of silent hysteria, *he's just the father of my baby.*

Oh, God. Not baby.

Babies.

Digging deep, Sophie faked a smile for the biggest gossip in the San Francisco library system. "I've known him forever. He's a close friend of the family."

Janice looked at her like she was nuts. "Friends? That's all you are?" She frowned. "None of my friends have ever kissed me like that."

Sophie shrugged, as if a kiss like that from a male friend was perfectly normal, then looked at her watch. "I'd better get inside."

Well, she thought as she walked up to the large front doors, perhaps there was an upside to Janice having seen Jake. At least that way, when she started showing, maybe she wouldn't have to explain as much. Her coworker would spread the word for her.

Fifteen

Jake screeched to a stop in his parking space behind McCann's.

Sophie was right. He was an idiot.

*What if their kids could barely read because
of him?*

A cold sweat broke out across his skin, thinking
of his kids going through what he'd been through.
School had been hell. He could still remember
sitting with the other kids in first, second, third
grade, watching them learn to read all around him.
But no matter how hard he'd tried, he couldn't get
the letters to make sense.

It was one more way he was worse than everyone else. He wasn't just the poor kid whose clothes
stank like his father's booze and cigarettes.

He was stupid, too.

Sure, numbers always added up easily for him, but words were a different story. They were part of everything. Throughout his years at school he'd cut more classes than he'd attended. And he figured they'd only let him graduate because the teachers didn't want to see his ugly mug for another school year.

How many times in those teenage years had he told himself it didn't matter? That he didn't need to know how to read in order to be a bartender?

It had been his lifelong dream to have a pub of his own but running a pub was a whole different ball game from merely working in one. And that was when he'd had to face the truth: if he didn't learn to read, there wouldn't be a chance in hell that he could keep the business afloat.

Man, he'd been an asshole with those first tutors he'd hired in secret, enough of a belligerent, angry twenty-one-year-old that they'd quit one after the other. Finally, he'd found one who seemed more amused by his antics than anything. Mrs. Springs had been in her sixties and was tough on him in a way no one had ever been before, almost as if she cared about whether or not he learned to read.

He still remembered the day things finally started to click. He'd planted a kiss straight on Helen's lips, but she hadn't been angry with him.

She'd hugged him instead…then told him the road was still going to be long and difficult, but hopefully worth it.

She'd been right about the first part, anyway. He'd continued to sweat it out with her, and then with other tutors after she'd retired. The bigger his business grew, the more contracts and the more correspondence he needed to deal with. People often commented on the way he did nearly all of his business on the phone or in person, rather than using email. They called it his "personal touch." He didn't care what they called it, just as long as no one ever guessed why he rarely used his computer for anything but spreadsheets and financials.

So, yeah, he could read. But it was still difficult to get through a book and he couldn't see himself ever doing it for fun.

Whereas Sophie lived and breathed books.

Please, God, he found himself praying silently, *let our kids get Sophie's brain, not mine.*

One of his waitresses saw him sitting in his car gripping the steering wheel for dear life, and gave him a nervous little wave before turning away quickly as she clearly realized her boss was losing it.

Not little by little, but in big, huge chunks.

Hearing that he was going to be the father of

twins by autumn had thrown him for the biggest loop of his life. Big enough that he hadn't been able to think of anything but chaining Sophie to him, and doing whatever he needed to do to make sure she didn't leave him, to ensure that she and his children would be healthy and cared for.

Jake started to get out of the car when his eye caught the corner of the thick book the pregnancy doctor had given them. He needed to read it, needed to know everything that could go wrong with Sophie's pregnancy, so that he could make sure nothing bad ever happened to her.

Of course, when he flipped through it, hundreds of tiny little words laughed up at him. *Just try to read me now,* each of those words challenged him. *Best of luck, loser.*

If Sophie ever found out that he could barely read—

He shoved the book off his lap onto the floor mat. He didn't have time to read it right now, anyway. His executive assistant had already called him repeatedly with reminders for the half-dozen conference calls he had scheduled for today. They were important meetings he would normally have given his entire attention to, budding emergencies at his newer sites that should have had him on the next plane out of San Francisco…rather than just trying to figure out a way to manage them so he didn't have to leave Sophie.

8:00 p.m.

If Jake thought she was going to pack up her things and be waiting for him like a good little girl, he was very much mistaken. As soon as he got to her apartment, she was going to give him a piece of her mind.

Just because they were having twins didn't mean he could treat her like she was his possession.

Sophie paced in her living room and stared daggers at the door.

9:00 p.m.

Seriously? He couldn't even get here on time to cart her away like a barbarian over to his place? That was how little she meant to him? Did anything hurt more than being forgotten? All her life she'd been invisible. Not just to Jake, but to everyone. How could a bookworm like her even begin to compete with her larger-than-life siblings? She'd never be a movie star, would never throw the winning pitch in the World Series, would never be the sparkling, stunning Sullivan twin.

Once Jake finally deigned to show up at her door, she swore that nothing was going to stop her from giving him a piece of her mind about what he could do with his six remaining days.

Okay, so maybe she was careening from one extreme to the other like a madwoman, but he could at least give her the respect of showing up less than an hour late to ruin her life.

10:00 p.m.

Sophie's righteous anger grew bigger, stronger with every passing minute until her cuckoo clock chimed 10:00 p.m. That was when it finally hit her—something had to be wrong. Jake had been too intent on controlling her life this morning to give up just a few hours later. Especially since he wasn't a man who ever gave up.

What if he'd been hurt? What if he needed her help and she'd been wasting precious time in her apartment thinking horrible things about him? She grabbed her phone and called him on his cell but it went straight to voice mail.

No one would know to call her if something happened to Jake. No one would know he was important to her, that she was pregnant with his children.

She didn't own a car since it was easy enough to rent one from the car share company when she needed one. But they were all out of vehicles for the night, and since Sophie didn't know the evening bus schedule very well, it took her far longer than she wanted to get to his house. All the lights were off and he didn't answer the door. She called the pub. The bartender told her Jake was there, but was in the middle of dealing with an emergency and couldn't get to the phone.

Twenty-five minutes and two bus changes later, she practically ran inside McCann's, pushing through a crowd of college kids and not caring that they clearly thought she'd lost her mind.

"Where is Jake?" She nearly grabbed the bartender's shirt to get his attention.

The scruffy man gave her the same look the college kids had. Like she should be on her living room clock with the rest of the cuckoo birds.

"He's in the back."

The last thing she expected was to see Jake in his office handing a tissue to a young woman with pink and blue hair. The girl blew her nose loudly just as Sophie saw that there were two other people in the room. The couple was older than Jake. Old enough, she realized, to be the girl's parents.

She skidded to a stop, but not fast enough for Jake not to see her.

"Sophie!" He said something to the couple, then got up and headed for her. He brushed his fingertips against her skin as he slid a lock of hair back from her face. "It's late. You know what the doctor said about rest. You should be sleeping."

"I couldn't sleep. I was worried when you didn't show up." She gave him a little half smile. "And I was mad at you for standing me up," she admitted. This time she was the one reaching for his face. How many times had she wanted to touch him like this over the years? Warmth flooded her as she realized she could do it now. "Now that I know you are okay, tell me what I can do to help while you—" she looked over his shoulder at the group gathered in his office "—deal with things."

"All I want is for you to get some rest." She was about to tell him she wasn't tired, that his day had to be a hundred times more difficult than hers, when he frowned at her. "How did you get here?"

"The bus." She didn't think it would be wise to mention the few dark blocks between the final bus stop and his pub.

He swore. "You should have stayed home."

Didn't he see? "I needed to make sure you were okay."

Jake still looked upset about her late-night jaunt through San Francisco's public transportation system, but rather than continue to rail at her, he threaded his fingers into her hair and tugged her closer so that her head was tucked in beneath his chin. "God, you're sweet." He pressed a kiss to her forehead.

Just then, the bartender burst through the door. "Customers are about to riot out here if they don't get some service soon. Betty is already way past what she can handle."

Sophie plopped her hand over Jake's mouth before he could reply. "I've got this." She didn't wait for Jake to agree before she grabbed a black apron from a peg on the wall and wrapped it around her waist. "Do you have a pad and pencil?" she asked the bartender.

He gladly shoved one into her hands and thirty seconds later she was in the middle of a steep learning curve on how to be a good waitress in an Irish pub as customers all but growled their orders at her and demanded endless refills.

Sophie had never been a part of something so noisy, so full of constant motion. No, she realized as she loaded a tray with frothy beers, that wasn't true. Growing up the youngest of eight had been just as noisy, just as full of motion.

No wonder she found herself loving every single second of it.

By the time Jake got a chance to pull Sophie from the pub floor, it was nearly 2:00 a.m. and they were on the verge of shutting down for the night. His bartender had popped his head in at one point to say, "You should hire that girl full-time," but Jake had still been focused on trying to get his young employee to agree to see a counselor. A full-on treatment program would be better, but he had enough experience with alcoholics to know that pushing them in the right direction usually made them do the exact opposite.

He'd always been careful to monitor his employees for substance abuse and to make sure all of his managers did the same, but Samantha had hidden it well. Well enough that it had taken her parents coming in and begging him to fire her for him to see what had been right beneath his nose.

He blamed himself, knew if he hadn't been so obsessed with Sophie these past months he might have seen the changes in Samantha's behavior.

The subject of his obsession was wiping down tables with a rag. She'd pulled her long hair back into a ponytail and wisps of hair curled around her flushed face. Her beauty took his breath away just as it always had, making it impossible for him to do anything but stare at her...until she went to lift one of the chairs onto the table.

"You shouldn't be lifting things." He took the chair from her and put it up. "I'll get the rest. Go lie down in my office."

He knew he should be thanking her for getting him out of a rough spot, that he should have already apologized for acting like a jerk that morning when he dropped her off at the library. Instead, he was barking orders at her.

But instead of railing back him, she simply said, "Is everything all right?"

God, she really was sweet. And far more forgiving than he deserved. No one had ever worried about him before. She was going to be the perfect mother...and wife.

Lord knew, she didn't deserve a life stuck with an idiot like him.

But there was no way he would ever give her up. Because he was exactly the selfish bastard she'd accused him of being.

He continued putting chairs onto the tables. "Not right now. But hopefully, it will be. I'm really sorry I didn't come pick you up tonight or call to explain, and that you were worried about me."

When was the last time someone had worried about him? His chest squeezed tight again as he thought about meaning enough to someone that they would come looking for him when he didn't show up somewhere he'd said he'd be.

"I was just heading out to your place when…" He shook his head, thinking about Samantha. She was a nice girl and he wanted to believe she'd overcome her addiction. But after living with an alcoholic, Jake knew just how hard that battle could be. And that you really had to *want* to stop drinking.

When he didn't say anything more, Sophie didn't push him for further explanations. Instead, she simply said, "Your employees all speak really highly of you."

"Owning a pub," he said, running a hand through his hair, "you've got to be really careful about things. Right from the start I always had strict rules for my employees."

"You mean all the easy access to alcohol?"

He nodded. "People can get hooked on it. Far too easily." And he couldn't live with himself if someone got hooked on drinking because they worked at one of his pubs. In fact, many of his key employees didn't drink at all. Just like him.

"I realized the other day that I've never seen you drunk before." Her eyes looked too deep into him as she said, "That's on purpose, isn't it?" He nodded and she put her hand on his arm. "I'm sure you've done everything you can to help that young woman. The rest is up to her."

He hadn't thought anything would help him feel better about tonight…but he hadn't counted on Sophie. The question was, he thought as she yawned, whether or not he could ever figure out how to become the kind of man she could count on, too.

"It's way past your bedtime." He reached out a hand to her and finally said what he should have long before now. "Thank you, Sophie."

She put her hand in his. "You're welcome." She smiled as she threaded her fingers through his. "I had fun."

He couldn't get a handle on what he was feeling as they walked out to his car in silence. And as she fell asleep almost the instant he pulled out of his parking spot, shifting in the seat so that her hand was on his lap, Jake was thankful for so much more than Sophie filling in for the night at his pub.

What, he wondered silently, had he ever done right to deserve even this one week with her?

Jake carried Sophie inside his house, loving the way she nestled in closer to him. He swore all he was going to do was tuck her in and make himself walk away, even though she was so soft, so warm.

But after he stripped her clothes and shoes off and laid her on his bed, before he could pull the covers up over her beautiful naked curves, she reached up and put her arms around his neck.

"Stay." She'd barely made her request when her tongue flicked out to lick his earlobe, just as he'd teased her when they were in the doctor's waiting room. Their morning together felt as if it had been a thousand years ago.

God, he'd never wanted anything more than to stay with her, but he couldn't forget what the doctor had said about getting enough food and rest. He'd already kept her up way too late, made her spend too much time on her feet, probably without nearly enough food for the energy she'd expended waiting tables at his pub.

"You need rest."

She finally opened her eyes and there was just enough light coming into the room from the moonlight to see the desire, the longing, in them.

"I need you more."

Jake did the only thing he could. He gave in to the urge to kiss her.

She moaned into his mouth as their tongues found each other. He wanted to be gentle, wanted to go slow, but with her curves already naked beneath him, Jake didn't have a prayer of doing anything other than filling his hands with her sensitive breasts, and then filling his mouth with them, one after the other as she arched into him.

Her breasts were so perfect they killed him, so soft and full, with nipples that simply begged for him to taste them. He couldn't imagine how he'd have a prayer of keeping his hands and mouth off them as her pregnancy progressed and they grew even bigger.

Maybe she was right, he thought as he kissed his way down past her breasts to her stomach. Maybe he did have a pregnancy fetish.

But only for Sophie.

He breathed in the sweet scent of her arousal as he kneeled on the floor to settle himself between her legs and she instinctively opened her thighs for him. Lowering his head to her already damp curls, he slid his tongue over her, then curled it into her. Her hands grasped his, and as their fingers threaded together, she cried out and bucked her hips into him.

One day he vowed to worship her like she deserved to be worshipped. Long and slow, stoking the flames of her desire until she was begging for release. But the self-control Jake McCann was so famous for had completely disappeared the first time he'd pulled Sophie against him and kissed her soft mouth. Tonight was no different and the only choice he had was to unzip his jeans with one hand before pulling her hips to the edge of the bed and driving into her like a man possessed.

There were no words between them tonight, no room for anything but heavy breaths and groans of pleasure. He filled his hands with her breasts again before moving them to her stomach.

He stilled at the realization of the lives she carried inside, and her eyes fluttered open. She covered his hands with hers and then looked up at him with a smile so full of love, his chest clenched tight enough that he actually thought his heart might shatter as he looked down at the beauty beneath him, wrapped tightly all around him.

Whatever control he might have been able to find to take her slower, to put her pleasure first, slipped from his grasp. He had to slide his hands to her hips, taking hers with him, had to grip her hard before thrusting in as far as she could take him. Her inner muscles tightened down around his shaft, and as the now familiar rush of her climax took hold, Jake threw his head back and came with a roar.

Minutes later, when he'd stripped off the rest of

his clothes and wrapped himself around her with Sophie already asleep against his chest, Jake had to softly say the words that had been burning a hole inside his heart for so many years.

"I love you."

Sixteen

Sophie woke up, all alone in the middle of Jake's big bed. As she yawned and stretched, something played in the back of her mind, a dream she'd had of Jake saying something important to her. She'd strained to try to make her recollection clearer, but she'd been too tired last night—and too sated from his incredibly passionate lovemaking—to remember the details of a fleeting dream.

In any case, the previous evening had been lovely. She'd had fun playing waitress for a few hours, but when she'd asked him to stay in the bed with her and he'd loved her so beautifully... well, it made her skin tingle all over just thinking of his mouth on her, his hands stroking her skin and his—

She blushed and pushed the thick duvet off.

After a quick shower and a little time with the toothbrush Jake had put out for her, she put on another one of his dress shirts.

She walked down the hall and into the living room, surprised to see Jake sitting at the dining table with spreadsheets laid out all across it.

"Good morning." She felt shy, all of a sudden, even though she was very happy to see him. Just like always.

He pushed up out of his chair. "Sleep well?"

"I always sleep well with you." She blushed again at what she'd just admitted.

Fortunately, all he said was, "Good. I'm glad. I made you a few things for breakfast." He brushed a kiss on her forehead before moving past her to the kitchen.

The first time he'd cooked for her, she hadn't wanted to admit how sweet he was. Now she wondered why she had ever tried to deny it. Especially when no man had ever wanted to take care of her like he did. Even the way he kissed her on the forehead was sweet. Almost as if he wasn't just with her for her body—or for the children growing inside of it—but because he actually cared about her.

She knew she needed to be smart and remember to keep her guard up against Jake for the next few days, until she'd fulfilled her side of the agreement and they both went their separate ways. But it grew more and more difficult to do that by the second.

Last night in his bed had been incredible. Passionate. Intense. Amazing. Especially when he'd stopped and put his hand over her stomach and looked into her eyes with wonder.

That should have proved what she knew was true, right? That he only wanted her here with him because of their children? But it had seemed just the opposite—that at least part of the reason he was happy with her being pregnant was because of *her*.

And then there was the way he'd seemed so glad to see her when she'd shown up at his pub last night. Or what about how he'd held her close after they had sex, even though he'd already had his pleasure and could just as easily have rolled over and left her lying there alone?

He broke into her jumbled thoughts, saying, "It'll just take me a minute to heat everything up."

Seeing the veritable feast he'd put together for her, she shook her head. "I can't eat all this." There were enough eggs and pancakes and fruit and sausage and toast to feed her entire family.

"You couldn't have eaten enough last night. I wanted to make sure you didn't go hungry this morning."

"You were there when I got on the scale at the doctor's office yesterday," she joked. "I'm not exactly wasting away."

He didn't smile. "You're perfect, Sophie."

She sank down on a chair at his kitchen's breakfast bar. *Perfect.* Had he just said that? And more to the point, did he actually mean it? Did he actually think that dull, *nice* Sophie Sullivan was perfect? Beyond the fact that she could have his children?

She swallowed hard, then looked over her shoulder toward the dining table. "What are you working on?"

He slid the plates of food into the oven's warming drawer. "We just put in a new tracking system for all of the pubs. There are a handful of bugs giving us trouble."

She was ashamed that it had taken her until last night to realize how hard he worked to build his business. Jake had always made everything look so easy.

What else didn't she know about him?

"How did you get started with the pubs?" She couldn't remember a time when he didn't own them.

He looked surprised by her question. "I guess you were pretty young when I bought and opened the first McCann's, huh? I've always worked in pubs, same as my dad. All that knowledge added up over the years, and when I got the chance to bail the owner of one of them out of a loan gone bad, I took it."

"How old were you?"

"Twenty-one."

"Wow, that's really young to own your own restaurant."

"I guess so," he said, "but by then I'd been working in pubs forever."

"You're good at making it seem so easy, but—" she nodded at the spreadsheets "—I'm starting to see just how much work it all is."

"It's just food and drink. Anyone could do it. Even a guy like me."

She frowned, not liking the way he was talking about himself, as if his incredible achievements weren't worthwhile. "Jake, you've got to see how amaz—"

"Food's up." He slid it across the breakfast bar.

She made a face at his habit of cutting her off every time it seemed like they were on the verge of something important. "It's so irritating the way you always do that."

He plated some food for himself, then came and sat next to her, saying nothing.

"Don't you even want to know what you do that's so irritating?" she demanded.

"Nope."

She almost laughed aloud. "You're such a guy."

"Thanks."

"It wasn't a compliment." She jammed some toast into her mouth and crunched it, lest she say something else she'd end up regretting later.

Jake looked at her with thinly veiled amusement. "You have some strawberry right here." He reached out and slid his thumb across her cheek, straight to her mouth, at which point Sophie shocked both of them by sucking the sticky pad of his thumb between her lips and licking off the jam.

His eyes darkened. "I came out here to work so that I wouldn't attack you again."

Her breath came faster as she said, "What makes you think I don't want to be attacked?"

He pulled his hand from her and closed his eyes like a man on the verge of losing it. "Sophie."

He said her name as a warning, but she knew he wanted her as much as she wanted him, could see it not just in the arousal that was starting to tent his pants, but in the taut lines of his face as he tried to control himself.

Not wanting to think, not wanting to face any of her worries for a little while longer, she quickly stripped off his shirt and let it fall to the floor. She couldn't believe how natural it was to not only get up and straddle his hips, but also to do it while completely naked.

"What about you?" She leaned forward and pressed her lips to the side of his neck, licking a path up to his earlobe before whispering, "Do you mind being attacked?"

"God, no."

Just as fast as she'd stripped and moved over him, he shoved his pants down and was inside of her. She lost her breath at the feeling of being connected with him like this, so full she felt as if she'd burst from the pleasure coursing through her veins.

She'd never have believed herself capable of something like having sex on a bar stool in the middle of breakfast, but being intimate with Jake was so natural. She wrapped her arms and legs around him and rode the waves of pleasure that crashed through her as he held her hips in his big hands and thrust up into her in perfect rhythm to her own downward thrusts.

She wanted to be with him like this for hours, to memorize the beauty of his rippling muscles beneath her, but when he moved one hand into her hair and crushed her mouth against his, she had no choice but to follow him over the edge...spiraling

off into a world full of brighter, more brilliant col-
ors than she'd ever seen before.

Sophie blew his mind. Not just every time they
came together, but in other ways, too. Like the way
she snuggled even closer to him, giggled and said,
"That was fun."

"Fun?" He did his best impersonation of a
wounded lover. "That's all I am to you?"

She giggled again, and with his shaft still inside
her, the vibrations felt good. Damn good.

"Oh!" Her eyes grew big as she felt him throb
inside her again. "I always thought guys needed a
little recovery time."

He was perpetually hard around her and knew
it would be a heck of a long time before he'd need
to recover from loving her before wanting to take
her again. But he had to think of more than just
himself and his needs now.

"You haven't eaten your breakfast yet."

When he saw that she was going to try to argue
and convince him to take her again, he very reluc-
tantly lifted her off his lap.

"I can see there's only one way to make sure
you eat." Instead of putting her on her seat, he
yanked his pants back up, then turned her around

so that she was sitting naked on his lap. He slid her plate over, forking up a bite of pancake. "Open up."

She shot him a surprised look over her shoulder, but when he slid his arms tighter around her waist, and growled, "Eat," she let him feed her the pancake.

After a few more bites, she said, "I've never eaten breakfast naked before." She shot him a naughty little grin. "I like it."

He realized he hadn't called her Nice in days, hadn't even thought of her nickname. It still fit her in some ways, but in others…

"Me, too."

She all but purred in his lap, and he knew if he didn't do something soon to take their minds off sex, he'd have her up on the kitchen counter in under thirty, her legs wrapped around his hips again as he drove into her.

Sure, her doctor had said that sex was fine. But there was no way the woman could have had any idea just how much sex he was talking about.

"Tell me when you decided to become a librarian." She seemed startled by his personal question, her muscles stiffening slightly on his lap as he rubbed his hand down her arm. "I remember you always had your nose in a book."

"I've always loved books," she said softly. "I

love being around them. I love getting lost in a story, a world. I love that I can become anyone, that I can live any fantasy."

The word *fantasy* should have filled the room with sexual tension again, but Jake had just realized what an idiot he was, just like she'd said the day before. He should have asked her anything else—about her family, or hobbies, or favorite food. Not books.

When she was in his arms he temporarily forgot the differences between them. That she'd gone to Stanford and he'd barely eked out a high school diploma by sweet-talking his female teachers into not flunking him.

Of course he wanted to know more about her. He couldn't spend this much time with her and not want that. But hearing about her love of books only served to remind him of the unbridgeable gap between them.

"I can't believe I've never asked you what your favorite book is." She grinned at him. "I've asked pretty much everyone I've ever met."

Jake moved her off his lap. "You probably need to get ready for work soon, don't you?"

She frowned at his abrupt personality change. "In about an hour."

Acting like he didn't realize he was being a

dick, he purposely turned his back on her and headed over to the pile of work he'd been sweating over before she woke up. "Let me know when you need me to drive you in."

The loud scrape of the bar stool's legs across the wood floor came a beat before Sophie said, "Is that really all this is to you? It's okay to have great sex all the time, but whenever I try to talk to you about *anything at all,* even something as ridiculously easy as your favorite book, you get to walk away without answering? How can you even think of marrying me if we're going to be strangers everywhere but in bed?" Hurt vibrated from her every word.

All he wanted was to make her happy…but he didn't have the first clue how to do that.

"I refuse to have a life like that," Sophie told him. "What's the point of going through the motions for a few more days when it isn't going to change anything?"

She fled to the bedroom. He was right behind her, and before she could slam the door on him, he shoved his shoulder inside and grabbed her hand. She'd been the one who just said she couldn't stand the way he shut her out, but couldn't she see that if she ran from him, if she closed off her heart to him, he'd be the one who'd end up utterly destroyed?

"Call the library. Tell them you're taking the day off."

She looked at him like he was certifiably insane. "What are you talking about? Why on earth would I do that?"

She tried to push out of his arms and he didn't want to let her go, but he knew it would be worse if he didn't. Damn it, he didn't mean to keep bossing her around. He was supposed to be using these seven days to woo her, not give her even more reasons to stay the hell away from him. But desperation to keep her near clawed at him, made it hard for him to clear his mind so that he could do the right thing for once.

"I want to spend the day with you."

Emotion flashed in her eyes and he prayed it was the renewal of hope, of the way she'd once felt about him. But all she said again was, "Why?"

"To give me the chance to prove to you that we've got more in common than sex."

"Jake, I don't think—"

He gritted his teeth and made himself say, "Agree to come and I won't touch you again today." Even though it was going to kill him not to. His chest clenched as he watched her consider his desperate request, and he knew he hadn't yet said the one thing he needed to say. "Please."

Seventeen

How had Jake known one of her favorite things to do was ride the cable cars?

Sophie couldn't help but smile as wind rushed through her hair. A child walking hand in hand with her mother down the sidewalk waved, and Sophie waved back.

The fact that he wanted to spend the entire day with her was surprising enough. But she hadn't expected him to head to Ghirardelli Square to buy two tickets for the most touristy attraction in all of San Francisco...or to hold her hand the entire time.

She was still wary of letting herself trust him again after the way he'd pushed her away that morning, but she couldn't stand seeing him still looking so tense as he stood beside her. Ever since she'd threatened to end their seven days early, that muscle in his jaw had been jumping.

She tugged on his hand so that he'd look at her. "It's been way too long since I've been on a cable car ride." She smiled at him. "Thank you."

She was glad to see some of the tension fade in his shoulders. "Whenever I see one I always think of you."

Surprise stole her breath at the same time that the cable car bumped over the road, tossing her straight into Jake's arms. God, she loved being there, always felt so safe when he was holding on to her.

She looked up into his beautiful face. "How did you know I liked cable cars?"

"You've always been important to me, Sophie."

His simple statement sent sparks of joy shooting through her system. Oh, it would be so easy to give in to them, but painful experience where Jake was concerned had her moving from the circle of his arms and saying, "Sometimes I forget you practically grew up with me and my siblings."

Rather than letting her go, Jake tugged her close again. "I spent a lot of time at your house. But don't try to tell yourself I didn't pay extra attention to you when I did."

He had?

He cursed out of the blue and released his hold

on her so that cold air rushed between them, instantly chilling her. "I promised not to touch you."

Sophie hated that promise. After so many years of not being able to touch Jake, then finally being allowed to give in to those powerful urges to be physically affectionate with him, it nearly killed her not to move back into his arms and kiss him the way she had over the past twenty-four hours.

But she knew why he'd made her that promise. It was too easy to get lost in the sensual sparks that always lit between them, so much easier than making sure they built a true connection, a real bond that would withstand the test of twins…and a possible life together as husband and wife.

She refused to let him go and reached out to take his hand. She wouldn't give that up, too. Not when it felt so right. Not when holding his hand was almost better than having sex with him.

Her body all but laughed at that thought, and she silently acknowledged that there was very little in life that was better than having sex with Jake McCann.

Just then, the conductor announced they were heading into Chinatown and her stomach immediately answered the news with a loud grumble that carried even over the sound of the cable car rattling down its tracks.

She grinned at Jake. "I think our kids like Chinese food."

Our kids.

The two little words reverberated through Jake's chest, holding steady in the center where his heart was beating too fast.

He should have made sure she ate more for breakfast. But instead of putting her needs first, he'd been too busy roughly taking her on the bar stool, then pushing her away as soon as they were done.

When the cable car stopped at the next light, he jumped down and reached for her. It didn't count as touching her if he had to make sure she got to the ground safely…even if he held on to her waist a few seconds longer than he needed to.

He was surprised when Sophie took his hand and started leading the way. "I know a place that has the best *cha sui bao*."

"Chasu-what?"

He loved the sound of her laughter. "You'll see." She shot him a happy glance over her shoulder. "I promise you won't be disappointed."

Thank God she was back to her normal self,

smiling and happy. Every time he did or said something to extinguish that joy in her eyes, he hated himself more and more. It was one of the reasons he'd stayed away from her as long as he had… because he'd known he would hurt her.

He hadn't spent much time in this part of Chinatown, where the tourists were. The parts he knew were the back alleys where the gangs came together. He hadn't rolled with that crowd since high school, but he still recognized the route through the narrow alleys. So when Sophie headed off the main street and started to turn down one of them, he had to stop her.

"There are plenty of places to eat on this street."

"None as good as the one I'm taking you to," she replied, clearly not understanding his concern.

Jake knew he'd spent too much of their time together dictating what she could and couldn't do. And she clearly wanted to take him to one particular place. So he let her lead them down alleys and back roads, keeping especially close to her, even though he couldn't understand how perfect little Sophie Sullivan knew her way around this part of the neighborhood.

Finally, she stopped in front of a bright red door and smiled at him. "We're here."

She pushed through the door and he saw that

it was a bakery, more industrial than a retail business.

A very thin, clearly exhausted middle-aged man looked up with a huge smile. "Miss Sophie!"

She let go of Jake's hand to give the man a hug. "Mr. Chu, I hope you don't mind us dropping by like this. Jake and I were in the neighborhood and I couldn't focus on anything but eating one of your steamed pork buns."

Jake knew exactly why the man looked so pleased. Sophie had always had that effect on people.

She looked over his shoulder at the kitchen behind him. "I hope we're not too late. I know how early you sell out."

But the man was already clearing off the small white plastic table in the corner, holding out the seat for Sophie as if she really were a princess. Jake shook the man's hand, and as he introduced himself, he knew what the guy was thinking as he studied him with narrowed eyes.

"You own those Irish pubs."

He nodded, saying, "I do," while making sure Mr. Chu heard what he was really saying: *I know I'm not good enough for her, but since I can't let her go, I'm going to do my damnedest to take care of her.*

Mr. Chu studied him before nodding once and disappearing into the back.

"What was that all about?" Sophie asked.

Jake shrugged as he put a stack of magazines on the floor and sat on the other chair. "How do you know this place?"

Before she could answer, Mr. Chu was back with tea. "How is Stanley's freshman year going?" she asked him.

"Good. Although he says none of the girls there are as pretty as his tutor."

She laughed out loud at that. "Let him know I miss him, too." She was still smiling as he moved back into the kitchen. "Stanley always was the world's biggest flirt."

Jake knew it was crazy to be jealous of a teenager, but just because it was crazy didn't mean he didn't feel it. Especially when he thought about the fact that she must have spent plenty of time alone with the kid if she'd been tutoring him.

"You have a full-time job. When do you have time to tutor kids?"

She blew the steam off her cup of tea. "Free time is overrated. I'd much rather be doing something I enjoy with people I care about."

Now he knew why he'd liked his tutor, Mrs. Springs, so much. It wasn't just because she'd been the only one he hadn't been able to scare away. It was because she'd reminded him of Sophie. Gentle, but with a spine of steel beneath that soft exterior.

"Besides," she said, "it's really all about my secret mission." She propped her elbows on the table and put her face in her hands. "I want everyone to love books as much as I do."

She was so beautiful, so pure, his chest clenched tight as he looked at her across the small table, knowing how badly he was going to disappoint her.

He might not be illiterate anymore, but books would never be fun.

And he would never love them.

Mr. Chu brought over a plate of steaming pork buns, then left them alone again. Sophie broke off a piece and held it out to Jake. "Here, you should have the first taste."

Thanking God that he'd never needed books to know how to give a woman pleasure, he wrapped his hand around her wrist to hold her hand steady as he put his lips around the food. He let his teeth graze her skin as he did so and was rewarded by the desire that lit her eyes.

"Good, isn't it?" she asked in a slightly husky voice.

"Give me another taste, princess."

She had to know what he was doing, that he was playing outside the rule book by touching her when he'd promised not to. But a moment later, she was back with another piece of the pork bun. Again, he made her part of their snack.

"Yes," he told her after he finally made himself let go of her hand, "it's very good." He slid the plate away from her and broke off a piece. "Your turn now."

She flushed, but didn't hesitate to open her mouth. At first he thought she was only going to take the food, but at the very last second her tongue came out to curl over his fingertip.

He barely bit back a groan. Why the hell had he made that stupid promise not to touch her?

Sophie felt happier than she had in a very, very long time. Just being with Jake, slowly walking hand in hand through downtown San Francisco, was better than any of the fancy evenings out she'd had with the men she'd dated before him.

Not, she supposed, that they were technically dating. No, they'd skipped right past that part, hadn't they? From one kiss to twins-on-the-way so quickly it made her head spin.

She was glad he'd insisted on this day together,

on wanting to prove to her that they were compatible outside of the bedroom. She flushed as she realized they'd had sex in far more places than the bedroom.

Still, she couldn't shake the sense that the tenuous connection she and Jake had been forging with each other had broken slightly when they'd been at the bakery in Chinatown. Something kept coming between them and she wished she knew what it was, wished that he would open up and tell her.

But she'd known Jake long enough to understand what would happen if she pushed too hard too fast. He'd shut down completely...and it would break her heart to lose him just when it looked like they might have a chance of making things work.

Her newly overactive bladder had her stopping in front of a Starbucks. "Nature's calling. I'll be right back," she told him, leaving him standing out on the sidewalk while she went to go wait in the surprisingly long line inside.

Jake was holding a fairly large plastic bag when she came back out. The only store anywhere near the coffee shop was one that sold cheap little tourist trinkets. Just the kind she absolutely adored, as a matter of fact.

But what could Jake possibly have bought?

Before she could ask, he grabbed her hand and

said, "If we run, we can probably catch that cable car before it heads back down the hill."

Hand in hand, they dodged people and dogs and garbage cans. Laughter and pure, unfettered joy bubbled up inside her at a side of Jake she hadn't known existed until now.

The cable car slowed down just long enough for Jake to lift her up before getting on behind her. The conductor seemed happy enough when Jake flashed their tickets at him and she figured he must recognize the McCann's owner like everyone else had so far.

"Where are you taking me?"

Instead of answering, he pulled her against him, her back to his front, breaking his promise again, thank God. She slid her hands along his forearms and leaned her head against his shoulder as the sights of San Francisco passed by them one after another. She closed her eyes and wished they could stay like this forever.

"Here's our stop."

Sophie felt groggy as she felt his breath warm against her ear, and realized she must have dozed off into a light sleep on the cable car, probably from the combination of the movement, her pregnancy…and finally being right where she'd always wanted to be.

Safe and warm in Jake's arms.

The wind had picked up, but the afternoon sun was still shining brightly. He'd taken her to a large strip of grass at Chrissy Field on the bay. To their right was Alcatraz, to their left the Golden Gate Bridge. In the middle of a workday there weren't many people out, just a few people flying kites.

"Do you remember coming out here when we were kids?"

Of course she did. "Lori and I had new kites, but mine ripped when she stepped on it before I could even use it." She paused. "You told me kites were for babies, but you made Lori share with me."

"I hated it when you cried." He stroked a hand down her cheek. "I still do." He pulled something long and colorful out of the big bag. "I wish I could have given this to you fifteen years ago."

"Oh, Jake." She could hardly believe it. He'd found a kite in the shape of a rainbow, so similar to the one she'd had as a child. "I can't believe you got this for me."

"I'm glad you like it."

"I don't just like it. I love it." *And you,* she thought. *I love you so much.*

He helped her tear open the package and soon the wind took the kite way up high in the sky. She had to run to keep up with it, and when she finally caught hold of it enough to look back at Jake, he was staring at her with that same wonder she'd seen on his face when they'd been making love and his hands had been on her belly.

This time she knew it couldn't have anything to do with the fact that she was pregnant with his children. But just because he'd stopped hiding his attraction to her, and the fact that he enjoyed spending time with her…did that necessarily mean he would ever fall in love with her the way she'd always been in love with him?

Eighteen

Jake saw Sophie shiver as the sun disappeared behind Alcatraz. He knew he should take her home, but he wasn't ready for their day together to end yet. He'd thought he was doing this for her, but the truth was, he couldn't remember a day where he'd had a more enjoyable time.

Her stomach growled again and she laughed. "I swear, it doesn't normally sound like there's a crowd in there."

"I should have fed you—and them—" he looked down at her stomach "—before now. Good news, I know of a pretty good place in one of the converted Fort Mason buildings just around the corner."

He loved the way she automatically reached for his hand for their walk across the grass into the parking lot where the old military base had been turned into galleries, shops and restaurants.

But when they got close to the restaurant, she abruptly stopped walking. "You can't be serious. I can't go into the fanciest restaurant in the city wearing this. And I'm sweaty from running around on the grass."

"I like you sweaty," he said in a low voice, but despite the answering desire that flared in her eyes at his reminder of how good it was to get sweaty together, he could see she was hesitant about where he was taking her. "You always look beautiful, Sophie. And we need to eat." He put his hand on her lower back and led her through the elegant entrance.

The maître d' recognized him immediately. "Mr. McCann, welcome. Please follow me."

Sophie was clearly startled by the greeting—and the fact that they were immediately seated at one of the best tables. He understood her confusion. A guy like him shouldn't be allowed within a hundred feet of a place like this. He should be in back washing dishes, not being led to one of the best tables in the place, with the most beautiful girl in the world on his arm. He didn't usually come to places like this, despite the fact that he knew most of the chefs in the city. He just never felt comfortable in them, never felt like he actually belonged there.

"Enjoy your meal. I'll let Chef know you're here."

Sophie lowered her voice to a whisper. "Did you have a reservation?"

She was so cute when her eyes went all big like that. So cute that he actually whispered back, "No."

Just then, his buddy Chris walked up to their table, smiling widely. Jake could see how much his friend appreciated Sophie's looks. She was by far the most beautiful woman in the room. The fact that she'd put absolutely no effort into it—and that she was utterly unaware of her effect on people—only increased her beauty.

"I'm so glad you're dining with us tonight, Miss—"

Sophie blinked up at the celebrated chef as she lifted her hand to his. "Sophie Sullivan."

She licked her lips, and as Jake watched Chris's eyes drop to her sinfully sensual mouth, he realized his mistake in coming here tonight.

He was going to have to kill his friend for looking at his woman like that.

"I'm very happy to meet you, Miss Sullivan."

"Please, call me Sophie."

"Miss Sullivan works just fine," Jake interjected.

Sophie looked mortified. "Jake!"

Surprise flickered in Chris's eyes as he looked between them. *You've got it right. She's mine. Forever. So you'd better back off—and quick.*

"It would be my pleasure to suggest the tasting menu tonight."

Sophie smiled that shy, radiant smile, and Jake had a sudden flash of what the rest of his life was going to be like, watching men fall at Sophie's feet. It was going to be hell.

What if their twins were girls? How was he going to protect them all?

Chris had more women at his beck and call than even Jake could keep track of. Something about the combination of gourmet food, a big ego and a few muscles seemed to make women salivate. But it was clear that if Jake stepped aside, Sophie would shoot straight to the top of the list, all the others instantly forgotten. She wasn't just beautiful. She was classy. Smart. And way the hell too good for him.

"The tasting menu sounds fine," Jake told his friend. "Now get lost."

Not missing a beat, Chris told Sophie, "It would also be my pleasure to suggest that when you get tired of this guy—"

Jake cut him off with a hard, "Later, Chris."

This time, thankfully, Sophie wasn't mortified. Instead, as Chris bowed to her before heading back into the kitchen, she started laughing, one of the sweetest sounds Jake had ever heard. Making her laugh would become his top priority.

"I can't believe how rude you were," she said, but she was still grinning. "I take it you know each other."

He buttered a piece of freshly baked bread and handed it to her. "I taught him everything he knows about washing dishes."

She bit into the bread, still chuckling, and he enjoyed watching her eat. He'd never taken care of anyone before, had never wanted that kind of responsibility. Now, keeping Sophie safe and healthy consumed his thoughts.

"I also taught him about women. He couldn't take his eyes off you."

Sophie blushed and looked at her plate. "He was just being polite."

"Don't you know the effect you have on men, princess? All your perfection, your elegance…you make us desperate to know what you'd look like sprawled naked beneath us in our beds, your silky hair tangled in our hands, your classy mouth begging us to—"

She kicked him under the table, hissing, "You can't say that kind of stuff here."

"Jesus," he said as he leaned forward to rub his shin. "That hurt."

"My brothers taught me how to deal with guys who wouldn't take no for an answer."

A violent vision of one of her brothers walking into this restaurant tonight and instantly knowing what he'd done to their baby sister was abruptly halted when Sophie exclaimed, "Oh, no, I just realized. I should have told Chris that I can't eat any soft cheese or raw fish."

Damn it, if he'd read that book the doctor had given them, he'd know that. But just thinking about trying to read all those tiny words on a subject he was already freaking out about made his head swim.

"I'll go tell him." He got up and pressed a kiss to her temple. "But if any of these guys try to hit on you, tell them—"

"—I'm taken."

She was so beautiful as she looked up and declared that she was his that Jake didn't care that they were in the middle of the most exclusive restaurant in San Francisco. He had to kiss her.

Her mouth was soft and warm beneath his and he wondered how he could be so stupid. Instead of taking her out, he should have kept her all to himself.

Her skin was beautifully flushed as he lifted his mouth from hers and headed for the kitchens.

"Sophie can't eat soft cheese and raw fish."

Chris looked up from plating a dish. "She's pregnant?"

Surprised that his friend got that from only one sentence, Jake nodded.

"Congratulations. She's gorgeous."

Jake hadn't told anyone yet, but suddenly he had to say, "We're having twins."

Chris whistled long and low. "Gotta let you know, you keep shocking the hell out of me. Especially since I've never seen you with a classy babe like that before." He cleaned the edge of the plate with his apron. "Since this is yours, I'll head back out with you."

Jake grabbed the plate from his friend. "I've got it."

"Fine. But don't screw up the presentation. I've got a reputation to preserve, you know."

"Yeah, for being an ass," he shot back, even though he knew it wasn't his friend's fault that Jake didn't fit into a place like this.

It was his own fault. He should have known better than to bring her here. All it did was show her exactly how poorly he fit into her world.

Sophie supposed she should have been mortified that Jake had kissed her like that in front of everyone, but even if she had been, she couldn't have missed the envious glances from the other diners. Especially the women, who clearly all wished they had a hunk who couldn't keep his hands to himself. Even the fact that she was wearing a totally inappropriate cotton skirt and sweater hardly bothered her anymore.

She looked up to see him coming back with a plate of food, and her heart swelled with love. They'd had such a perfect day together so far.

But when he sat down he seemed a bit crankier than he had a few minutes earlier. She was getting used to his often gruff manner, the way he liked to be in control all the time. Something had obviously happened when he'd been back in the kitchen with his friend.

Ignoring the food, she said, "What's wrong, Jake?"

He didn't answer, just held out the plate and said, "You need to eat."

The easiest thing would be to get angry at him

again for pushing her away. But she was tired of that pattern. It was time for a change.

"Today has been great," she said softly, "but it's got to be about more than cable cars and flying kites."

Sophie waited for him to say something, but his face remained carved in granite. She sighed. It seemed like they'd come so far today, but had they really?

But then, he finally said, "Everyone is wondering what the hell a guy like me is doing in a place like this with a girl like you. I should be washing your dishes, not sharing them."

She'd never seen his vulnerability so clearly before. Had never actually believed that he had any vulnerable spots at all. She'd thought she knew him so well, after all these years of having a crush on him.

But maybe she hadn't really known him at all, hadn't known that he'd be a man who would claim an unplanned child with such enthusiasm…or appreciate a simple girl like her who didn't shine and shimmer like the rest of her siblings.

"I've spent so much of my life feeling like I didn't fit in. My brothers and Lori were so much bigger, so much brighter, than I could ever be.

But now—" she paused, met his dark gaze "—I feel better."

He couldn't have looked more surprised. "You do?"

She nodded. "It's nice to know that you feel like just as much of a misfit as I do."

"*Misfit* is one word for it," he said, but there was a darkness to his words that he couldn't disguise.

It was the in she'd been looking for and she couldn't let the opportunity pass. Not when she felt so close to him…and wanted to be so much closer still.

"I know we practically grew up together, but I don't really know much about your childhood."

"Trust me, it's not interesting." He shoved the appetizer at her. "Seriously, Sophie, you need to eat."

"You know everything about my childhood. It's not fair that I hardly know anything about yours." She realized she needed to play her trump card. "I'll eat if you'll talk."

"When was I ever stupid enough to think you were a pushover?" He nodded to the food. "Fine. Start eating and I'll talk."

She worked to hide her smile as she bit into the red and yellow beet salad, knowing Jake would be shocked to realize just how cute he was when he was being tough and irritated with her.

"My mom left when I was a baby, found some guy who could give her more than a cheap apartment and a lifetime of waitressing. She didn't want anything to do with us. The next time she showed up, I was six. She needed money. Turned out her meal ticket was a loser, after all."

Sophie couldn't hide her shock. "What happened?"

"My dad kicked her out. I was at school when it happened. Never even saw her. She was better off away from him. He was a drunk. Died when I was eighteen from liver damage."

He was rattling off the facts as if they were from someone else's life, as if they didn't matter, as if they didn't hurt him. But she knew they did, that they had to have wounded him. Deeply.

How could it not hurt to have been raised with such neglect? Sophie had tried so many times in the past two and a half months to guard her heart against him. It was smarter. Safer.

But how could she be on guard against a boy who'd had a terrible childhood, but had turned into a wonderful man despite it all?

Somehow she managed to hold in her emotions, knowing he'd mistake sadness over how awful his childhood had been for pity. More food came just then, and after the waiter walked away, she reached for her fork as though everything were perfectly fine, while forcing a small smile onto her lips.

"And here I thought losing my kite made for a rough childhood."

She nearly cheered when her comment surprised a laugh out of Jake and he began to eat, as well. "Having all those brothers giving you anything you wanted must have been pretty tough, too."

"Do you have any idea what it's like to be guarded by six older brothers?" She made a face. "All the boys at school were too scared of them to come near me. I didn't have my first kiss until I went away to college, if you can believe it."

"If anything ever happened to you, they would never have forgiven themselves for not protecting you better."

"I hate being treated like I'm breakable. I'm sick of everyone thinking all I am is some *nice* girl who can't take care of herself." She was on a roll now and couldn't seem to stop herself. "I'm so much more than that, but no one ever wants to see it."

"I see it, Sophie."

Surprise had her fork clattering to the plate. "You do?"

"Of course I do. How could I not see how strong you are? How resilient. The way you adjust to changing circumstances that would give anyone else whiplash. You're so much tougher than anyone would ever guess." His mouth curved into a smile that stole what was left of her breath away. "And, on top of all of that, you just happen to be the sexiest woman I've ever known."

She rolled her eyes. "You almost had me going up until that last part."

"I almost ruined your brother's wedding, you know."

She couldn't follow his train of thought, how they'd jumped from whether or not she was sexy to Chase's wedding. "Ruined it? How?"

"I wanted to kill every man who looked at you in that pink dress. And there wasn't a guy there who didn't look. All that blood in the middle of their party…" He shook his head. "It wouldn't have been pretty."

"But you never noticed me, not until the wedding when I wore that dress and had the makeup artist make me up."

His eyes were dark, his face as serious as

she'd ever seen it. "Trust me, I noticed you before that. A long time before that."

"Are you up for one more destination?" Sophie asked a little while later as they were leaving the restaurant.

Attraction had buzzed between them as they ate the rest of their meal, and all he could think of was taking her to bed. Come midnight, when the day was officially over and he'd made good on his promise, he could finally touch her again. And, oh, the ways he was going to touch her…

But when she gave him one of those beautiful smiles that had always made his heart beat faster and said, "There's something I want to show you. It's not far from here," how could he not agree to whatever she wanted?

Hand in hand, he let her lead them down the waterfront toward a large gray building. She reached into her bag and pulled out a key card, holding it in front of the electronic lock. It clicked open and she pulled on the door.

"You're showing me a swimming pool?"

She grinned again, saying, "Among other things," as she pulled him toward the next set of doors, which led to the locker rooms and then, finally, the pool.

She kicked off her shoes and dropped his hand to reach for the hem of her sweater.

"Sophie? What are you doing?" It was a stupid question. He knew exactly what she was doing. He just couldn't believe it.

"Getting undressed."

Hallelujah!

She pulled her sweater over her head, then quickly took off the top she'd been wearing beneath it. Her skirt came off next, until she was standing in front of Jake in only her bra and panties.

"Do you need help taking off your clothes?"

Didn't she know he could hardly put together a coherent thought when she was standing in front of him looking that good?

"We're not supposed to be here after hours, are we?"

She cheerfully shook her head as she reached for his T-shirt and started to pull it up. "Nope."

She deftly pulled his shirt off, but when she put her hands at the top of his jeans, he had to know, "Have you done this before? With anyone else?" If she had, he'd hunt the guy down and beat him to a pulp. Sophie was his, damn it. She'd always been his, even if he'd never let himself get close enough to claim her until she'd shown up at his doorstep in Napa and seduced him.

Just as she was seducing him now.

"I've always wanted to go skinny-dipping," she said as she worked his zipper down and shoved his pants off. "But you're my first."

And your last, he thought as he tore off the rest of his clothes, shoes and socks.

He'd promised her a full day with no sex and he'd made it this far. Skinny-dipping with her was going to kill him, but hell, even if he couldn't touch her, he could still look.

"It's not skinny-dipping if you've clothes on, princess. Turn around." When she did as he asked, he brushed aside her long hair to unclasp her bra, then pushed it from her shoulders so that it fell to the ground. Even her back was beautiful, her skin so smooth, so perfect.

Jake couldn't remember ever needing to touch anyone the way he needed to touch her. But, somehow, he kept his hands, and mouth, to himself as he moved down to one knee. His hands were shaking as he reached out to hook his thumbs into the sides of her panties.

Needing a moment to compose himself before he pulled them down and bared every last inch of her beauty, Jake closed his eyes and tried to think of anything but Sophie.

Only, without his sight, his other senses leaped to the forefront, and despite the smell of chlorine from the pool, taking in Sophie's soft and sweet scent made his breathing speed up even more.

He heard Sophie suck a sharp breath before asking, "Do you need help taking that off?" in a husky, clearly aroused voice.

He couldn't have formed the words *yes* or *no* for the life of himself at that point, so he simply made himself yank her panties all the way down her legs.

And Lord, when he opened his eyes just in time to see her step out of them, he came as close to the edge of reason as he ever had.

Yes, he'd seen her naked already, more than once by now. But instead of dulling his desire for her in any way, the knowledge of just how perfect her curves were turned his desire into pure, out-and-out greed.

And a yearning unlike anything he'd ever felt before.

"Sophie," he said in a raw voice, his mouth just inches from her luscious rear end, "you'd better jump in before I break my promise."

"Not without you." As she pulled him up to stand beside her, her eyes fixated on his erection and she smiled. "I'm glad you like my skinny-dipping idea so much."

Jesus, it was going to break him, getting in the water with a naked Sophie and not touching her. Not kissing her. Not making love to her.

But he'd do it, damn it, because he'd given her his word…and because he needed her to know how much he cared about her. Not just as a sexy woman, but also as the person he wanted to spend the rest of his life with.

On three, they jumped in together and Sophie's laughter was the best sound in the world as she splashed up from beneath the water. The next thing he knew, she had wrapped her arms and legs around him and he was holding her up in the water.

Oh, man, was she soft. And wet.

He wanted to run his hands over every inch of her skin.

The way his erection was throbbing against her belly, it wouldn't take more than the slightest shift of her in his arms to be inside all that heat. If this was her way of testing him, he would dig deep to prove to her that he was up to the challenge.

Even if it killed him.

"It's been a perfect day so far," she whispered into his ear just as her tongue licked out against his earlobe, "except for one thing."

He could barely get out the words "What would make it perfect?" when he wanted her so bad he was about to lose it with nothing but the feel of her naked curves bobbing slightly in the water against him.

"This."

Sophie bit down on his earlobe just as she impaled herself on him. He couldn't remember ever feeling anything so good. Or so right.

"Now," she said on a gasp, "it's perfect."

"Better than perfect, Sophie. Nothing is as good as you are."

Finally, he was able to give in to the shocking pleasure of kissing the sweetest mouth he'd ever tasted. Lips so soft, so warm, as they parted, taking and giving in equal measure. He could feel her strength, her lithe muscles, as she wrapped herself tighter around him and used the strength in her thighs to ride him in the water.

He'd thought she was too fragile, too easily breakable for him, for his needs, for his past. But she met every thrust in equal measure, met every stroke of his hand across her gorgeous skin with her hands on him.

For so long he'd wanted her, and every time they came together he only wanted her more. He'd never get enough of her passion, the way she all but vibrated with desire in his arms as she opened herself up to him.

He'd told himself he didn't need anyone, and especially not her. But he'd been wrong. He was a liar of epic proportions.

Because there was nobody he needed more. No one who would ever fill his heart—and soul—the way this beautiful woman in his arms always had.

She lowered her head to his shoulder, her lips and tongue and teeth moving against his skin. He could feel how fast, how frantic, her heart was beating against his. He had to grip her hips tighter, had to hold her closer as he drove deeper inside her warmth, coming closer and closer to heaven with every stroke of hard flesh against soft.

She gasped out his name, and as their combined sounds of ecstasy rebounded off the swimming pool's walls, unbelievable pleasure blurred with pure love and became one and the same.

Nineteen

Sophie woke up sprawled across Jake in his bed. Her head was resting right over his breastbone, his heart a strong, steady beat in her ear. They'd come back from the pool and all the "exercise" they'd done in the water had made both of them ravenous. Especially her, considering she was eating for three now.

They'd rummaged through his pantry and made a feast out of corn chips, salsa and a box of raisins. Dinner at his friend's restaurant had been delicious, but sitting cross-legged on Jake's living room rug munching on chips with a man she adored while a really bad movie played on cable was exactly the kind of evening she'd dreamed of sharing with the man she loved.

She vaguely remembered closing her eyes for

a few minutes and then the next thing she knew he was carrying her into his bedroom and she was curling up against him and falling back asleep. At some point in the middle of the night, she must have wanted to get closer, and just climbed on top of him. He was so big, so warm, and she loved that she could lie on him like he was her own personal island.

Not, she figured, that he much minded being her new mattress, if the enormous erection pressing into her stomach was any indication. That made two of them who didn't mind it, she thought, as all that hard male muscle beneath her quickly brought her from sleepy to aroused in a matter of seconds.

For all the years she'd dreamed of being in bed with Jake, those visions had always been of Jake touching her, Jake kissing her, Jake making love to her. But yesterday at the pool when she'd taken the lead with sex, he'd loved it. But even more than that, she'd loved the way he'd begun to share pieces of himself with her the previous night. Their physical connection was undeniable. Could their emotional connection become just as strong, too?

Was there a chance that Jake would keep letting her in, bit by bit, until he actually shared his whole heart—and soul—with her?

She ran her fingertips over the strong muscles

of his shoulder, tracing the veins and sinews just below the surface of his skin. Sophie feathered her fingers from collarbone to biceps, wanting to memorize Jake from feel alone, already putting together a mental map of his masculine perfection. She was also glad for the chance, at long last, to really study the tattoos on his tanned skin. What, she wondered, did each one of them mean? Jake wasn't a man who did anything without a reason, and she couldn't imagine the tattoos had been painless. Regardless of how tough he acted, he was flesh and blood like anyone else.

Being able to touch Jake at her leisure like this was such a gift. But it wasn't nearly enough to whet her ravenous appetite for more of him. She didn't just want to know the contours of his body with her hands, she wanted to feel them all against her lips, wanted to know the taste of him on her tongue.

She shifted her head so that she could press her lips to his breastbone. His body was so solid, so strong. He smelled so good and he tasted even better. She shifted again, just enough to lift her head from his chest so that she could lick him, barely managing to hold back a moan of pleasure as she laved his slightly salty skin. No wonder men were so fixated on women's breasts. Already, she was an addict, could spend hours with her mouth on him, her tongue, her teeth, all vying for superiority.

Slowly shifting her weight, she moved her legs to either side of his hips and let her weight fall to her knees on the mattress so that she could kneel above him and feast her eyes. That was when she realized his dark eyes weren't closed.

"You're awake?"

His mouth curved into a sexy smile. "Do you actually think there's a guy alive who could sleep through that?" His hands curved over her backside, gently squeezing the soft flesh there. "I've been awake since you made me your body pillow a couple of hours ago." He chased his words with the slow drag of his hands from her hips to her waist.

"Poor baby." She smiled down at him, loving when he was playful like this. "I should make those sleepless hours up to you, shouldn't I?"

His eyes lit with surprise—and heat—at her soft words, just a beat before his fingertips skimmed the bottom of her rib cage and his hands curved over her breasts, his thumbs brushing over her already erect nipples. She wanted to keep focusing on him, on the heady adventure of exploring his body, but when he touched her like that she couldn't keep her spine from arching her deeper into his hands. Nor could she keep in a low moan of pleasure at how good his touch felt.

His shaft was hugely erect between her thighs and her body moved into position over it as though they were connected by magnets, so that she could glide over him, back and forth, until her breath was coming fast.

Jake looked from her breasts in his hands to the slick, aroused vee between her legs, then back up at her face. When their eyes met, it sent an even deeper, stronger wave of pleasure through her than having him between her legs did.

"God," he said as he listened to her breath catch, "I love the sounds you make when you come. I love to watch you come. Do it now for me, princess. Ride me all the way there, just like this."

Every time she was with Jake, Sophie disappeared deeper and deeper into the sensual spell he wove around her. She'd never thought she could be this woman, one who brought herself to climax while her lover urged her forward, had never imagined she would break into the swim center to skinny-dip with him.

Then again, she'd never felt this safe before, had never had a man look at her as though she was the only person in the world who mattered.

The intense appreciation in his dark eyes sent

her hurtling over the edge. As she ground her pelvis into his, and his fingers played over the taut peaks of her incredibly sensitive breasts, Sophie realized she wasn't *nice* anymore. But she wasn't *naughty,* either.

She was simply a woman who finally understood how deep pleasure could run when she was with the right man…especially when love was bringing them together as much as hormones and attraction.

She leaned down over him, then, and their mouths met in a tangle of desire, tongues slipping and sliding, teeth catching on lips. Waves of ecstasy crashed into her, through her, over her. Her orgasm seemed to go on and on forever, spiraling higher and higher before leaving her muscles loose and limp. Even then, despite the way his shaft was still hard and throbbing between her legs, he simply stroked her hair, her back, as she worked to catch her breath.

"Mmm." She couldn't get her brain around anything clearer than that little hum of pleasure. Still, any minute now, she was sure he'd roll them over on the bed, push her legs open and take her in a deliciously dominant way. And, oh, how she'd enjoy every second of it.

But even after she could breathe normally again,

even when she realized his muscles had tensed up so much that he was nearly a living, breathing rock beneath her, he didn't move.

She lifted her head from the crook of his neck and brushed the damp strands of hair from her face so that she could see him properly. "Aren't you—?" She paused, blushing despite the fact that they were already naked and she'd just climaxed in cowgirl position over him. "Don't you—?"

His mouth captured hers. "Yes." He kissed her again, the thrust of his tongue the perfect window to his desire. "God, yes."

Suddenly, Sophie was struck with an idea that she never would have dared to see through before. But being with Jake made her feel brave. Moving off him, she slid off the bed and went to her bag to pull out a couple of hair clips. Within seconds, she had her long hair pulled off her face into a tight bun. She rooted around for the nonprescription glasses she kept with her to wear to important meetings—when she needed to make sure her brains were the only thing people noticed.

Ah, there they were. The big, thick rims were perfect.

She turned around to face Jake and had to laugh aloud at the look on his face. Lust mixed with horror.

"Sweet Lord, you're every twisted librarian fantasy I've ever had come to life." His voice sounded strangled as he looked down at her naked body, then back up to the bun and glasses. "I don't know if this is a good idea. I'm pretty much on the edge already, here, Sophie."

"Not Sophie." She squeezed his huge erection before letting herself stroke up, then down, the skin that had been stretched smooth. "Ms. Sullivan."

"Is that your librarian voice?" When she nodded, he groaned. "This is officially my new favorite game." She glared at him and he added, "Ms. Sullivan. Ma'am."

"Game?" She crawled back onto the bed, straddling him again and leaning down to lick up the side of his neck. "Do you think this is a game?" She sank her teeth into his earlobe before moving to the other side and giving it the same treatment. "Or this?" She pressed her hands flat over his chest, covering his pectoral muscles. "What about this?" She lowered her head to his chest to lick and nip at him and he reached for her.

But instead of letting him pull her up over his body, a surge of feminine power came over Sophie. She'd reduced big bad, lady-killing Jake McCann to a puddle of desire. That was how much he wanted her…and, oh, wasn't it just lovely to finally be wanted?

Before he could stop her, she moved down his incredible body to experience something she never had before, but suddenly couldn't live without for another second. Seconds later, warm, thick male flesh greeted her tongue. She hummed her pleasure at how good he tasted as she circled the broad head of his erection before opening up her mouth and taking it inside.

Jake's fingers threaded into her bun so tightly that Sophie was held captive over him, but she didn't care that she was no longer in charge, didn't even care about playing the "sexy librarian" role anymore. She threw off the glasses and gave in to the shocking thrill of giving Jake pleasure as he thrust up into her mouth. He'd wanted her to come above him earlier and now all she wanted was for him to do the same for her, just like this.

"I need you here." His words barely pierced the thick fog of her lust. "Right here with me."

A heartbeat later he was pulling her up and then down over him, causing her to lose her breath completely as he filled her all the way up. If it had been just her body he was filling, then maybe she would have been able to handle it, but the way he was looking at her, like she was his every dream, every single fantasy come to life, had tears springing to her eyes even as her body began to explode around his.

"Now," he urged as he grew impossibly big inside her and her inner muscles instinctively clenched around him. "Come with me."

Sophie threw her head back and held on to him like she was going for rodeo queen and he was the prized bull that was going to clinch her the title. Jake's roar of pleasure set every nerve in her body to tingling as she called out his name.

When she could finally rouse her brain to working again, she realized that somewhere in there he must have rolled them over to cradle her in his arms.

For several minutes, they remained connected, two sweaty, panting people wrapped around each other. Sophie felt she could stay like this forever. No need for food or clothes or words. Just Jake's arms around her, his heart beating against hers.

Jake had spent his entire life on guard against pain, failure, disappointment. Being with Sophie made him want to stop bracing himself for the inevitable fall, made him want to give in to a hope he'd sworn as a kid never to let himself feel again.

"Can I ask you something?" She was slowly

tracing the inked armband around his biceps with the tip of one finger.

He tensed before he could will himself not to give his discomfort away, and she pressed a kiss to his chest. "Don't worry, it's nothing bad. At least, I don't think it is."

She lifted her face to look up at him and his breath caught at how beautiful she was. He kept thinking that, after all these hours they were spending together, he'd get used to it soon.

Considering he'd never been able to get used to it as she'd grown from girl to woman in the past twenty years, he supposed he should just man up and accept that he never would.

She was that beautiful to him.

"What is it?" he said, the realization of just how powerfully the woman in his arms rocked his world making the words come out harder than he intended.

Fortunately, she didn't flinch. Sophie had never been afraid of him. Even when he'd thought that might be better for both of them, even when he'd been rough with her, she'd risen to every challenge he'd given her. And then some.

"I was just wondering about your tattoos." She slid the tip of one finger over the Celtic dragon tail that ran from his back to his lower rib cage.

"They're beautiful. I'm sure they must have hurt, so you must have really wanted them."

Being drilled with a needle for hours hadn't hurt nearly as much as his father's punches had. At least the tattoos had made him feel stronger. Tougher. As though the Celtic warriors of the past were in the wings waiting to help him when he needed them most.

"Tell me what they mean." At his continued silence, she lifted her eyes to his again. "Please."

Did she know that he could never refuse her anything if she looked at him like that and asked so sweetly? Did she have any idea just how tightly she had him wrapped around her little finger, that even as a bitter ten-year-old boy he'd been utterly captivated by her? Every year that passed since they were kids had only made her allure stronger... and his need for her more undeniable.

"That one is a Celtic dragon."

"We're always so busy with——" She blushed and he found it impossibly sweet that even after having wild, unbridled sex, she could still be shy around him. "I've never really had a chance to see the whole thing up close." She slid her fingertips over the tattoo, her breath warm on his skin. "It's amazing. What does it symbolize?"

He'd never shared the symbolism, or his reasons, with anyone else. Had never even been tempted before now. Before Sophie.

"One who conquers the dragon."

She slid her fingers from his ribs, up his torso to his upper arm. "What about this band around your arm? What does that stand for?"

"The strength of a warrior."

Again, she moved across his skin, lighting a fire everywhere she touched. "And the leprechaun on your forearm? Why does he have his fists raised?"

He would have shut her down if he thought he could get away with it. But he knew with utter certainty that she wouldn't leave it alone until she had all her answers. And if he didn't give them to her, she'd just look them up in one of her books.

Anyone who thought Sophie Sullivan was a pushover was the real idiot.

"Leprechauns are fighters."

"Funny, I always thought they were more like rascals hiding a pot of gold." She moved her hand up his chest, to his right shoulder. "This one looks like a shield."

"It is."

She cocked her head to the side, and asked, "No four-leaf clovers anywhere?"

"I've never believed in luck." Or any of the other

things that the four leaves represented, like hope, or faith.

Or love.

Sure, he'd loved Sophie nearly his whole life. How could he not? But he'd never believed anyone could love him back…never thought there was a chance that luck, hope and faith would barge into his life by showing up on his doorstep in Napa.

She placed her hand flat over his heart and looked up at him. "Strength. Symbols of battle. Warriors. Shields."

He could hear the sadness she'd been trying to hide from him in the restaurant when he'd told her about his mother and father. She moved onto her hands and knees and crawled over him.

"Can we pretend you have one more tattoo, right here?" She pressed a kiss over his heart and left her lips pressed against him.

He couldn't answer, couldn't speak, couldn't do anything but pull her closer so that he could kiss her. He would have kissed her forever if he could have, would have simply stayed here in this bed with her and pretended nothing else existed but her.

"Thank you for answering my questions," she added in a husky voice when he finally let her go.

"If I wasn't almost late for work already, I'd thank you properly."

She pressed one more soft kiss to his lips, then went to take a shower.

Jake remembered what Chase had said on his wedding day—that Chloe was worth so much more than one-night-stands and random hookups. Jake hadn't believed it, but now he knew the truth: one of Sophie's smiles, her gentle kiss—along with the love she'd once declared to him—meant a million times more to him than anything else ever would.

Twenty

Jake and Sophie stood on the library steps half an hour later. She had kept her hair up in that hot little bun, and as he kissed her goodbye he tangled his fingers in it to pull it loose.

"Knowing you're in there today looking like that would mess with my head really, really bad." Her librarian role-play that morning had been one of the hottest things he'd ever experienced. "You don't have your glasses with you, do you?"

He loved the sound of her laughter, so carefree, so pretty. But then, her smile turned to uncertainty. "Jake, would you come inside with me today?" When he didn't immediately reply, she said, "I loved spending time with you at the pub. It's nice to be able to picture you at your desk going over spreadsheets or bossing around your employees like a tyrant." She looked up at him with impossibly big beautiful eyes. "I thought maybe you'd like to know about where I spend my days."

Jake knew it was long past time to stop being such a wimp. Libraries weren't his thing, but he couldn't avoid them forever.

"Well," he said slowly, "if you'll agree to put your hair back up and have your way with me in a dark corner…"

Sophie smacked his arm and exclaimed, "Jake!" but the grin she couldn't quite contain along with the sensuous way she ran her hand down his arm before threading her fingers through his as they headed up the steps to the front door told him the truth about how much she liked his teasing.

He held the door for her, but she stopped and sucked in a breath, squeezing his hand tight.

"Sophie? What's wrong?"

She shook her head, taking a couple of breaths before saying, "Nothing. Just took the stairs a little quick, I think." She tugged him into the building, her color back, thank God. "Isn't it incredible?"

Jake had to admit the building was impressive. The domed ceiling in the main room had to be at least three stories tall. At some point someone had painted murals on it and even a nonreader like him could easily guess that they must be scenes from classic literature.

"Sophie, hi!"

A woman he assumed was a coworker practically ran up to greet them. Sophie's hand stiffened in his for a split second and he pulled her closer to him.

The woman's eyes darted between them. "Is this your...*friend?*"

The urge to claim public possession of Sophie was nearly impossible to hold at bay. But their week wasn't up yet. And this would be a good chance for him to see where she was in making her decision about letting him stay in her life. The way she'd made love to him this morning had given him a piece of the answer.

It wasn't until Sophie squeezed his hand and turned to him with a radiant smile that he realized he'd been holding his breath. "This is Jake." She never looked away from him for even a second as she said, "My boyfriend."

There was no point in trying to stop himself from kissing her. After keeping the kiss way shorter than he wanted to out of respect for her job, he held out his hand to her coworker. "Great to meet you."

"Wow, it's really nice to meet you, too. I can't

believe Sophie has been keeping you a secret all this time. Aren't you the owner of the McCann's pubs?"

He was sure Sophie didn't realize she'd put her free hand over her stomach just then. Two more secrets would—soon—be revealed, whether she wanted anyone to know or not.

Sensing that she wasn't entirely comfortable with this woman, he said, "Yup, that's me. Come in for a beer on the house sometime," before turning to Sophie and saying, "why don't you show me around before I have to get going to my meeting?"

The woman's eyes remained on them as he steered her in the opposite direction. "Thanks for getting us away from her," Sophie whispered.

He'd felt the same way when she was bailing him out of the mess at his pub earlier in the week. Was this how it would feel to parent two kids together?

He liked being a team with her.

Hell, he liked doing anything at all with Sophie.

At her desk, she locked her bag into the bottom drawer, then offered, "You take the chair for a minute. There's something I want you to see." Standing behind him, her hands on his shoulders, she said, "Isn't it the best view in the whole world?

There isn't anything you couldn't learn, nothing you couldn't be in here."

He was looking at thousands of books, at people reading and learning. He'd been to the top of the Eiffel Tower and looked out over the grid of Parisian streets, had explored the pyramids of Egypt, had been blown away by the blue-green water that stretched on seemingly forever from the beaches of Thailand. He hadn't thought any view could top those.

But that morning in Sophie's bed, he'd known just how wrong he was when she'd smiled at him.

He would never love being in a library, given his problems with reading…but that didn't mean he didn't comprehend, or appreciate, just how important this world was to Sophie.

"I've got to get story time going in a few minutes," she told him, pointing over to a group of young children and their mothers who were gathering on a colorful rug. "I'd love it if you'd stay a little while longer."

Jake knew he was already taking up too much of her time, on top of the way he'd monopolized her the past few days. Plus, his phone had been continually jumping in his pocket for the past half hour with calls from his assistant, who worked out of the McCann's headquarters downtown, about all the meetings he'd been flat-out ignoring. He wanted to chuck his phone across the room and watch it shatter, but he could only ignore the demands of his business for so long. Especially now that he had more than himself to think of.

Still, he couldn't leave just yet. Not when the chance to sit and stare at Sophie a little longer was too good to pass up.

"Sure. I'd love to see you in action."

He was rewarded with another one of her radiant smiles. "Maybe you could even read to the kids?"

Panic hit him at her innocent suggestion. It wasn't that he couldn't make it through a kids' book. Of course he could. But reading aloud in front of people? What if he got stuck on a word? What if he stumbled over a sentence? What if he was so distracted by Sophie's nearness that the letters took control of his brain the way they always used to instead of the way he'd forcefully trained them to behave?

No.

No way.

He shook his head, trying to act like it was no big deal that he didn't want to help her out with story time. "They came to hear you."

She frowned at his refusal. "Okay. But if you change your mind, just let me know."

He nodded, even though the odds of that were about as good as being able to throw snowballs in hell.

She introduced him to a handful of people as they made their way across the large room. He heard the pride in her voice every time she introduced him as her boyfriend. Guilt slashed through him, stronger now than ever before. He should have gone with her to tell her family everything as soon as she'd informed him that she was pregnant.

But he'd been too much of a coward. Again. He'd been too afraid that they'd see just how unworthy he was of her and try to keep him from her before he had any chance at all to convince her to marry him.

Sophie drew him over to an open seat and leaned over to whisper, "Stop looking so hot. The moms are going to be too busy staring at you to hear a word of the stories."

He knew just how that went, considering he could hardly make sense of what she'd just said to him with her soft hair brushing over him, her sweet scent washing over him and her curves pressed lightly into him.

"I'm glad you're here." She pressed a soft kiss

to his lips before turning to greet the children like old friends she'd been dying to see again.

Jake watched little boys and girls happily surround her, even the babies crawling from their mother's laps to get closer to her, and his heart turned all the way over.

Everyone in his life was so predictable, but not this beautiful woman who was reading so animatedly from a book about an elephant and a pig who were playing with a ball. As the children laughed with her when the elephant lost the ball, he realized Sophie Sullivan was the only person who had ever kept him on his toes.

He couldn't imagine anymore what life would be like without her. Without her spark. Without her laughter.

As a girl, she'd been sweet and he'd been charmed despite himself. As a woman, she was sensual and bright, sexy and sweet, a thousand contradictions wrapped up into one irresistible package.

He'd asked her for a chance, for seven days to prove that he had what it took to take care of her and their children. She'd given him that temporary gift and now he needed to give one back: the support of her family at a time when she needed it the most.

Jake took one last, long look at the beautiful woman who had gone from role-playing "naughty fantasy librarian" to "silly piggy" in the span of one short morning and knew there would never be a better reason for the hell he was about to willingly walk into.

Sophie looked up from the book she had just finished to see Jake blow her a kiss before walking away. The women at story time practically sighed in unison.

She couldn't stop the smile from growing on her face as she admired his broad back, his narrow hips, the way the tips of his dark hair curled just the slightest bit over his collar. Things had changed between them in the past twenty-four hours.

He'd asked for a week, but it looked like he was going to beat it by a mile.

No doubt he'd enjoy rubbing that in, she thought with another grin.

She said goodbye to the little girls and boys and their parents, then went back to her desk just as a ten-year-old boy walked up. "I need to write a book report about Abraham Lincoln, but the only book I can find on him is this one." He held up a thick, dusty tome that she doubted she'd want to read herself.

Something about the boy reminded her of Jake. Not because of any physical similarities, but more his manner, the way he held himself. She'd met Jake at this age and he'd been larger than life to a worshipful five-year-old.

"I don't read all that fast, or that good," the boy told her, his cheeks flushing slightly at the admission.

Again, she couldn't help but be reminded of Jake. And the slightly panicked look in his eyes when she'd asked him to help read to the children.

"Do you know if there are any other ones that are smaller? With easier words?"

She smiled at him. "There sure are. Follow me."

But as she helped the little boy find the books he needed, she couldn't stop thinking about Jake and the fact that he hadn't been in the library until today, and she hadn't found a stash of books anywhere in his house yet. She didn't expect everyone to be as addicted to books as she was, but in her experience, unless someone had major reading disabilities, they could usually find something they enjoyed reading.

Just then, a wave of nausea hit her and she lost the train of her thoughts. Her muscles were suddenly achy and, for the first time since she'd gotten pregnant, she needed to sit down. She grabbed for the nearest step stool and sank down onto it as she took a few deep breaths. Who knew morning sickness could hit so far into the first trimester?

Then again, she thought with a small smile, nothing about this pregnancy, or the man she loved, was all that conventional, was it?

And she wouldn't have it—or Jake—any other way.

The sun was setting by the time Jake finished the endless meetings he'd been blowing off all week and headed across town. He found Zach Sullivan in the private garage off the main Sullivan Auto building, under a dinged-up old Ford truck from the twenties he was obviously rebuilding from scratch.

Zach spent enough time on the ground to recognize most people by their shoes. "Be out in a sec," he said to Jake.

How long had he known Zach? For more than twenty years they'd backed each other up during fights, made sure the other guy made it home in one piece if he got tanked, cursed and cheered on sports teams together. But one thing they'd never done together was to sit down and share *feelings*.

A week ago—hell, two and a half months ago—Jake should have come clean about Sophie. He wasn't willing to be a lying coward for even another five seconds.

"Sophie and I are together."

Zach slid out from beneath the car so fast he was practically a blur. "What did you just say?"

The menace in Zach's question was all the more impressive for how steady his voice was. Almost as if he were asking for a glass of water.

"Your sister is pregnant. We're having twins."

His friend's hands were on his throat a millisecond later. "I'm going to kill you. And no one is going to give a damn."

Jake figured Zach was right about one thing at least: no one should give a damn if he died. But Sophie would care. His kids would care.

Thinking of them made him strong enough to fight Zach off as his friend came at him ultimate-fighting-style. Nothing was off-limits. Not nuts or teeth or hair or feet straight to the gut. Jake had expected this, would have been pissed at his friend for doing any less to defend his sister. Those expectations didn't make it hurt any less, unfortunately. And even in strict self-protection mode, he still had to get a couple of good slams in on Zach just to try to remain upright.

Both of them were bleeding in separate corners of the garage when Zach spat, "I've knocked a lot of guys to the ground for messing with my sisters before, but I never thought you'd be one of them. No one will ever be good enough for my sisters. How could you have laid even one finger on Sophie?"

"I shouldn't have." But he had. Over and over. And he refused to even think of giving her up now. He wouldn't do that for anyone, not even the people who had helped raise him, who had given him a home and a family to go to when he wouldn't have had anything else without them.

"I'm marrying her."

"Look," Zach snarled, his nostrils flaring, "Nice had a crush on you. You took advantage of it. Now she's pregnant. Don't make things worse by mar—"

"Sophie is more than one goddamned word!"

Jake's voice was loud enough to carry out of the garage, but he didn't care who heard him. It was time her siblings started seeing the real Sophie Sullivan the way he did. As more than Nice.

"Yes, your sister is *nice*. And sweet. And kind. But she's also cool and risky and willing to put herself on the line when anyone else would be running for cover. She's more woman than I frankly know how to handle, but I'm going to work like hell to try to keep up with her and our kids."

If it had been anyone else, Jake would have walked away. But Zach knew every crappy thing he'd ever done, and was the only one who knew he hadn't been able to read until he was ten...because his friend was the one who had tried to teach him how to wrestle letters into words.

"I love her." The three words he never thought he'd have to admit to anyone sounded like they'd been raked over gravel. "I've always loved her."

Jake tried to prepare himself from Zach's leap across the room to kill him. Instead, Sophie's brother slumped back against the wall and said, "I know."

Jake's jaw would have hit the floor if he hadn't been holding it to try to keep the bones together.

Zach held up two fingers in front of his own face and worked to focus on them, dropping them with an irritated scowl. "You've been in love with her since we were kids." Zach yanked himself to his feet. "Smith is going to lose his mind over this. They all are."

Jake knew full well this was only the first of many beatings to come at the hands of the Sullivans. He used a tool cart to pull himself up. "She's worth it."

"Of course my sister's worth it." Zach scowled.

"I just can't believe I've got to write another speech. Nearly killed me writing the last one."

"You wrote Chase's wedding toast ahead of time? It was the worst one I've ever heard."

"Get ready to hear an even worse one."

That wasn't the least bit funny. He wouldn't let Zach do anything to upset Sophie. "I'm going to write your speech for you and you're going to say it word for word. And," Jake warned his friend, "I promised Sophie I would let her tell your family about the pregnancy when she was ready, so don't screw up her big announcement by saying anything to anyone before she does."

Zach looked down at Jake's curled fists and shook his head. "My brothers have been losing their minds, one by one, over women. But seeing you like this…over my sister." Zach opened a metal drawer and uncovered his hidden liquor cabinet. He poured himself a large shot of Scotch and downed it. *"Love,"* he sneered.

Zach was pouring himself another shot as Jake headed back to his car to go tell Sophie that he loved her.

He always had.

And he always would.

Twenty-One

Sophie was walking down the hallway to her apartment, flipping through the mail she hadn't picked up all week, when she heard a low voice say, "Sophie."

"You surprised me," she squeaked as she almost dropped the stack of mail. "Oh, my God, Jake!" The bills and advertisements fell from her hand.

He looked as if he'd been mugged and beaten in an alley, covered with bruises and drying blood from his forehead to his chin.

"It looks worse than it is." He touched his jaw. "Probably should have gone home to clean up first." Even with the bruises and the cuts all across his face, he was impossibly beautiful as he asked, "Any chance you know how to bandage up a guy after a fight?"

She knew she should unlock her door and take him inside, but she needed to hold him right that second. She opened her arms and he walked into them, pulling her tight against him.

"It's so good to see you," he said into her hair. "So good to hold you."

She didn't know how long they stood like that in her hallway. All she knew was that she didn't want to ever let go of him. Everything had seemed so perfect this morning, like maybe there was a chance that they were going to get their happily-ever-after.

Not moving her head from where it lay over Jake's heart, she asked, "Who did this to you?"

Jake finally pulled out of her arms. "Let's go inside."

She frowned. That wasn't an answer.

Her hands were shaking slightly as she slid her key into the lock, but she worked hard at remaining calm as she moved into the kitchen, found a clean hand towel and turned on a stream of lukewarm water to wet it. God, she hated knowing Jake was hurt. He was so much bigger than she was, but she wanted to protect him, wanted to make sure he didn't know any more pain in his life than he already had.

His voice came from behind her. "I went to see Zach tonight."

She spun from the sink, forgetting she had the wet towel in her hand and flinging water on her walls. "Why?" But she knew why. "You told him about us, about my pregnancy, didn't you?" When he didn't deny it, pain moved through her as she said, "How could you? You promised me you'd wait. You promised you'd let me figure things out first." She loved him—would always love him— but she was so angry with him right now. "Why ask for a week if you weren't actually going to give it to me?"

"You keep wanting to hold on to this *week* thing, but after yesterday, after this morning, you know as well I do that things are different between us now."

"Different? *Different?* How different could things be if you're still acting like you run the world and the rest of us should just blindly follow your every last command?"

He scowled at her and even then he was so beautiful her heart skipped a beat. "I'm not going to keep hiding the truth from your family."

"The *truth?*" She scowled back, even fiercer than he had. "And what truth is that, exactly?" She moved her hands to her hips as she faced him down. "That you have zero respect for my wishes? That you just take whatever you want, whenever you want it? That it is so important to you to lock me into marrying you that you had to go behind my back to tell my brother you made the mistake of sleeping with me and getting me pregnant?"

"You want to hear the goddamned truth?"

Jake had never raised his voice to her like this before, but then again, neither had she. Until now when she practically yelled, "Of course I do, but you wouldn't know the truth if it slammed into you like one of my brother's fists!"

The abrupt silence that followed was unlike anything she'd ever experienced before. One heart-beat turned to two and then a dozen, and with every second that passed the ache grew bigger. She was trying to figure out what to say, how to possibly make things work out for the two of them, when Jake's expression shifted.

Suddenly, she knew what he was going to say.

"I'm in love with you, Sophie."

Sophie would never forget this moment, the wet towel in her hand dripping onto the kitchen floor, the ticking of the clock on the wall…and the way Jake's eyes were so full of love that it turned out she hadn't actually needed him to say the words, after all. Sophie had waited for this moment her whole life…but even in her wildest dreams, she hadn't thought it would be like this, while they were screaming at each other.

"I've been in love with you since we were kids, since the first time a pretty little five-year-old girl looked up at me and asked me if I wanted to play dolls."

Finally, she found her voice again. "You said no." The words, the memories, came before she could clamp down on them. "You said you wouldn't play dolls with me if someone was holding a gun to your head. You scared me." And thrilled her in equal measure. Even then, she'd known he shouldn't be talking about guns to a five-year-old girl, but Jake didn't play by anyone else's rules. Whereas, Sophie had rarely played outside those rules…until Chase's wedding, when she'd chucked the rules in for desire.

And love.

"I only said that stuff to you because I hated the way I felt when you looked at me. The way I still feel every time I'm with you. Hell, Sophie, I feel it every time I even think about you, like I've finally found something, someone, who matters. Only, I've never had the first clue how to hold on to you. Or how to be worthy of you."

How long had she wanted to believe she mat-

tered to him? To believe in impossible love becoming possible?

Jake's arms came around her as he sat on a
kitchen chair and pulled her onto his lap, the wet
towel squishing between their bodies. "I know I
screwed this up. Big-time." He brushed a trail of
moisture from her face. "I'm an idiot, remember?"

"No," she had to say, "you're not. You're anything but that, Jake."

But it was as if she'd never spoken. "Let me
make it up to you." He stroked her hair, pulled her
closer. "Please don't be mad at me. Don't push me
away. Even if I deserve it."

Loving and hating someone at the same time
was crazy. Sophie knew that. But she'd never been
able to stop the way she felt about Jake.

All at once, the week full of highs and lows, of
excitement and fear, of joy and anger, came crashing down on her. She didn't want to think about
the ramifications of what he'd just done by talking to Zach, couldn't even begin to process what
it would mean to really and truly have Jake's love.

All she wanted was to feel.

"I need you." Her throat was thick with emotion. "Make love to me."

Maybe, she thought as she tossed the towel to
the floor and frantically fumbled with his belt

buckle, it would be easier to believe him if they were skin to skin, connected by flesh and heat and pleasure. Maybe then she'd be able to actually hold on to his words of love instead of feeling like they were simply skidding past her, flying out of reach before she could catch them.

"Sophie, you know I want you. I always want you." But instead of helping her strip his clothes off, he put his hands over hers. "But we don't have to do th—"

"Please."

She didn't want to hit the pause button, couldn't stand it if he tried to be rational rather than just taking her. She yanked his zipper down and pulled his shirt from his pants a beat before he finally gave her what she wanted and unzipped her skirt to push it down her hips. She shoved his jeans down to his thighs, then kicked off her shoes. His fingertips grazed the bare skin of her stomach, pulling her sweater over her head right before she yanked open the buttons on his long-sleeved shirt. A heartbeat later she was straddling his hips and sinking down onto him, her eyes closing as she took him inside.

Yes, this was exactly what she needed right now. Pleasure to replace her confusion. Ecstasy to replace the fear.

And yet, she remembered too late that sex with Jake had never been simple, had never just been about pleasure. They'd always been such a perfect fit, their bodies utterly in tune with each other even during that first stolen night in Napa.

But this time it wasn't just attraction that joined them, it wasn't just the spark of arousal that made everything feel so good. It was the possibility that the magic between them was more than skin-deep, more than just hormones and unavoidable passion.

"Sophie." Jake groaned her name and she was caught in his dark gaze as he stilled her frantic movements over him with strong hands on her hips. "You're so beautiful." He moved a hand to cup her breasts, tilting up to run his tongue over each nipple. "I love you. So, so much." A flood of pure desperation pulled them closer together, wrapping around them as Jake buried his face against her chest and they shuddered against each other.

When Jake led her into the shower a few minutes later, she got a chance to see the full extent of the damage he'd incurred from his fight with her brother. In addition to the horrible bruises all across his jaw and over one eye, the ribs on his right side were turning black-and-blue.

"I can't believe Zach did this to you." She gently cleaned the cuts with a soft washcloth and soap, hating the way Jake winced at the sting.

"You're his sister. He feels like he's let you down by not protecting you from a guy like me."

Anger welled up inside her again, not just at Zach for what he'd done to Jake, but at her entire family. "Why don't any of them realize I can take care of myself?"

"Don't fault them for loving you."

But she was shaking her head. "Is it really love if there isn't trust there, too?"

Jake went completely still. "Sophie, I—"

He cut himself off, and when she looked up at him she saw his eyes flashing with emotion he'd tried to hide so many times before.

But then his hands were on her hips and he was turning her away from him before saying, "I've always wanted to wash your hair."

She knew what he was doing, avoiding yet another conversation they needed to have. About trusting each other not to do things like go to her brother behind her back. But his fingers massaging her scalp felt so good that she simply didn't have the strength to make him stop.

"Close your eyes."

She was already a step ahead of him, her eyes

having closed the moment he'd started washing her. Suds and water ran down her shoulders, over her body, as he cleaned every inch of her skin, his touch so gentle, so sweet. Especially over her stomach.

"You've grown bigger already."

She couldn't miss the reverence in his voice. Maybe another time she could have made another pregnancy fetish joke, but not now, not when his joy was so pure. So honest.

"I can't wait to watch you grow even rounder, even softer."

Her stomach growled loudly and he turned off the water, wrapping her in a towel. "Sounds like it's time to feed you again."

"I have some eggs and cheese in the fridge." She felt like her voice was coming from a mile away, like she was standing on the outside of her bathroom looking in at the two of them.

Jake lowered his face to hers and kissed her so softly it was more of a breath than a kiss. "I'll get working on dinner while you get dressed."

After he pulled his jeans back on and left the bathroom, she stared at herself in the foggy mirror. The blurred, partial image facing her was a perfect manifestation of how she was feeling.

She'd just gotten exactly what she'd always

wanted. Jake McCann had told her—repeatedly—that he loved her. She should be ecstatic. She should be leaping around her apartment in bliss.

What was wrong with her?

She felt like a block of cement had taken up residence in the pit of her belly, right between the two fetuses she'd seen on the ultrasound screen just a few days before. She hadn't felt quite right all day, actually, had chalked it up to morning sickness.

Jake looked up with a smile as she joined him. "Perfect timing."

She took a seat beside him at her kitchen island, where he'd set the full plate. She picked up her fork, speared some of the eggs and blew on the steam rising even though the thought of food made her feel like puking.

"Sophie? Are you all right?"

Jake had moved beside her, was looking at her with deep concern etched across his face.

She tried to smile to reassure him, but all she could say was, "I'm just tired. Really, really tired."

"Damn it, I knew I shouldn't have dragged you all over the city yesterday."

She didn't resist as he picked her up and carried her into the bedroom. Her limbs felt terribly stiff and heavy, exhaustion taking her over head to toe at almost the exact moment her head hit the pillow.

* * *

Jake sat in a chair in the corner of Sophie's darkened bedroom and watched her sleep, each breath she took pulling and tugging at his chest as if he were breathing with her.

He had sworn he'd never let himself feel this way, that he'd never let himself care about someone this much, that he'd never ask for help again. He could still remember the day he'd come home to ask his father for help. He was in fourth grade and it was getting nearly impossible to fake his way through class every day.

"I can't read."

His father had looked at him with disgust. "It's your mother's fault. The stupid bitch couldn't even give me a kid with brains."

Jake had turned and run from their apartment before he could shame himself even more with tears. It was easier, after that, to skip out of class on reading days. Until the day he'd been put on a project with Zach Sullivan. The cocky little jerk had everything and Jake had hated him on sight. He hated Zach even more when he flat-out told Jake they weren't going to skip the book report they were supposed to be doing together.

Jake remembered how cool he'd try to play it. "Books are for losers."

Zach had seen right through him. Maybe there had been other people who had guessed, but none of them had dared call Jake on it. Not flat-out like Zach had. "You can't read, can you?"

Jake threw the first punch, but Zach was barely a beat behind him. The two boys had done a pretty good job of smashing each other up before the teacher had pulled them apart. Zach's mother came to the office to take her expelled son home. But they'd heard the secretary say that no one was coming for Jake, and before he could figure out how to get out of it, Mary Sullivan had both of them in the backseat of her station wagon. A few minutes later they were sitting in front of a huge plate of cookies with tall glasses of milk. The book they were supposed to do their report on—*The Lion, The Witch and the Wardrobe*—sat on the table between them, along with a thick blue dictionary that had clearly seen plenty of use.

"Let me know if you need any help, boys."

Mary Sullivan hadn't yelled at them, hadn't smacked Zach or called him stupid. She didn't smell like booze, either. Jake couldn't believe anyone like her existed, couldn't stop himself from fantasizing about what his life could have been like if he'd had a mother like that.

After Mrs. Sullivan left the room, he'd been

coiled into a tight ball of nerves and bravado, expecting Zach to smirk and rub in his stupidity, but all the guy did was shove a chocolate chip cookie into his mouth and open the book to start reading it out loud, spitting chunks all over the pages.

Zach never brought up his reading problem again, but somehow they always ended up working on reading projects together after that.

He'd met most of the Sullivan crew later in their backyard when they were playing touch football. Lori swept into the middle of the group at some point, demanding the attention of her big brothers, wanting to know who *the new boy* was.

He couldn't imagine having six siblings. How great it would be to have someone to play with all the time. And then, from the corner of his eye, he saw her, Lori's twin. The other little girl should have looked just like Lori, but he would never get them confused. Not even when they were five years old.

She was sitting in the corner of the yard beneath a large oak tree, with a big book open on her lap. But she wasn't looking at the book.

She was looking at him, her eyes big as she stared at him.

He'd never seen anyone so still. So calm. Or so pretty. Sophie Sullivan had looked like a princess from one of those movies he snuck in the back door of the movie theater to see sometimes.

Sophie shifted on the bed just then, as if she were reaching for something. *For him.* She frowned in her sleep before putting her arm around a pillow and hugging it close to her.

Trust.

If there was anyone he wanted to trust, it was Sophie. But after a lifetime of hiding the truth from everyone, keeping secrets was what he did best.

Never share.

Never trust.

Never give anyone another chance to say you're nothing but the stupid son of a whore and a drunk.

But this time, Jake knew, everything was different…because he couldn't stop himself from loving Sophie. And he'd never wanted anything more than for her to love him back.

Which meant he would have to tell her soon, have to warn her that their children might not be able to do the one thing that came so easily to her.

Moving restlessly in the chair, his eyes caught on the book sitting on her dresser nearby. *What to Expect When You're Expecting.*

Reading it tonight would be torture, but that fact wasn't going to change. There would always be too many words, and he'd always have to work like hell to try to get them to make sense in his head.

But if anything was worth the pain and suffering of making his way through an entire book, it was Sophie…and the children they'd have in the fall.

Picking up the book, Jake used every trick to keep his brain focused, moving from one word, to one sentence, to one paragraph, to one page. As the minutes turned into hours and he turned the pages one after the other—and the endless warnings and risks of pregnancy rained down upon him—Jake actually found himself wishing he was that ten-year-old kid again, who couldn't read at all.

Twenty-Two

Sophie had slept the night through, but she didn't feel rested. Her eyes felt gritty, her mouth dry. She knew the reason. Jake hadn't slept with her, hadn't wrapped his big, warm body around hers and held her close. Even in her sleep, she would have known if he'd been there.

But he had never come to join her in the bed.

Where, she wondered, had he gone? Back to his house to rethink the love he'd offered her the night before?

She was so lost in her dark musings that she almost didn't notice Jake sitting in the corner of her bedroom. She sat up in bed so quickly that everything spun for a few moments. "You're still here?" Her throat sounded as raw as it felt.

"I've been here all night."

He was wearing his jeans from the night before and his hair was standing up on end as if he'd been pulling at it. He looked tense, horribly so.

Despite the fact that she felt like she was coming down with the flu, she pushed aside the covers and was about to get on her feet to head across the room to him when he said, "Have you had coffee since you've been pregnant?"

She frowned at the strange question. "Yes."

His mouth tightened. "Have you been around cats?"

Why was he treating her like this? Like she was a defendant on the witness stand. One who had done everything wrong.

"Yes."

"What about heating blankets or hot tubs? Have you used either of those?"

Obviously, his random questions must be related. But to what?

"Why are you asking me these things?" Everything was hurting now, worse than it had before. She leaned back into the headboard, pulling a pillow up over her lap to hold on to.

He lifted something off his lap. It was the *What to Expect When You're Expecting* book. "I just spent the entire night reading this."

Oh, no. The doctor had warned them about the

book, but Sophie hadn't thought much of it. Now she saw she should have known Jake would do this. He was so protective of her—and the twins she was carrying—that he'd let all of the book's warnings spiral completely out of proportion.

But before she could say anything to calm him, he was up out of the chair, holding the book open. "You're getting a new doctor. I can't believe she told us sex is fine. Right here it says twins need tons of extra care when you're pregnant."

"Jake," she said in what she hoped was a patient but not condescending voice, "my mother had eight kids. Everything's been going great so far with my pregnancy. That's all worst-case scenario stuff. I know what to be careful about."

"Then what about this? 'Deep penetration can cause bleeding.'" She could see the panic on his face as he thought back to every time they'd had sex. "If you knew that already, then why the hell have you let me keep taking you like an animal? I couldn't have been in any deeper last night. Or in the pool."

Knowing he was worried, she tried not to lose her temper again. "Show me where it says that." He only wanted what was best for her, she tried to remind herself, but he looked bigger, tougher, than ever as he got up off the chair and held the book open in front of her.

But when she read the passage he was referring to, she was too tired to keep her irritation with him at bay. "*Occasionally.* It says deep penetration can *occasionally* cause bleeding and not to worry about it unless it happens!" Exhaustion turned to pure frustration as she shot out, "Can't you even read? Or do you just make up words to suit your bossy purposes?"

A wave of nausea mixed in with her frustration, but even as she worked to ride out this horrible new onset of morning sickness, she could feel the air in her bedroom cool by a good dozen degrees.

In all the years she'd known Jake, she'd never seen him look like this—so cold, so distant.

"Funny, here I was working out a way to tell you," he said in a hard voice, "but you've already figured it out."

She could hardly breathe with him looking at her like that. "What are you talking about?"

"I can barely read!" he growled. "That's what I'm talking about."

Her brain raced as she tried to make sense of what he was saying. Jake McCann had always had her heart, from the first moment she'd seen him playing football in the backyard with her brothers. He'd been larger than life, even with that dark shadow following him, calling to her to clear it away with sunshine. With love. But until this week when he'd insisted they spend time together, she hadn't known just how hard his childhood had been, or the details of how he'd built his amazingly successful business from scratch.

And she definitely hadn't known he had a problem with reading. He'd never mentioned it, had never even hinted at it. Even if the thought had occurred to her, she would have instantly dismissed it because of all he'd accomplished.

Shaking her head in confusion, she said, "But you just read that entire pregnancy book."

"Ten years with tutors is the only thing that got me through that goddamned book. I'll never love books, Sophie. *Never.*" His expression grew even grimmer. "You were right, back in the doctor's office, when you called me an idiot."

The look on his face when she'd said that to him came back to her as clearly as if it had just happened. Riddled with guilt over the unintended pain she'd caused him, she said, "Oh, my God, Jake. No. I didn't mean that, you know I didn't."

She didn't want to fight with him…and she definitely didn't want to hurt him. More than ever before, she needed to be able to think clearly to convince Jake that she loved him. Especially now that she knew she'd said the absolute worst thing she could have said.

"I was scared and stunned that day in the doctor's office when I said that horrible thing," she tried to explain, "but I could never think that you were—"

"Sure you could," he cut in, not letting her finish. "Because it's true." He looked more fierce—and bleak—than she'd ever seen him. "Don't you see why I tried to push you away, to keep you from getting stuck with a guy like me? You could have had anyone, Sophie. And then when I just couldn't stay away from you, don't you see why I worked so hard to hide it from you? So you wouldn't find out what you'd gotten stuck with."

Pain shot through Sophie at the fact that he hadn't trusted her with something that mattered so much, that he'd gone out of his way to make sure she didn't know something so important about him. And just as bad, that he'd truly believed he wasn't good enough for her. It all hurt so bad that she had to put her arms around herself to try to keep herself from crying out at it.

And yet, despite her pain, wasn't it true that she'd been too wrapped up in her accidental pregnancy, in hopes and dreams and her fears that

Jake would never love her back the way she loved him, to uncover Jake's long-held secret? Because if she had only figured out what was going on, then maybe she could have helped him deal with it. Not the reading part, since he'd clearly worked through that on his own, but everything that came with a history of illiteracy. The fear. The shame.

Now she was finally able to put it all together. The fact that he didn't have any books in his house, no magazines or newspapers, either. All those months they'd met to work out various details about the wedding, he'd never written anything down. He always just stored the information in his head, even things she knew she'd forget if she didn't take notes. That time they'd been talking about his pubs over breakfast, when the conversation had turned to her love of books and she'd asked him about his favorite book, hadn't he immediately pulled away from her? Not to mention the strange way he'd reacted when she asked him if wanted to read one of the books at story time, the flash of terror in his eyes lingering long enough that she'd almost asked him if something was wrong.

"I love you," she whispered. "I love you so, so much, Jake. You should have told me. You should have trusted me."

She thought she saw him wince at the word *trust,* but then his features blurred before her.

"You keep telling me you've loved me all this time, but you've loved a goddamned fantasy. Not the man I really am. Take a look at me, princess. Take a good long look."

Sophie tried to focus on Jake's face, wished she could get the words out to tell him it wasn't true and that she did see him for exactly who he was, the good and the bad. And she loved all of him.

Unconditionally.

"I *do* know who you really are," she said, barely able to pitch her voice above a whisper.

"Really? You know me?" He snarled each word at her. "Did you know my father was a drunk and the thing he liked best when he was drinking was to beat me black-and-blue? Did you know that one day it was so bad I grabbed a knife and made him bleed? Did you know that when he finally drank himself to death I didn't care, didn't shed even one goddamned tear for him?"

She tried to open her mouth to tell him the reason she didn't know any of those things was because, for all his courage, for all his incredible strength, he hadn't taken the risk of sharing his life with her and trusting her to love him, anyway...

but she couldn't get her brain to send out the right messages to her lips.

"We both know you can't love a man like me. I was never going to be a father for a reason. I shouldn't be one, shouldn't pass these screwed-up genetics on to a couple of innocent kids. But you couldn't leave me alone, could you? You couldn't just let me love you from a distance forever and keep you safe from me."

Forever? Had he just said he'd loved her from a distance all this time and that he'd love her forever?

"I should have never tried to convince you I was worth marrying. Or that I could hack being a father to two kids. We both know you're all better off without me."

Wanting so badly to give him comfort, to wrap her arms around him and convince him to stay, she forced herself up off the bed as she said, "Please don't go. I love you."

But instead of her words of love making everything better, his expression only darkened further.

"No," he said in a horribly dark voice that sent shudders through her, "you don't love me. You only love a fantasy that doesn't exist. A fantasy that will *never* exist."

He turned away from her to walk out of the

room—*to leave*—and somehow she found the strength to reach for him. But just before she could make contact with his retreating back, the ground swayed, and pain shattered her midsection.

Everything went black.

Twenty-Three

Jake paced the hospital waiting room.

Please, God. Please take care of Sophie. Please give her back to me so that I can spend the rest of my life making everything up to her.

He'd given up on prayers as a young boy when they hadn't stopped him from being hit, or filled his stomach when there was nothing to eat. It had been up to him to save himself. To work for the money for food. To spend as much time as he could in safe places, like the Sullivans' house. To build a multimillion-dollar business from scratch.

But all his hard, bullheaded work, his stubborn drive to succeed, couldn't help Sophie now.

He should have noticed how pale she was when she woke up, that she hadn't been moving quite right, but he'd been too busy yelling at her. Too busy pretending he knew everything, just like he always had.

A frantic call to 9-1-1 had brought the paramedics to her apartment within minutes, but it hadn't been nearly soon enough. Bile rose in his throat at the memory of the blood between her thighs.

He'd held tightly to her hand in the back of the ambulance while giving the paramedics every bit of information he could about her pregnancy, about her schedule the past week, anything that could have led up to this horrible event. He hadn't spared himself, had confessed everything, the too-frequent sex and even yelling at her just moments before she collapsed.

He hoped a part of her knew he was there with her. That he'd never leave her side as long as she wanted him there. And that he was sorry for every single thing he'd ever done to hurt her.

She should have looked small, fragile, on the gurney, but even with dried tear tracks across her cheeks, and such pale white skin, she held him spellbound. Nothing could ever take away Sophie's serene strength. Her beauty was more than skin-deep, was more than the way her eyes and nose and mouth were shaped, was more than the curves and contours of her body.

Her beauty was in her bravery. Her intelligence. Her nonjudgmental curiosity about life.

And, most of all, the size of her heart.

He nearly lost it when the nurses wouldn't bend the rules. He wasn't her husband, and not only would they not let him go back to her, they also wouldn't tell him a damn thing about how she was doing. But he knew he needed to let them, let the doctors help Sophie.

It was the only reason he could have possibly let her go.

As soon as she was wheeled into the back, Jake took his cell phone out of his pocket with shaking hands and called Zach to let him know Sophie had fainted, that she might have miscarried. It wasn't long before Zach pushed through the doors, his mother and Lori a step behind him.

"Is she okay?" Jake had never seen Zach look this off balance before, every last trace of his cocky behavior gone.

"I don't know. I'm not fam—" His voice broke on the word he might have used if only he'd been able to prove to Sophie that he could be a good husband and father, rather than screwing everything up. "I've asked a hundred times, but they won't tell me anything."

Zach and Mary immediately went to speak with the receptionist, but Lori remained with him.

Sophie's twin reached out to grab his hand, and before she could say a word, he was confessing everything about the morning's argument, the way pain had crossed her twin's face before she'd fallen into his arms. And then, the horrible bleeding...

Lori squeezed his hand, tight enough that he had to look at her. "My sister's tough, Jake. So much tougher than anyone knows."

Why wasn't Lori tearing him apart?

"Go find out what's going on," he told her in a gruff voice, knowing he didn't deserve to be pouring out his guts all over her.

But Lori didn't let go of him. Just like her twin, she was one of the only people who didn't jump at his unilateral orders.

"Sophie always believed in you. No matter what you did, what you said, none of it made any difference. My sister wasn't ever going to change her mind about loving you."

"She was wrong. I'm not good for her." He'd wanted so badly to prove to her that he could be. No one had ever failed so badly. "This proves it."

"You're here, aren't you?"

"I was *yelling* at her," he told her again as something warm moved down his cheek. At first he didn't know what it was, because he hadn't cried since he was a kid. Not since that last beating when he'd grabbed the knife. "She wouldn't have fainted if I hadn't—"

"Seriously? You think she's in here because you were yelling at her? I yell at her all the time. Sophie doesn't give a crap about yelling. After growing up in such a big family, I'm sure she barely even notices it."

A part of him heard what Lori was saying, but the other part—the voice in his head that said he wasn't good enough for the woman he loved—had been around so much longer. "She deserves a guy who can give her a perfect life. No yelling. No bossing her around. No crazy hours at work. No screwy past."

"Don't use this not-being-good-enough-for-her crap as an excuse to leave her hanging this time." Lori Sullivan was fierce. "If you're going to step up to the plate, step all the way up, Jake."

With that, she strode away to find out what her mother and brother were learning from the receptionist, leaving Jake to reel.

"It's really sad, isn't it?" A couple of young hospital residents were walking past him to the coffee machine against the wall. Jake was certain one of them was the nurse who had taken Sophie into the back. "Man, this job is a bummer when people lose their babies like that."

"I know. I never know what to say."

The young woman shook her head. "I don't think there was anything we could have said to make this better for that woman. Not when it all happened so suddenly, and especially now that she can never have kids."

"God," the other resident said with a shiver, "can you image that happening to you?"

Sophie felt a warm caress on her cheek and would have smiled if she could. *Jake was here. Everything would be better now.*

"I love you so much. And I'm so sorry. So damn sorry."

She finally managed to open her heavy eyelids and saw that Jake's cheeks were wet, droplets clinging to his eyelashes. His sorrow, the fear in his eyes, held her speechless. Along with the way he was looking at her.

With pure love.

"I wanted those kids, you know how bad I wanted them. But you're everything. *Everything.* It doesn't matter if we can never have kids. All I need is you. If you'll have me. If you'll trust me and let me trust you from here on out."

Finally, her tongue came unstuck. "Jake?"

She tried to sit up to put her arms around him, but the sharp bite of pain had her gasping instead. Jake's arms came around her, holding her so gently, as if she were broken. The pain medication they'd given her made her feel heavy, fuzzy. But she needed to tell him.

"I heard the nurses talking outside." Every word he spoke was racked with deep pain. And loss. But still he stroked her hair as if he were afraid she'd break apart any second. "I should have been here with you when they told you about the miscarriage."

No, God, no, he couldn't think that—

Her tongue felt thick as she said, "It wasn't a miscarriage. They weren't talking about me."

The hand that was stroking her hair stilled. "Sophie?"

He pulled back to stare into her eyes. She watched relief war with disbelief on his face, as if he didn't want to give in to hope again, only to have it come crashing back down harder.

"But the blood, I saw the blood."

She pushed down the sheet and took his hands in hers, placing them over her stomach. Her eyelids felt like they had lead weights hanging from them, but she had to explain. "I have a fibroid in my uterus." She hoped she was making sense with the drugs still moving through her system. "A really fast-growing one. That's why Marnie didn't catch it earlier when she was concentrating on finding heartbeats. They're going to take me in for surgery to get it out."

He looked down at their hands, linked over her. "So you're—they're—" His tears fell even faster now, only these ones were tears of joy.

"Yes."

She was crying now, too, but when Jake kissed her she forgot their tears, the hospital…everything but how much she loved him.

And that he loved her, too, just as much.

"Excuse me, sir, you can't be in here. I need to finish prepping Ms. Sullivan for surgery right away."

She knew that fierce look Jake gave the nurse oh-so-well, and loved that Jake was willing to fight any battles he needed to for her. For their children. He was going to be the most wonderful father. The most loving husband.

As he argued with the nurse, telling her she could take it up with Sophie's mother in the waiting room if they needed proof that he belonged with her, that she *needed* him, she held on to his hands…and knew that everything was going to be okay, after all.

Twenty-Four

In the twenty-four hours after Sophie came out of surgery, the entire Sullivan clan invaded the hospital. She'd never been so suffocated by their concern as they hovered over her...or felt so loved. Through it all Jake stayed beside her, his hand holding hers, his strength bolstering hers as they fielded her brothers' reactions to seeing their baby sister with a man they had thought would never be able to love.

How, she wondered for the thousandth time, could they not have known Jake loved with his entire heart, with every last piece of his soul?

Desperately wishing she had a moment alone with Jake to finally tell him everything that was in her heart, as soon as the door finally closed behind Gabe, Megan and Summer, she said, "Jake, there's so much we need to tal—"

Her brother Smith pushed through the door before she could finish her sentence. She knew he had walked off the set in Australia the moment her mother called and caught the first flight back to the U.S. His arms immediately came around her and he held her longer than anyone.

So many times Smith had been like a father to her, and after working to stay strong with the rest of her siblings, she couldn't keep the sobs from coming when her favorite brother's arms were around her. She'd spent so many years hoping and dreaming of a life with Jake. It was still hard to believe that everything she'd ever wanted was finally hers.

Her brother held her until her tears stopped. His expression was at once fierce and full of love. "We'll all take care of you and the babies. You don't have to marry him, Sophie."

Smith spoke as if Jake wasn't in the room, as if she wasn't still holding his hand. She knew Jake wanted to confront her brother, but she also knew he loved her enough to trust her to make Smith understand how she truly felt.

She brushed her tears away before reaching for Smith's hand with her free one. "I love Jake. I love him with all my heart. And I want to marry him. Not because I'm pregnant. But because of who he is. And what he means to me."

Smith finally acknowledged his onetime friend with a scowl that would have had anyone else scurrying from the room to find a hiding place. But after what Jake had lived through with his father, she knew Smith was wasting his time trying to intimidate him.

"You were just crying like your heart was breaking in half," her brother pointed out. "You don't have to pretend with me, Soph."

She could feel Jake vibrating with the need to leap to her defense, with the instinctive urge to claim her, more than ever now. And still, he held his silence and her hand as he backed her up every step of the way.

"I'm not pretending. I'm happy, so incredibly happy, that my big brother has come all this way to see me. To make sure I'm okay, which I am." She smiled at Smith as she said, "And to give me his blessing." She squeezed her brother's hand. "Please be happy for me." She looked at Jake, then back at her brother. "Be happy for both of us."

Smith stared long and hard at Jake, and Jake stared right back, neither man backing down. Finally, Smith turned back to her. "If this is what you really want, I'll try to be happy for you."

Jake's voice came as a warning to her brother. "She's mine, Smith. And no one hurts what's mine."

Knowing the man she loved had tried his best to let her fight this fight herself, and that she wouldn't change one single thing about him even if she could, she told her brother, "Jake is right. I am his. I've always been his. And I always will be. I want Jake." She glanced down at her stomach. "I want the babies we made together." Knowing it was time to finally say what she'd held back from her family for far too long, she said, "And I want you, I want everyone in our family, to accept that I'm more than just your *nice* little sister who can't take care of herself."

The silence between them stretched out for a long while before Smith shook his head and said, with a slightly rueful expression, "I always thought your nickname was all wrong."

That was all it took for laughter to bubble out of her. "Just as long as no one comes up with any for my kids," she warned him.

Smith took a deep breath and he glanced down at her stomach. "Twins, huh?" He looked amazed and so proud her heart turned over with love. "You're going to be one heck of a parent, Soph."

As he leaned forward to kiss her cheek, she whispered, "I had a lot of great teachers." She held his hand even tighter. "Especially you."

And then, from out of the blue, Smith held out his hand to Jake. "Welcome to the family."

Mary Sullivan walked in just as Jake said, "Thanks, Smith. You don't know how much that means to me."

Smiling at everyone despite the fact that she was clearly choked up, Sophie's mother said, "I'm so glad you two finally figured out that you're meant to be together."

Sophie gasped in surprise. "Wait a minute, you mean you knew all along that Jake and I would end up in love?"

Mary Sullivan beamed at her. "From day one, honey. Just like Jake did, didn't you?"

She could see how much her mother's approval meant to Jake as he squeezed her hand tight. "It was all I ever hoped for, Mrs. Sullivan."

Mary smiled at the man who had captured her beloved daughter's heart. "Actually, Jake, I'd much rather you called me *Mom*."

* * *

At long last, Sophie's mother and brother left, with a promise to be back first thing in the morning with all of her favorite treats. The door hadn't quite closed behind her brother, but she couldn't wait another second to turn to Jake and ask, "Did you mean what you said? That you'd been loving me from a distance all this time?"

"I only have eyes for you, Sophie. But I never thought I deserved you."

"Can't you see how magnificent you are?" she said softly. "Because I've always seen it. I'm just so sorry I didn't see more, that I wasn't there for you when you needed me most."

"You couldn't have seen it. Not when I've spent twenty years honing my ability to hide my problems with reading from everyone. Especially you."

She watched as his fears surfaced in his eyes, and while she didn't ever want him to be afraid, it meant so much that he was no longer hiding his true emotions from her.

"What if I'm a horrible father just like mine was? What if all the hard work in the world won't change that? And what if our kids have the same problems I do?"

"I know you're nervous about becoming a father, but I'm scared, too. I wasn't planning to become a mother yet—or to have two at once. All we can do is make a vow to each other to stick through the good times and the bad and figure everything out together." She stared into his beautiful dark eyes, knowing it was long past time to say, "Ask me again, Jake."

"Sophie?"

"Ask me."

He dropped to one knee at the side of her bed. "Sophie Sullivan, I love you. I've always loved you. I always will love you. *Forever.*"

She didn't even try to keep her tears from falling. "I love you, Jake McCann. Always." She felt the wonder, the magic, the beauty, of knowing true love had been waiting for them all along. *"Forever."*

His mouth captured hers in a kiss so sweet her heart soared.

He reached into his pocket and took out a small blue box she couldn't believe he'd been carrying with him all this time, just in case she was ready to agree to his proposal.

"Marry me, princess."

His proposal was still more of a demand than a question, but Sophie wouldn't have Jake any other way. She loved every bossy, sweet, dominant, comforting, overly protective, loving part of

Jake's soul. Sophie had never felt like an outsider in her own family, but until Jake, she'd never truly felt like she belonged, either.

His love had made her whole.

He opened the box to show her the ring and she lost what was left of her breath. "Oh, Jake." The center stone was a bright, beautiful yellow gem surrounded by a ring of diamonds.

Looking up into his eyes, she smiled even as tears slid down her face. She could never change his past. But with her support—and her boundless love—she hoped that one day he would finally put it behind him, where it belonged.

She had to kiss him, had to hold him, giving him her answer—the *Yes* she'd been longing to say all her life to one man, and one man only—from within the warmth of his arms.

Two months later...

Sophie smiled, happily singing along with one of Nicola's songs on the radio as she drove from the library to Jake's house. Even though she'd always been perfectly happy with public transportation, especially in the city, where she could easily get wherever she needed to go, he'd insisted on buying her a car. Life with Jake was sweeter than she could ever have imagined, but given that he was still the dominant man she'd fallen in love with so long ago, she'd quickly learned how to pick her battles. A car wasn't worth fighting over.

She'd recovered well from the surgery to take out the uterine fibroid, but even though Jake had been loving and just plain wonderful during the past two months, she'd missed the wild part of him. They'd made love, of course, and it was always amazing, but she could tell he was holding back out of fear that he might hurt her or the babies in some way.

She tilted the rearview mirror down to take one last look at herself before she got out of the car. During her lunch break she'd been inspired to go out and buy a soft pink, long-sleeved dress. Sure, she knew she wouldn't fit into it in a few weeks, but she loved the way the soft fabric slipped and slid against her skin. It reminded her of the way Jake touched her, so gently, so sweetly…so wickedly.

She'd seduced Jake McCann before, and she was beyond excited about seducing her fiancé again. Especially after he'd showed her his new tattoo last night, a Celtic knot that symbolized the never-ending path of life, faith…and love. He'd had the artist thread her name through the design, worn right over his heart.

Taking a deep breath, she rang the doorbell instead of using her key.

Jake opened the door a few seconds later, a dumbfounded yet lustful expression on his face. "Sophie?"

She'd never forget that night in Napa when she'd stood on a different doorstep and begged to come inside. "I know you think you need to be careful with me, but the doctor said I'm fully healed now." Her voice grew husky. "I need you, Jake. Badly."

He pulled her inside and she was immediately enveloped in his delicious heat, but despite the fact that he clearly wanted her just as much as she wanted him, she could tell from the hard set of his mouth—and the fact that he was keeping a bit of distance between their bodies—that he was going to be a hard sell.

Well, she'd just picked her battle. And there was no way he was going to win this one, thank you very much. One day he'd finally accept that his self-control was no match for the intensity of their connection. In the meantime, she thought as the heat from his skin and muscles warmed her all over, she'd just have to prove it to him one night at a time, making her case over and over until he finally gave in.

"Stop trying to deny it, Jake," she said in a husky voice. "You need this just as much as I do."

He didn't argue with her, just simply said, "I'll make you come, princess, as many times as you need." He looked like he was about to burst with the need to do just that. "But I can't be rough with you. Not if it means hurting you again."

"I know what you're trying to do," she told him in a soft voice. "You're trying to make all the decisions for both of us again. But it's not going to work." Heat jumped into his eyes, along with the emotion he no longer tried to hide from her. "I want you exactly the way you are. Rough around the edges. Commanding. Exciting." She licked her lips. "And I'm willing to do *anything* to prove it to you."

She worked to control the laughter that threatened to spill out at how adorable he was as he tried to fight the inevitable.

"You'll do anything to prove it to me?" His expression had finally changed back to the wicked lover she'd begun to miss lately.

"Anything," she repeated as she reached for the buttons on the front of her dress and began to undo them. Jake's eyes held hope, desire and so much

love in them that it took her breath away as she
pulled open the front of her dress.

She loved the way her name fell as a ragged plea
from his lips, loved the way his eyes ate up the
fullness of her much-larger-than-usual breasts, the
swell of her stomach. She pushed the dress from
her shoulders and let it fall to the floor.

"I'm yours, Jake."

Sophie was everything to Jake. Despite all the
ways he'd been longing to take her in the past two
months, he'd known going slow, easy and gentle,
was what she needed as she healed from her surgery. They had *forever* to make their way through
everything else he wanted to do with her.

Tonight, however, he could see she needed—
and was finally ready for—more.

Thank God.

The air was already heavy with desire, and the
promise of incredible pleasure. He loved the way
her body felt against his as he pulled her into his
arms. The softness of her skin, the gorgeous swell
of her breasts against his chest, her rounded stomach pressing against him. She was his perfect fit
in every way, the only woman he could have ever
dared to be completely honest and open with.

And the only one he ever wanted in his bed again.

He scooped her up into his arms and she wound her arms around his neck, laughing as he carried her into the bedroom. "You're going to have to start lifting weights soon if you want to keep doing this."

He pressed a kiss to her stomach as he laid her down on the bed, almost knocking over the pile of colorful children's books on the side table. He and Sophie had a standing date at the bookstore once a week to select books for their children. He could hardly believe it, but he actually enjoyed reading when Sophie was in his arms, and he couldn't wait for their children to be there, too. The fact that his little girl *and* his little boy were growing inside of Sophie still blew his mind.

Jake ripped his clothes off in record time, then moved into her outstretched arms. She offered him her mouth and she tasted so sweet he had to take and take and take, even though he'd been planning to do nothing but give. He cupped her breast with one hand, her hips with the other. God, how he loved filling his hands with her, could spend hours running his fingertips over every inch of her skin. Even better was the way she begged for him to do more than touch.

His thumb caressed her breast and when she begged, "Jake, please," against his lips, he was too close to the edge himself to make her plead any more than that.

Every time they made love, Jake gave silent thanks for the way she opened not just her body but her heart to him. Later, he'd use his hands, his mouth, to slowly bring her to the edge—then over—again and again. He finally believed in forever.

But he needed her *now*.

Cupping her face in his hands, he crushed her mouth beneath his as their bodies became one. Their limbs were wrapped tightly around each other as they moved together in the perfect rhythm they'd always had, until he was swallowing her gasp of pleasure in a wild kiss as he fell with her over the edge.

Jake was certain nothing could be more amazing than lying with Sophie after they'd made love, with her nestled into the crook of his shoulder, her hand laid over his heart, his on her stomach. But then, he felt it, a ripple of movement under his palm.

"Did you just feel that? Did they just kick for the first time?"

Sophie's smile was radiant, and so full of love it stunned him every time.

"Yes," she said as she lifted her face to his and kissed him, "they did."

Epilogue

As Sophie Sullivan stood at the entry to her mother's backyard in a lacy white wedding gown that proudly showed off her baby bump, she knew she'd never been happier in her entire life. Everyone she loved—her brothers and sisters and cousins and friends—was here to celebrate with her and Jake.

Considering what pregnancy hormones had been doing to her lately, she was pretty darn proud of the fact that she hadn't cried yet and ruined her makeup. Yes, she knew it was going to happen, probably the second she started walking down the aisle that her mother and sister and niece-to-be Summer had strewn with rose petals of every color and saw Jake standing beneath the shade of the big oak tree waiting for her to pledge herself to him. Lori swore she'd used completely waterproof liner and mascara when they were getting ready earlier, but Sophie still rarely wore makeup and wasn't sure she trusted it to hold up and keep her from looking like a raccoon during her vows.

Vows. She and Jake were about to make wedding vows to each other.

Her heart swelled so big she thought it might actually leap out of her chest and run up the flower-strewn aisle to the man who had stolen it when she was just a little girl. She'd had so many dreams for a future with him, and now she knew how good it felt when they all came true.

When the breath she took shook, Smith, who would be walking her down the aisle, gently rubbed his hand on the small of her back and she leaned into him. He'd always been there for her, the big strong boy, and then man, who would never let anyone hurt her. He might have been one of the biggest movie stars in the world, but when Sophie looked at him, she only ever saw her beloved big brother, never the celebrity he had become.

As they waited for the *Wedding March* to begin, the sun momentarily moved behind a cloud. When it emerged again, it lit up the tree fort that she and her siblings had had so much fun in as kids. Jake had almost always been there with them… and she'd never forget that he was the reason she'd mustered up the courage to climb it as a five-year-old girl who was far more interested in reading stories than getting skinned knees.

Darn it, she thought as she sniffled, that was all it took. Just thinking about that day, the challenge in Jake's eyes which had her climbing up so high into the huge oak tree to discover a completely new perspective on the world, and she couldn't stop herself from tearing up.

It figured she wouldn't have any time to compose herself, because that was right when the *Wedding March* started up.

Smith tucked her hand into the crook of his arm and looked down at her, love and warmth shining down on her from his deep blue eyes. "Sophie—"

Great, his voice was breaking on just her name. If he said anything more, she'd be a complete blubbering mess by the time she got to Jake.

Smiling at him through the tears that she was only just barely keeping at bay, she squeezed his arm. "Take me to Jake, Smith. I'm ready."

She'd been ready forever, and now—*finally*— she would be Jake's wife.

Smith pressed a kiss to her forehead and then the two of them started the slow procession through the crowd of friends and family who were standing and smiling at her.

She didn't hear another note of the *Wedding March,* couldn't hear anything but her heart pounding in her ears, couldn't see anything but Jake waiting for her by the base of the old oak tree looking as happy, and as madly in love, as she'd ever seen him.

He was standing close enough to the tree fort that what had once seemed so big, so high, to her as a little girl, now looked small by comparison to his six-plus feet and incredibly broad shoulders.

As soon as their kids were big enough, they would be building a tree fort in their own backyard. And she and Jake would play Pirates again, just as they had so many years before.

At the end of the aisle Smith pressed a soft kiss to her cheek, and then he was putting her hand in Jake's.

Sophie looked down at their linked hands, Jake's so big and tanned, hers smaller, yet just as capable. They made a great pair.

A perfect pair.

Just as she'd always known they would.

She looked up at Jake and when he whispered, "I love you," to her so softly that only she could hear it, she went up onto her tippy toes and whispered it right back, before kissing him.

Everyone laughed at the way they were doing

everything out of order by kissing even before they'd made their vows, but Sophie knew out of order was what worked for the two of them.

A one-night stand...and then seven days and nights together that turned into forever love.

Getting pregnant with twins...and then getting married.

And as Sophie took her place beside Jake to say their vows, she knew she wouldn't change one single thing.

Zach Sullivan yanked at his tie. Damn, he hated wearing ties, but he figured he could suck it up for an afternoon, considering it wasn't every day one of his little sisters got married.

The past year had churned out a seemingly endless supply of Sullivan weddings and pregnancies. First Chase had gotten married and had a kid on the way in a matter of weeks, then Sophie pulled the same thing from out of the blue. Even Gabe and Megan were now engaged. Only Marcus and Nicola were still slightly sane, but Zach wouldn't be surprised if Nicola showed up sporting a huge diamond ring one of these days. Marcus had just officiated Sophie and Jake's wedding, mere months after he'd done Chase and Chloe's. If things kept up like this, he was going to need someone to cover for him at his winery.

Zach had expected Sophie to want a big wedding, a splashy Sullivan celebration where every relative and friend on the planet would be invited. Instead, here they were in his mother's backyard, like so many other Sundays. The only real difference from their usual Sunday brunch was his sister's long white dress and Jake's monkey suit.

When, Zach wondered, had Sophie grown up? And how long would it take him to see her as anything other than the baby sister that he needed to protect with his life? He'd choked up more than once while she'd been walking down the aisle and then when she and Jake had exchanged vows, but pretty much everyone at the wedding had been sniffling and pulling tissues out of their bags. All of his brothers looked like they were having a heck of a time keeping it together, actually. Lori, of course, cried up a storm as her twin took the marriage plunge.

Five months pregnant, Sophie was prettier than ever, especially in her wedding dress. He could see how happy she was, but Zach still had a hard time thinking of Jake with Sophie. Even though the bride and groom looked like the most mismatched couple on the planet—the big guy with the tattoos

and the classy brunette—Zach was starting to realize that Sophie gave as good as Jake dished it
out. Better, usually.

As the chairs were cleared so that the dancing
could begin, Lori walked over and handed him
a beer. "Wanna make a bet on who's the last one
standing? You or me?"

Zach loved his twin sisters equally, but he'd always understood Lori better. She thrived on speed.
Excitement. Breaking the rules. Just like he did.

"You looking to give away your money, Naughty?"

She stared at him over the rim of her glass as
she took a sip of Marcus's finest bubbly. "Haven't
you learned yet—it's always the cocky guys who
think they're so safe that fall the farthest."

Zach rarely backed down from a challenge. Especially not one that was this easy to win. Knowing there wasn't a chance that he was going to fall
in love with someone against his will, Zach Sullivan held up his bottle of beer to clink it against
his sister's champagne flute.

"Game on."

* * * * *

Meet The Sullivans...

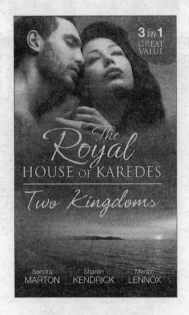

Discover more romance at

www.millsandboon.co.uk